Lightning lit up the sky and Cay took hold of her hand.

Sasha's eyes were wide and frightened when he looked into her face. Gently, he turned her loose.

"This, too, is part of living in the Keys," he declared. "It's a part that will either nourish you or break you. The stormy side of the people here. The secrets we hold. It is the price that some of us pay."

"You make it sound ominous. I think it's beautiful." Sasha looked up at the sky.

"Yes, risk can sometimes be beautiful," Cay agreed. "The beauty lies in the uncertainty. The thrill. But it takes a lot of courage to walk that path. I've learned to play it safe."

"Are you telling me you're a coward, Cay Ellis?"

"Perhaps."

"But I know that's not true." She thought of how he rescued her from the storm.

"When it comes to some things. When it comes to you," his voice was husky as his face descended, "perhaps I am a coward."

Other Avon Contemporary Romances by
Eboni Snoe

TELL ME I'M DREAMIN'
WISHIN' ON A STAR

EBONI SNOE

A Chance On Lovin' You

AVON BOOKS
An Imprint of HarperCollinsPublishers

This is a work of fiction. Names, characters, places, and incidents either are the product of the author's imagination or are used fictitiously. Any resemblance to actual events, locales, organizations, or persons, living or dead, is entirely coincidental.

AVON BOOKS
An Imprint of HarperCollins*Publishers*
10 East 53rd Street
New York, New York 10022-5299

Copyright © 1999 by Eboni Snoe
Inside cover author photo by Terry L. Ford
Published by arrangement with the author
Library of Congress Catalog Card Number: 99-94798
ISBN: 0-380-79563-9
www.avonbooks.com

First Avon Books Printing: September 1999

Avon Trademark Reg. U.S. Pat. Off. and in Other Countries, Marca Registrada, Hecho en U.S.A.
HarperCollins® is a trademark of HarperCollins Publishers Inc.

Printed in the U.S.A.

WCD 10 9 8 7 6 5 4 3

To Ida Scott-Falls, Mary Falls-Scott
and Annie Falls-Moore
for their support in a time of need

It was as if the mighty hand upstairs had flipped a coin. But as Sasha Townsend long ago realized, the ultimate power never uses coins. It uses people's lives. This time, a heads up had appeared for her life.

Sasha had never owned land before. A town house with a zero-sized lot, yes. But not three acres of land. It might not be much to many folks, but to Sasha the Floridian property appeared to go on forever.

The impact of what she saw was startling. This was the first time she had actually seen her inheritance, walked on it, and each step turned into an exploration. The sloping ground was a precious thing beneath her. The air smelled so promising. If it were possible, Sasha believed she could have tasted abundance on Magic Key.

Sasha wasn't exactly a nature lover, but something here moved her as she gazed up at the sky. Was it joy? Perhaps. But Sasha and joy had parted company so long before it was difficult for her to know.

Part of it was her fault. She was thirty years old and couldn't think of anyone who was really close to her. Sasha had come to believe that most people were insincere. They said things they didn't mean, motivated perhaps by an ulterior motive or just plain nosiness. From Sasha's experience, on a scale of one to ten, ten being perfection, human nature would score a three. As a younger woman it pained her to admit it, but with time a callus had hardened the tender spots in her heart.

As a result she had created a life no bigger than a shoe box. It contained the school where she taught and the town house where she lived with her ailing mother. Eight years before, directly out of college, Sasha had taken the first position offered in her hometown of Gary, Indiana, in order to take care of her mother, Leslie. Any other relationships were mere shadows. Men had come and gone, and through the years she had loved and lost. But it hadn't taken Sasha long to decide she did not favor loss, so she cultivated the feminine skill of only appearing to give her heart. Those were times Sasha was not proud of, but she held no regrets. Those times allowed her to give her life to her mother. Now, after Leslie Townsend's death, the chance to truly live had opened up for Sasha.

A few months before, the idea of inheriting land from the "other side" of the family would have been laughable. But the cosmic wheel of fortune had been spun, and what was once laughable was now reality. Much to her surprise she inherited the property from the Bethels, estranged relatives on her father's side of the family.

Sasha did laugh now, and she broke into her own celebratory dance. She whirled across the flower-filled field, stopping only when her sandal sank into a puddle of mud. She felt dizzy, and the landscape seemed to continue to spin around her, but she was aware of how different the area appeared from before. The trees were thicker, the wildflowers profuse, and there were reeds above the moist, dark earth. It was a natural habitat for any creature that favored dampness, and Sasha immediately considered the possibilities. She stepped back, but she was already ankle-deep in murky water.

"What in the world?" Sasha spun around. She was standing in a muddy stream that originated at a tiny fountain bubbling out of the earth. "Well look at that. It's coming right out of the ground," she exclaimed. "Just like the springs at the Pure Spring bottled water plant where I took my class."

She hiked her purse onto her shoulder and put her sunglasses on top of her head. *Why is there a natural spring here?* she questioned. *The island is surrounded by salt water. There must be an underground river running beneath the Key,* Sasha rationalized.

Excited, she cupped her hands above the tiny spout and sipped. The water was unusually sweet. "Mmmm, this is good," she said as a feeling of euphoria surfaced. "Oh, my. I don't know what's happening, but this is wonderful," Sasha murmured as she closed her eyes and surrendered to it. . . .

When Sasha opened her eyes she was lying on her back and someone—a man—was looking down at her. She attempted to focus on his face, but it was useless. She closed her eyes again.

"I thought you would be coming around soon. How do you feel?" a deep voice penetrated the pleasant fog.

"I feel . . . I feel," Sasha repeated, her lips barely moving. "I feel wonderful."

"Wonderful? Is that right?" There was a pause. "You should feel lucky as well," the man continued. "I don't know why you tourists insist on visiting Magic Key. There's nothing here for you. Anything you'd be looking for is across the way on Big Pine." His voice lowered almost to a grumble. "Roaming around these Florida Keys without a clue is not a smart thing to do. One day somebody's going to get hurt."

"Tourists, m-m-m, who's a tourist?" Sasha opened her eyes again. This time she caught a glimpse of the man's shoulders before she closed them. *They are so broad,* she thought as she floated away.

"Nope. Don't do that," he commanded.

Sasha felt herself being picked up and cradled in the stranger's arms. "What . . . what are you doing?" she questioned as she wondered who the stranger was and what his motives might be.

A tinge of fear sparked, but Sasha noticed how warm and comforting his body felt, and how easily she fit within his arms. No one had carried her in their arms since she was a child, and she opened to the warmth. *How wonderful it would be to feel like this all the time*, she thought. *This is security. This is peace.* All too soon she felt herself being propped up against a tree.

"How much of the damned water did she drink?" the man muttered to himself. "You would think she'd have better sense—"

"Wha-what did you say?" Sasha emerged again and tried to clear her head. She didn't like the tone of his voice or the things he was saying. "Sense? I've got plenty of sense," she replied groggily.

"So you understood that, did you?" The words came from another direction. "I guess you're doing okay."

Sasha put her hands up to her face, then pressed her temples with her fingertips. "I'm doing just fine, thank you." She hoped she sounded indignant but she wasn't sure. "It must have been the combination of the heat and the water. This isn't like me. Maybe the water had some salt in it after all." Sasha removed her hands from her head.

"This isn't like you," he repeated with obvious cynicism. "Well, whoever you are, you need to be careful while you're out here exploring these Keys. You'll find yourself in all kinds of predicaments."

"I can assure you I can handle anything that comes my way," Sasha replied. She focused on the man who was giving her a hard time. A colorful shirt was draped around his neck, and the ends dangled against his mahogany chest. He wore thigh-high cutoff jeans, and Sasha thought, with legs like that, he had to be a runner. She expected him to be barefooted, but his feet were covered by a nice pair of white-soled shoes.

"I think if I examined you as thoroughly as you are examining me, you might be insulted," he said in a low voice.

Sasha looked up at his face. He was the most handsome man she had ever seen, silvergray highlights and all. "From where I'm sitting, your body was the first thing I saw." She shaded her eyes against the bright sunshine. "I didn't mean anything by it." Then Sasha recalled how it felt to be carried in his arms and she wasn't so sure.

"I must confess, if I looked at you that way it would mean plenty." His eyes remained steady. Sasha met the challenge in them before looking away. Feeling silly and at a disadvantage, she began to get up.

"I don't think that's a good idea," he advised.

She heard his warning just as the intense floating sensation returned. "Whoa-oa," she said. Sasha eased herself back down to the ground.

"By now it should be obvious that water was poured by the devil and no good will ever come of it." The words were filled with loathing. "But you'll be okay. Just sit still for a little while longer."

Sasha closed her eyes and massaged her temples. "Is there something in it?" she asked.

She waited for an answer, but all she got was silence. Sasha opened her eyes. The man was gone. She searched the field and the edge of the forest; there was no one there.

Testing, Sasha moved her head back and forth. She could feel remnants of the euphoria. In hindsight, she knew drinking the springwater had been an impetuous thing to do, probably even stupid. Was the spring toxic? Did it have salt in it? Or had she fainted?

"That was really a dumb thing to do," Sasha chided herself as she thought about the stranger and how dangerous the situation might have been. "My purse?" She grabbed her side. The purse was hanging there undisturbed.

Sasha looked toward the sun as she wondered why she'd passed out. True, it was quite hot, and being from the North, she was unaccustomed to this kind of heat. Her excitement over discovering the spring probably hadn't helped, either. Perhaps the combination of heat, excitement, and the water had brought on the fainting spell. Slowly, Sasha got to her feet. She felt a little out of sorts, but other than that she felt fine, even energized.

The strange incident monopolized her thoughts as Sasha made her way back to the small stucco house situated on the property. When she sat down on the front stoop she realized the walk had helped her make up her mind.

Sasha had toyed with the idea of moving to Magic Key ever since she received the inheritance, but she didn't know how to make it work. Now the land had provided the answer. It possessed a saleable natural resource: springwater.

Sasha thought over the changes she would have to make during the next month or so. Moving from Gary to the Keys would be quite a change, and starting a bottled water business would be no small feat, either. Still, Sasha felt accomplishing those goals would be nothing compared to the hardships she and her mother had endured during her last years. Hardships a person as loving as her mother did not deserve.

The incident at the spring ran through her mind as she watched a troupe of butterflies fluttering in the field. Once again, Sasha wondered who the mysterious male visitor was. His clothes told her he was one of the locals, perhaps someone who worked on either the docks or on a fishing boat, although there was something distinguished about him.

Sasha stood, walked over to her rental car, and pulled her sunglasses down over her eyes. She took one last look at her property before she climbed inside the vehicle and headed toward the seven-mile bridge.

Chapter 1

Six weeks later . . .

The two weeks prior to her move had been a mess. In the end Sasha managed to rent her furnished town house and give notice at Ernie Pyle Elementary that she would not be back to teach in the fall. Everything she needed to start her new life was packed in a small U-Haul trailer when she crossed the seven-mile bridge that spanned the Keys.

But once she'd arrived, settling in on Magic Key was easy. It was a quiet place that felt far removed from the larger neighboring island, Big Pine. If it hadn't been for the occasional passing of vehicles on a distant road, Sasha could have envisioned she was alone there.

A wall of forests that surrounded her property on three sides heightened her feeling of isolation. It was a welcomed feeling for the time being, for the five-room house and the land had been maintained with tender loving care. She could feel that care emanating from the pastel-shaded furniture, the unique decorations, and the pruned key lime orchard.

Florida agreed with Sasha. In one week her skin had evened to a smooth, maple syrup brown, and her natural shoulder-length hair seemed to thrive in the tropical environment. There was plenty of physical work to do, and Sasha believed she could not help but firm up and become stronger.

An exuberant sun had shown its face every day, but that didn't stop Sasha from spending her time clearing the land around the spring. Her vision of a bottled water business consumed her; it was her future and her inspiration. As she worked in the heat, it was hard for Sasha to imagine how her ancestors were able to stay in the fields from sunup to sundown. Hers was a labor of love, but without technology and the occasional breaks under a tree with some ice-cold lemonade, Sasha didn't believe she could have done it.

Now, at the day's end, she stood at her front door and looked up at the setting sun. Her body ached and her hands were sore, and all she could think about was a nice, cool shower. She was halfway to the bathroom when the knock came.

"Yes?" She peered out the door to see an elderly man standing on her stoop.

"Are you the person who lives here now?" He tried to look around Sasha into the house.

"Yes, I am."

"This was stuck in your mailbox." He handed her a piece of paper.

"Thank you." Sasha glanced at the flyer advertising a local attorney, then up at the man who remained where he stood. "Can I help you?" She noticed the envelope in his pocket.

"I was told to give you this."

"What is it?" Sasha took it and turned it over.

"I don't know, ma'am. I was just told to give it to the person living in the Bethel House."

Sasha opened the envelope and looked over the letter that was addressed "To Whom It May Concern": "You are being asked to cease all land-altering activity at 340 Bimini Lane. This letter officially summons you to Guana Manor." She stopped. That name was familiar. Then Sasha recalled that *Guana Manor III* was the name of the sloop she saw during her first visit to Magic Key. "Look, I don't know what this is, but I think you've got the wrong house. This is three-forty Route Nine."

"That's what it used to be until Hazel allowed Precious to turn the Bethel House into her special place. No, ma'am, I don't have the wrong address."

"Precious?" Sasha looked puzzled and shook her head. "Who is Precious?"

They stared at one another.

"So, I'm sorry." Sasha refolded the letter and placed it back into the envelope before handing it to the man. "There's been some kind of mistake. This might have been Precious's . . . place, but it isn't anymore."

He accepted the envelope but continued to stand on the stoop.

"I've got to go now," Sasha said as she closed the door. "Have a good day." How strange, she thought as she walked toward the bathroom, where she began to remove her clothes.

Sasha treasured the early-morning hours. It was a peaceful, quiet time when she sipped coffee and listened to the sounds of dawn. And at Bethel House she finally felt as if she'd come home. She didn't know how to explain it, but there was something comforting about the house that made her feel as if she was not alone. Maybe because she was surrounded by the possessions of her Aunt Hazel Bethel. Sasha had not expected to feel so comforted. After living with her mother for so many years she had feared living alone would be lonely. But nothing was further from the truth. The house itself seemed to waken with the prisms of sunlight that reached through the windows every dawn.

In spite of her contentment, Sasha was keenly aware of how uncertain her future was. She knew the inheritance would carry her only so far, and she wondered where she would be in five years. Would her bottled water business be thriving? Would she still be alone, if not lonely? She hoped not as she closed her eyes, but the thoughtful moment was disturbed by another knock on her front door. Sasha was astonished to discover that the man from the day before had returned.

"Good morning," he said with a slight smile.

Sasha was so outdone she didn't know if she should speak or shut the door in his face.

"This *is* the right house, ma'am. And I was

told to show you this." This time he held out a document headed "The Bethel Agreement" along with another letter.

"Do you realize it's seven-thirty in the morning?" Sasha asked.

"Yes, ma'am, I do. I thought it was a little early, but I was told to bring this over right away." He looked uncomfortable. "Most of the folks around here tend to get up real early. They want to get things done before noontime. It's just too hot to work outside after that. You have to wait to almost dusk."

Sasha lowered her fiery gaze. She knew this man wasn't to blame. He was only a messenger. She opened the screen door and took the document. "All right. I'll look it over, and if I think it's necessary I will get back to you. I guess whoever is trying to contact me, their name and address is on the letter?" She glanced at the top and bottom of the page. In the center, "Guana Manor" was embossed in a metallic black; an address was underneath it. The name "Cay Ellis Jr." was printed at the bottom.

"Um-m." The man cleared his throat. "I was told to wait and escort you over."

"Escort me over. Now?"

The man nodded. His eyes were apologetic.

Sasha could feel her anger rising. What could be so important that this Cay Ellis would practically get her out of bed to be escorted to his house? Sasha scanned the document. It was an agreement between the Bethels and the Ellises. "But what does this have to do with me?" She shook the paper.

"Ma'am, it's my place to—"

"Never mind," Sasha snapped. She opened the letter again. It claimed the Ellises had the right to legally stop her from clearing the land around the spring: "We will have a restraining order drawn up against you if you do not accompany Mr. Knowles to Guana Manor this morning."

"*You* are Mr. Knowles, I presume," Sasha questioned.

The elderly man nodded. Sasha read on. " 'We hope to resolve this matter in a way that's satisfactory to all.' They have to be kidding. This agreement is practically a hundred years old!"

"If I should say so, ma'am, I don't think they're kidding. The Ellis family is a pretty powerful force around here. I haven't known them to kid too often."

Despite how trite the man sounded Sasha could see he was sincere. "Where is Guana Manor?"

"Just down the road a bit. The Bethel House and Guana Manor are the only two houses on Magic Key. Magic Key basically belongs to the Ellises."

A sinking sensation stirred in the pit of Sasha's stomach. She had come to Magic Key to get away from the blatant disparity between the haves and the have-nots. Yet here she was being thrust into a familiar battle. But Sasha was a fighter. She had fought long and hard to get her mother the medical care she needed. She never gave up trying. She never lost faith, even until the end. Her sense of inner strength crystallized and she would fight again to keep what was rightfully hers. "Okay. If they want to see me I want to see them," Sasha proclaimed.

She gathered her keys and her purse as Mr. Knowles waited beside a vintage 70s Cadillac with the passenger door wide open.

Minutes later they went past a nearly hidden Keep Out! Private Property! sign that introduced the road to Guana Manor. Sasha was surprised the house was so close. The evenly paved road defied the pinewood forests on both sides, snaking its way through the tall trees until it opened onto manicured grounds. She hadn't been prepared for such a display of wealth, and Sasha found herself leaning close to the windshield. Automatically, her body armed itself with adrenaline, preparing her for whatever lay ahead.

She studied the landscape. It was a masterpiece of finely trimmed hedges and flower gardens. A fountain stood in the center of the garden. Beyond, a white, three-floored stucco building gleamed. Its rose-colored porticos offered shade to the occupants of the mansion who chose to venture outside and lounge in the wrought iron furniture beneath them. It was picturesque to say the least. A far cry from Sasha's town house in Gary, and an outright shout from her five-room house no more than three miles away.

Mr. Knowles pulled up behind an SUV parked at the apex of the semicircular driveway. He got out and began to make his way to Sasha's side of the car, but she got out be-

fore he could help her. Sasha wanted the Ellises to know she was not expecting any
handouts, nor was she a pushover. She
wouldn't allow them to take what was rightfully hers.

It was cool and quiet inside the mansion as
Mr. Knowles led Sasha to a sitting room. During the short walk she could sense that Guana
Manor was a class act that smelled of lemon
oil with a hint of patchouli. It had been a long
time since Sasha had been intimidated, but intimidated she was as she sat on a striped chair
with its twin facing her on the opposite side
of a glass table. She browsed through a spread
of *Black Enterprise* and *People* magazines as the
minutes ticked away. By the time she was on
her fourth magazine Mr. Knowles reentered
the room.

"I'm really sorry. I had no idea you were
still sitting here waiting. Would you like something to drink? A glass of water? Some ice
tea?" he offered.

"No, I don't—"

"Olive," a voice spoke over the intercom.

"No, Mr. Cay, it's Baltron."

"Is someone waiting for me in there?"

He looked at Sasha. "Yes, there is."

"I'll be there right away."

"Yes, Mr. Cay," he replied. "It won't be
long now," he reassured Sasha before he disappeared.

Moments later a man entered the room looking at his watch. "I wish someone had told me
you were coming," he said, striding across the
floor.

"Are you Cay Ellis?" Sasha inquired.

"Yes."

"Then you should have known I was coming. You're the one who told me to come." His memory and his inconsideration were appalling.

"I don't know what you're talking abou—I remember you." He pointed. "You're the woman I found laid out in the field a few weeks ago."

"Laid out in the field!" Irritation and shame washed over Sasha. "I'm amazed that you remember something that happened weeks ago when you can't remember sending someone to my house to get me at seven-thirty this morning."

"I beg your pardon?" His tone was clipped.

"That's right. Here is the letter and the paper to prove it." Sasha tossed the papers on top of the magazines.

"I don't need to see your papers." Cay Ellis stood poised with his hands in his pockets. "I did not send for you or anyone else."

"This is ridiculous." Sasha threw up her hands. "So you don't know anything about this?" She pointed toward the letter and the document as a slim, well-kempt woman entered the room.

"Oh, here you are, Cay darling," she said, diverting his answer. "And who have we here?" She placed a perfumed hand against her cheek.

"I'm Sasha Townsend," Sasha replied, attempting to calm herself. "I was given this document this morning"—she passed it to the woman—"and this letter demanding that I come to Guana Manor. It has Mr. Ellis's name at the bottom, but he claims he did not send for me." Sasha threw Cay Ellis a challenging look.

"He didn't," the woman replied. "I did on behalf of my father-in-law, Cay Ellis Jr. I'm Sherry Ellis." She offered Sasha her hand.

Sasha noticed a large diamond and wedding band. "Oh, I see."

"Then why isn't Father down here to meet her?" Cay Ellis interjected.

"He's not feeling well, Cay. I wanted to tell you under more appropriate circumstances"— she glanced at Sasha—"but I didn't know you were back."

"I got in about an hour and a half ago. How is he?"

"He's fine," she hurried on. "If I had known you were back I would have had Olive prepare a special breakfast for you." She touched his cheek.

Sasha looked away. She didn't know why. A wife could touch her husband any way she wanted.

"I'm okay," he replied. "What is this about?" Cay pointed at the papers.

"The Bethel property," Sherry answered. "Ms. Townsend is doing some things over there that I know you wouldn't approve of, so I—"

"I inherited that land a few months ago," Sasha spoke up. "I've got the legal documents to prove it . It's my property, and I should be able to do whatever I want with it."

"You inherited the Bethel property?" Cay questioned, looking deep into Sasha's eyes.

"Yes, I did." Her steady gaze wavered under his probing.

"But I thought there was no inheritors."

"Obviously, there is," Sasha retorted.

"But it's not that simple, Ms. Townsend," Sherry Ellis stated. "The agreement makes it clear that although the Bethels have lived on that land for several generations and the house was theirs, the land actually belongs to the Ellises."

"What?" Sasha exclaimed.

Sherry Ellis turned away from Sasha and looked at Cay. "Baltron told me someone had been working on the property. So while you were gone I talked to Papa about it. I hate to say it, but he was in one of his moods. Although he did manage to tell me the original Bethel Agreement is in the family's files and has been there from the moment it was signed. So I thought it would be best to send Ms. Townsend this letter"—she gave him the paper—"in light of all you've been through."

Sasha watched him read it.

"You are clearing the land around the spring?"

"Yes." His question caught her off guard.

"Why? What do you plan to do?" he interrogated.

"I don't think that's any of your business," Sasha replied.

"I'm making it my business," he said sharply. Then he softened his approach. "If you don't mind."

"I was told she applied for a business permit." Sherry massaged her wrist. "You're planning to start a bottled water business, aren't you, Ms. Townsend?"

Sasha squinted. "How do you know that?"

"It's a matter of public record," Sherry informed her.

"A bottled water business." Cay Ellis's tone lowered substantially. He walked over and looked out the window. "That water should never be sold."

"And pray tell why is that?" Sasha couldn't believe how deep the Ellises had gotten into her affairs.

"You don't recall what happened to you? I had to literally pick you up after you sampled it."

With his close proximity Sasha remembered how natural it had felt to be in his arms. Their gazes held, and she knew he was remembering, too.

"So you two have met before?" Sherry asked, folding her arms.

"Yes," Cay replied.

Sasha collected herself and defended her actions. "There is nothing wrong with the water. I had it tested. It's not toxic and there's no salt in it."

"I didn't say there was anything wrong with it," Cay corrected her. "I said it should never be sold."

Sasha felt as if they were going around in circles. She decided to take another approach. "Look, I'm sorry you feel that way. I simply have a different opinion. And since the water is on my property, I have a right to do whatever I want with it."

"So you intend to go ahead with your plans?" he asked in a deceptively soft voice.

"It's my land," Sasha replied. "I can do whatever I want."

Silently, Cay Ellis studied Sasha's face before he looked away. "Sherry."

"Yes."

"You say we have the original document in our legal files."

"That's what Papa told me."

"Then I think you need to give that copy back to Ms. Townsend so that she will be familiar with the terms." He looked directly at Sasha as she took the papers. "I want you to know that I am of the opinion that the Bethel land cannot be altered or capitalized on in any way. I'm telling you that as the proprietor of Guana Manor and the owner of that land. Since I am acting in my father's stead, I prohibit you from doing any further clearing of the land around the spring."

Sasha couldn't believe what she was hearing. When she recovered from her shock she replied, "Well, I must tell you, Mr. and Mrs. Ellis, it has not been a pleasure meeting my new neighbors." She gave a fake smile. "It's a shame that we've gotten off to such a rotten start, but if this is the way you want it, that's the way it's going to be. You can be certain I'm going to seek legal advice on this, and I believe you don't have a chance in hell of winning with this ancient agreement." Sasha started for the door.

"Ms. Townsend," Cay called.

Sasha turned.

"There are a couple of things you're wrong about. I always have a chance, and"—he paused—"Sherry is my brother's widow."

Sasha and Cay locked gazes for the last time as Sherry watched with apparent interest.

Chapter 2

Sasha watched the legal secretary's fingers fly over the computer keys. Her desk was neat, and her voice professional when she answered the inner office telephone.

"Attorney Williams will see you now. Just go through the door." Her head bobbed but her hands never left the computer keyboard. "He's in the first office on the right."

"Thanks," Sasha said as she got up. She glanced at the clock on the wall. It was nearly lunchtime and she was hungry, but she had to take care of business first.

"Ms. Townsend," a man in his thirties said as he got up from behind his desk and extended his hand, "I'm Attorney Williams."

They settled down on opposite sides of the desk.

"What can I do for you?"

Sasha handed him the copy of the Bethel Agreement. "Have you seen a document like this before?" She was so anxious she couldn't wait for his answer. "This agreement claims the property I inherited is not mine. It says, to settle an old score, the Ellises gave my house to my relatives, the Bethels, but they didn't give them the land. According to this I don't own the land my house sits on."

"Well . . . can't say I have heard of this in particular, but with the folks down here all kinds of pacts were created to settle old island business. Caribbean Islands, I mean." He studied the document. "Did you know some of these Keys were settled by folks from the West Indies?"

"I've heard a bit about it," Sasha replied, not interested in a general history lesson at the moment.

"Well, it's a big thing down here in the Keys. All the people born here call themselves Conchs. I consider myself to be a Conch." A smile lit his average features. "But a while back, you had to be a descendant of the original Bahamians who settled the Keys to bear that label. This Key, Big Pine Key, was settled by a group of Bahamians. The Ellises were one of the families."

"So is that supposed to intimidate me?" Sasha was beginning to feel more and more like an outsider.

"Nope. Just thought you might want to know." He looked up at her, then back down at the paper. "But I tell you right now, I know the Ellises, and I know them pretty well. They're a big name in these parts. Even though they've had Guana Estate on Magic Key for at least four generations, they carry a pretty big stick in the entire Big Pine Key area."

"I get the picture." She reached for the document.

"Wait a minute." He pulled the paper toward him. "I just like to size up my opponents before I take them on. That's all. I'm not saying this to scare you away."

"So is this agreement legal?"

"It's got some legs to stand on, but I think they're pretty weak." He tapped his pen on the desk. "You know, these Keys are full of subcultures. Folks like to hold on to the past. It gives them a solid foundation to work from. People like knowing their beginnings. I'm talking about the Bahamians. They are proud of their heritage. But of course I don't need to tell you this. You're part Bahamian yourself. You've got to be. You inherited the land from Hazel Bethel. I'm assuming she's a relative of yours."

"She's a relative of mine, but I didn't know she was Bahamian until now."

"What d'ya mean?" He gave her an uncertain look.

"I didn't know the Bethels were Bahamians."

"But you're in the family, aren't you? You inherited the land." He leaned back as if he were questioning Sasha's credibility for the first time.

"Yes, I inherited the land. Hazel Bethel was my aunt. Her brother, Amos, was my father. But he and my mother never married." Sasha folded her hands in her lap. "It's a rather complicated story."

Attorney Williams chuckled. "Most family

histories are." He sat forward again. "So obviously, you didn't know anything about this agreement when you inherited the property."

"No, I didn't. As a matter of fact, I didn't know anything about it until this morning, when I was *summoned* to Guana Manor."

"Summoned? How so?" One eyebrow went up.

"I don't know what else to call it. This guy shows up at my door at seven-thirty this morning with this letter." Sasha slid the letter toward Attorney Williams. "I didn't know what the legal repercussions would be if I didn't obey, so I went."

"Uh-huh. So what is it? The Ellises want you out of the house and off of the property?"

"No, that's not it. Cay Ellis wants to stop me from starting a bottled water business using the natural springwater on the property."

"That is a mighty big project for a single woman to take on, don't you think?" Attorney Williams pulled at his mustache.

"We've got to get something straight right now if you're going to represent me." Sasha's patience had run out. "I came here because I'm new to the area and I don't know anyone. This bizarre situation was thrown at me this morning, and I knew I needed an attorney, fast. Your promotional flyer was stuck in my mailbox and I called you. Now, if you've got something against taking this case, it's fine. It's okay. But I don't plan to spend my time convincing you that my starting a bottled water business is a good idea."

Attorney Willams nodded. "You're right.

Sometimes I just get too caught up in these things." He adjusted his tie before proceeding. "So the Ellises don't want you to disturb the land."

"To be honest with you, I'm not sure. Cay Ellis Junior . . . no, he must be the third," Sasha corrected herself. "Cay Ellis the third doesn't want me to do anything with the springwater. That's what seemed to get his goat. He acknowledged there was nothing poisonous in the water, but he says it should never be drunk or sold. Sherry Ellis just wanted to do whatever he wanted. It was rather strange. I thought she was his wife, but then he tells me she's his sister-in-law."

"Yes. She was married to his half brother, Wally." Attorney Williams got up and walked over to the window. "It looks like that tropical storm is rolling in."

Sasha suddenly noticed that the natural light in the office had dimmed. "It sure does," she agreed, looking at the gray-tinted sky through the glass.

"We always get hit with storms. It's part of the price you pay for living in paradise. It's part of the Key's history, just like the stories. There are all kinds of stories floating around." He stuck his hands in his pockets. "One of the stories claims that water is part of the Fountain of Youth Ponce de León discovered. Another one claims the water flows from an underground system that was used on Atlantis." He faced Sasha. "You ever heard of the continent of Atlantis?"

"Yes, I've heard of it, but isn't that a myth?"

"As far as a lot of people are concerned, the jury's still out on that. You've got geologists and all kinds of professionals still investigating it. Of course, other folks think they're wasting their time."

"You don't believe those stories, do you?" Sasha sensed she might have picked the wrong attorney. Perhaps she'd acted too quickly.

"I'm a native of these parts. I've seen some of everything, so I don't rule out anything," he rushed on. "But I think what's important to you is that I can free you up from this agreement." He leaned over and studied the papers again. "That is, if the Ellises don't produce any other legal document proving the land is theirs. It might take a little while, because the Ellises are pretty big stuff around here and they have some influence with the courts." He turned the agreement over. "But you can get a fair shake at the law in these parts, so I think it can be done."

Sasha smiled slightly. "Good. I guess that's all I needed to hear."

The room fell silent.

"Give me about a week and I'll have a report for you," Attorney Williams assured her. "Make sure you leave your phone number with my secretary so I can contact you if I need to."

"All right." Sasha stood up. "What will your fee be for this, Attorney Williams?"

"Let me see what all this will entail." He rubbed his chin. "But it shouldn't be more than three hundred dollars." They walked to his office door.

"I've got one more question for you," Sasha told him.

"Yes?" His eyebrows knitted together.

"Can you recommend a good place for me to have lunch?"

"I sure can." He smiled. "It's got to be Myers Seafood Café. Once you leave out of here, you go back up to the main intersection and turn right. Keep straight and you'll see them on the left-hand side."

"Got it." Sasha reached out to shake his hand again. "Thank you."

"Thank you," Attorney Williams replied.

She had eaten some of the best seafood chowder she'd ever had, and the sky looked ominous as Sasha climbed into her Mazda. The storm that had been threatening earlier was quickly moving in, but Sasha felt at ease about the business with the Ellises. Attorney Williams was a little offbeat, but Sasha felt he could handle the job. As he said, he was a Conch, this was his territory, and she believed he knew the ins and outs of the system, legally and politically.

Thunder rumbled in the distance as Sasha pulled up in front of her house. She had anticipated working on the spring, but when she looked at the sky she knew rain was imminent. There was plenty for her to do inside and around the house in the meantime. Sasha unlocked the front door.

She had barely stepped inside when a powerful smell surrounded her. Her eyes began to burn and she began to cough. It was the smell of bleach—and an awful lot of it. She couldn't believe what had happened. Someone had deliberately vandalized her house!

Instinctively, she covered her nose with the sleeve of her blouse as she looked around the room. Bleached-out white trails crisscrossed the old couch and the overstuffed chair. The clothes that were stacked on the couch were ruined as well.

Each breath was difficult as she entered her bedroom. There was more evidence of the destructive bleach on her bed and inside her closet. Finally, the fumes became too much. Sasha hurried to the front of the house, threw open the door, and stepped into the fresh air. Her hands covered her eyes as she gagged and coughed. The rain that began to fall was a welcome relief.

Sasha's eyes continued to burn even after the coughing stopped. Gratefully, she gulped the clean air. She gazed off into the distance as she thought about who might be responsible. Sasha didn't have to think long. No one but Cay Ellis could be behind it. It made no sense that a man of his status would get involved in this kind of prank, but there were no other suspects.

The rain began to fall faster. By the time Sasha reached her car the rain was coming down in sheets and the wind was gaining strength. She was wet and furious when she jumped inside the car and closed the door behind her.

"So the Ellises think they can do whatever they want because they are big stuff in the Big Pine Key area," Sasha fumed. "They obviously felt powerful enough to wreak havoc with my life, and they didn't feel there would be any ramifications, either."

Sasha had experience with the heavy hand of people in power who didn't care how their decisions affected those beneath them. Her mother could have benefited greatly from specialized medical assistance, but the people at the HMO office said they could not bend the rules. They knew her mother would suffer, but they didn't care. It didn't matter that it was a life-or-death situation. To them she wasn't a human being, she was a financial liability. Sasha recalled how she surrendered all her pride in seeking help for her mother. She had left no stone unturned, but in the end there was no help to be found.

Sasha had felt broken, defeated. Yet it was her mother, knowing any day could be her last, who reminded her, "Your intention and your effort were the most important things. They are the seeds for the rest of your life. You may not see the results when you think you should, but they will come, and you will have grown because of them." Sasha never forgot the strength and wisdom her mother possessed in the dusk of her life.

She gripped the steering wheel as she visualized her mother's face. "Cay Ellis is not going to get away with this," she declared. "I won't be able to get the law to do anything because I can't prove he was behind it. But I can give him a piece of my mind, and I'm going to do it right now."

Chapter 3

The rain was relentless and driving was difficult. By the time Sasha pulled up in front of Guana Manor the wind sounded like a pack of wolves on the prowl. Her white clothes stuck to her body as Sasha rang the doorbell again and again.

A heavyset woman answered the melodious chimes. She inspected the doorbell button as if Sasha might have damaged it before she addressed her. "May I help you?"

"I don't think you can, but speaking to Cay Ellis might do me some good," Sasha replied.

The woman was surprised by her frankness. "Oh . . . do you mean Cay Ellis Junior or Cay Ellis the third?" She lifted her chin as she made the differentiation. At that moment a heavy spray of rain caught Sasha from behind and splattered the woman's face.

"It's Cay Ellis the third," Sasha told her, cringing from the onslaught of water. "May I come in? If you haven't noticed, I'm getting soaked standing here."

The woman hesitated, wiping her eyes. "I-I

33

guess so," she stammered before she stepped aside.

Sasha felt the woman might not have given in so easily if her own face had not been drenched. She watched as more rain blew inside before the woman muscled the door closed with her shoulder and her weight. "I'll go get Mr. Ellis." She dabbed her face with her apron as she walked away.

Rivulets of water poured onto the rug where Sasha stood. She removed the Scrunchy that was at the end of her ponytail puff and attempted to smooth and tighten the style. She could hear voices approaching. The woman's words were barely audible, but Cay Ellis's rich tone was clear.

"Well, who is it?"

"I don't know, Mr. Cay. She was ringing the doorbell as if Satan himself had a hold of her hand. I was afraid she would break it."

"You didn't ask her name?" Cay Ellis persisted.

"I didn't have a chance. There she was, standing there like a wet chicken demanding to come in."

Cay Ellis III and the housekeeper emerged from the hall. The woman hushed accordingly.

"So it's you." He stopped a few feet away from Sasha, one hand in his pocket, the other arm hanging casually at his side.

"You didn't expect to see me again so soon, or did you?"

"No." He paused, pointedly studying her drenched appearance. "I can't say I did."

"Well, you should have. Did you honestly

think I wouldn't do anything?" Sasha tried to keep the water running down from her hair out of her face. "Obviously, you didn't think anybody else would do anything, either."

"Olive"—Cay Ellis motioned with his head—"go get Ms. Townsend a towel, please, and bring the bathrobe from the second guest bedroom as well," he called as the housekeeper went to do his bidding.

"I don't want it. I've already seen a display of your kind of hospitality," Sasha defied him. "You're insincere and a hypocrite, and I don't want your handouts."

One of his eyebrows went up. "Ms. Townsend, you're soaked to the skin," he said huskily. "And I am sincere."

"I don't believe you."

"That's your choice."

They looked into each other's eyes. His were dark enough to disappear in, and there was no way to ignore the spark of something between them that had nothing to do with anger. It perturbed yet excited Sasha.

Sasha tore away from his gaze and surveyed the opulence of Guana Manor. She shook her head. "I don't understand. You have everything you could possibly need and more here. Why did you—"

"Yes, Guana Manor is beautiful," Cay interrupted her, "but sometimes things aren't as simple as they seem."

"I see this as a simple matter, Mr. Ellis." Sasha knew they both could feel the pulsing energy passing between them. "And I don't want to go off on any tangents. As rude as this sounds I don't know your history, and I don't want to know it. I want us to focus on the subject at hand."

"That's going to be rather difficult to do," he said, his eyes hooded.

"And why is that?"

"It's rather hard to concentrate seeing you as I see you now."

"What?" Sasha said, confused.

Once again his eyes perused her body, but this time when they reached her face there was a definite fire beneath their depths. "I am human, Ms. Townsend, no matter how you may paint me."

Sasha looked down. The rain had made her white poet's shirt and stretch pants transparent. This time her habit of not wearing a bra was of major consequence. Still, Sasha's gaze didn't waver when she looked back at him, covering herself with her arms.

"So are you still not taking handouts?" His eyes were impenetrable, but one side of his mouth tilted upward.

"No, I'm not." She swallowed, and held her position.

"So you've solved my dilemma," he replied. "Part of me wanted to offer the bathrobe to you because I thought it would be the proper, neighborly thing to do. But the other part of me . . ."

The clicking of Olive's heels stopped Cay Ellis from going any further. With a look of disdain, the housekeeper handed the robe and the towel to Sasha. She continued to stand there, obviously curious about what was transpiring.

"I believe Baltron needs you in the kitchen, Olive," Cay informed her.

"Baltron isn't—" She stopped and pursed her lips. "All right. Excuse me, please." Olive turned away, unhappy with her dismissal.

Sasha felt ashamed, but she couldn't let Cay Ellis know it. "Why did you have someone pour bleach inside my house? On my clothes? Everything is ruined," she accused. "Then I come over here and you act like the concerned neighbor."

"Bleach?" His features were a mirror of confusion.

"Yes, bleach. Perhaps you don't know what bleach is, since you obviously never have to use it. You just get others to do your dirty work," Sasha added sarcastically as the wind rattled the windows and the foyer darkened by degrees.

"I didn't send anyone to the Bethel House," Cay Ellis replied.

"How did I know you were going to say that?" Sasha slapped the towel against her leg.

"Maybe because it's true."

"Well, Mr. Ellis, if you didn't send anyone, who did?"

"I don't know."

Sasha's frustration level reached its maximum. "And I don't know why I'm here. No, now, that's not true. I do know why." She locked into his gaze. "I didn't think the law would do anything about the vandalism, but I had to speak up for myself and let you know you had no right to do it," she proclaimed. "Yes, I'm new here. I've only been here a week. I don't know anybody, and this stuff between the Bethels and the Ellises . . . I never heard of it until yesterday. But I do know you had no right to send somebody into my house to do what they did."

"As I told you before"—his tone remained steady—"I had nothing to do with that."

"This is ridiculous." Sasha headed for the door.

"Where do you think you're going?"

"I'm going home." Sasha placed her hand on the knob and pulled.

Immediately, Cay Ellis prevented Sasha from opening the door. "Didn't you hear the weather report? A hurricane will be making landfall within the next twenty-four hours," he announced. "We have massive flooding in this area. By now it will be impossible for you to drive back to the main road. The land slopes near the entrance of Guana Estate. Water fills up very fast there. I'm surprised you didn't encounter any flooding on your way over."

"Well, I didn't. And I'll be the judge of when and where I can drive," Sasha replied. She could not imagine staying at Guana Manor for another moment. Cay Ellis's ability to lie to her face made Sasha uncertain about even more drastic methods he might use to keep her from commercializing the spring. But if she didn't open the business, how would she take care of herself? It would be very difficult to find work in such a small community, and it wouldn't be long before she'd run out of money and have to leave Magic Key. Sasha took off the bathrobe and held it out between them. "Now let me out of here."

Cay Ellis looked at Sasha's determined expression, took the robe, and stepped away from the door.

Sasha bolted into the rain.

From the window, Cay watched Sasha struggle to get into her car. It took both hands to open the front door, but moments later her red Mazda was swallowed up by the torrential rain.

Cay had never seen so much determination in a woman's eyes before. Not even in Precious's eyes while she was alive; she had possessed an independent spirit, too. It was one of the reasons he'd married her. But as her obsession took her further and further away, Cay knew that same independent spirit had contributed to her death.

Still, while she lived, Precious had been a light in his life. During their brief years of marriage she had been happy, and for the first time in years Cay had been content. Theirs was an unorthodox union for sure. They had never shared the physical union that most couples shared, and Cay had never expected it. It was his way of trying to make amends for his family's extraordinary appetite for things of the flesh and other worldly desires. But in the end it hadn't mattered. His life remained an outgrowth of what he had tried to deny, the Bethel Curse: an unfulfilled life where death loomed if that unfulfillment was threatened.

No one could ever be close to him without being enveloped by its darkness . . . not even a soul as bright as his wife, Precious.

His mouth set into a grim line as he wondered if the day would come when he was no longer a prisoner of the past. He thought of Sasha Townsend's determined face. She was very much planted in the present and looking forward to her future. Maybe that accounted for the magnetism between them. She was a free spirit who refused to be chained by anything. He was a man chained from birth. Opposites attract, and he could not deny the attraction he had for her.

Cay recalled how Sasha's dark eyes flashed when she realized he could see her breasts through the rain-soaked shirt. She did not cower or appear to be shamed. For Cay, her attitude only heightened his awareness of her physical beauty. If he touched her, would he be able to feel her love for life? he wondered.

But touching Sasha in the way he wanted to was out of the question. She wholeheartedly believed he was responsible for the Bethel House's being vandalized. He stared at the blanketing rain. He had told her the truth. Something like that simply wasn't his style. He didn't fight his fights in such a manner. He didn't have to. He, like the rest of the Ellises, allowed the Ellis fortune to do all his fighting for him. If he really set his mind to it, he could influence the right people and tie the Bethel property up in court for maybe a year. Eventually, he might not win, but by then Sasha

Townsend would probably be broke or so discouraged that her bottled water idea would have passed.

Cay watched the pine trees yield to the wind like weeping willow branches. The walkway in front of the house had become a shallow stream, and the rain was so dense he could not see the tiles beyond it.

"I thought I heard you talking to someone, Cay," Sherry said as she descended the stairs.

"I was. Sasha Townsend was here."

"Why?" Sherry's voice was blank.

"Someone poured bleach inside her house. She thought I was responsible." He continued to stare out the window.

"That goes to show what kind of person she is." She stepped down onto the Italian tile floor. "Thinking that you would stoop to something like that. You're above that kind of trickery. It sounds like some island foolishness to me. Olive and Baltron will be claiming the *chiccharnie* did it."

"Island foolishness?" He turned to her. "Be careful, Sherry. My roots are in the islands. I'm not going to stand here and allow you to belittle my people's beliefs."

"You know that's not my intention, Cay." She stood beside him. "I love the Bahamian culture. There are many things about it that I find fascinating. I wish I had been born to it."

"Did Wally know that?" His eyes became hooded.

"I-I guess so," she stammered. "If he didn't, it wasn't my fault."

"He was your husband. You could have reassured him just like you reassured me," Cay said quietly.

"I'm sure I did." Sherry touched his arm. "I just haven't been right since Wally died. You know, in a way I'm still grieving for him."

"No . . . I didn't know." Cay looked at her hand on his arm.

"Why are you so distant?" Sherry's laugh was brittle. "Did you allow that Townsend woman to upset you?" She turned toward the window with a flounce. "Anyone who would be stupid enough to come out in this storm isn't worth the bother."

Cay studied the jagged lines of lightning in the sky as an image of Sasha's frightened face surfaced. Somehow he knew she was in trouble. "Once again, Sherry, I disagree with you." He walked over to the front door and opened it, leaving water and wind in his wake.

~

Chapter 4

Cay was grateful the man had talked him into buying an SUV. The vehicle was heavy enough to stand up to the wind, and because of its height the rising water on the road only reached the middle of the tires. He leaned toward the windshield as he drove, his lights on high beam. The familiar road seemed longer than usual. Cay knew it was because he was anxious.

The land began to slope, and the water began to move faster. He hoped Sasha Townsend had made it past the main flood point, but with the way things looked, her chances were slim. Cay rounded a bend and thought he saw red in the distance. As he advanced his heart quickened. It was the Mazda. And if his vision served him right through the heavy rain, the car had stopped with the water just below the windows.

Sasha couldn't believe how fast the water was rising both inside and outside of the car. There was at least six inches of water on the floor, and she could see the water lapping at the window on the driver's side.

Everything had happened so quickly. In the beginning, the Mazda had been able to navigate the water pretty well. The water was deep, but not too deep, and Sasha believed she could make it home. Then the landscape must have changed, because the water grew steadily deeper before the car cut off. She had only been sitting there for mere seconds before the water starting coming inside. The next thing Sasha knew she could hear it lapping against the car door, and now it was clearly at the base of the windows.

Sasha was scared. She could feel the force of the water rocking the small vehicle, and she knew the car could be swept away. She put her feet up on the seat. She needed to get out and get out fast. Sasha tried to think the situation through, but the water was beginning to soak the car seat. Panic-stricken, she reached for the door handle, and that's when she noticed the steady beam of light. She looked out the rear window and saw headlights.

Cay Ellis stopped before he reached the point where the water would be considerably deeper. Before he climbed out of the vehicle, he secured one end of the heavy rope he had with him around his waist and then tied the other end to the luggage rack on top of the SUV. He couldn't help but think how luck had to have been with them, as he was not a man to believe in the positive forces of the spirits. Normally, he would not have had a rope. He only had one now because the captain of his new cabin cruiser had overstocked his craft. Cay had brought the rope back with him from the marina that morning.

He knew he didn't have much time, so he worked quickly and steadily. There would not be a second chance, and the sailor's knot had to hold. Cay jumped down into the water and prayed Sasha Townsend would have the fortitude to stay inside the vehicle until he reached her. The way the water was rushing, if she climbed out, she would probably be swept away.

Sasha couldn't see anything but the two headlights. She waited for them to come closer, but they didn't appear to be moving forward. She tried to calm her nerves as she judged the two orbs. Finally, Sasha determined the lights were not moving and the deep water had changed the driver's mind.

Her shoes were covered by water, and outside the car water was splashing against the middle of the window. Panicked, Sasha decided to climb through it. She began to roll the window down but realized it would be impossible. The water was too high. "I've got to get out of here! If I wait any longer it may be too late!"

Sasha grabbed the passenger bar with one hand, then reached for the door handle with the other. With her adrenaline surging, she took a deep breath, turned the handle, and pushed. The water did the remainder of the work when it rushed inside the vehicle. Sasha could feel the car giving way when the door was forced open, but she continued to hold on to the passenger bar. Just as she thought she and the Mazda would be swept away, a strong pair of arms grabbed her around the middle.

"I've got you," a voice yelled above the water. "Let go of the car."

Sasha recognized Cay Ellis's voice. He had come to help her. Her mind and emotions churned, but Sasha did as Cay instructed. "I've got you," he repeated with his lips pressed reassuringly against her ear.

The force of the water pushed the car sideways, and Sasha and Cay followed behind it. Cay locked his arms around Sasha's waist as they held their heads above the water. They were victims of the current until the rope ran out before they were jerked backward suddenly.

"Hold on," he yelled. Sasha pressed against him, holding on to his arms. The whiplash was short but powerful. Once it was over and they were somewhat stable, all of Sasha's energy seemed to drain away. Involuntarily, she closed her eyes. She could feel Cay's breathing. It was as rapid as her own.

"We're not done yet," he told her.

"I never would have guessed," Sasha quipped.

"What a time to find out there is a jokester beneath that fiery exterior. A *chiccharnie*," he spoke in her ear. "But now I need you to help us out. You've got to turn and face me. I need you to hold on to me so I can pull us back to the SUV."

"All right." Sasha's voice was shaky, but she began to maneuver herself within Cay's arms right away. It was moments before she was staring into Cay's rain-soaked face as he repeated, "Don't worry. We're going to be okay."

Sasha nodded her head. "I know. I know."

Sasha clung to Cay until they got to the SUV. Once it was in reach she grabbed hold of the door handle and climbed inside. Breathing hard, she watched Cay untie the rope from around his waist, remove it from the luggage rack, then toss it into the water. When he settled down beside her he dropped his chin to his chest and closed his eyes. Sasha sat beside him in silence. She didn't know what to say. Cay had risked his life for her. No one had ever dared so much. The bad image she had of him tumbled with the weight of it.

"That was a close call, wasn't it?" he said.

"Yes, it was," Sasha said softly.

He gave her a sidelong look; a slight smile touched his lips just as Sasha began to shiver.

"Cold?"

"Yes." Her teeth chattered.

Cay reached behind them and grabbed a navy blazer off the backseat. He gave it to Sasha. "Why don't you put this on."

By now she was having the shakes from a combination of things: chill, relief, gratitude, and more. She followed his suggestion. "Thank you." The two words seemed so inept, but at that moment Sasha was afraid to say more. She was on the verge of saying things she feared she might regret later.

They drove back to Guana Manor in silence as the storm continued to raise its voice in a combination of wind, rain, thunder, and lightning. When they arrived at the house Cay came around to open Sasha's door. She waited and allowed him to assist her. Exhausted and soaked, they approached the stairs together.

Cay placed a protective arm around Sasha's shoulder as they forced their way up the stairs.

"Cay! Are you all right?" Sherry ran to him as they entered the house.

"I'm fine." He closed the door with difficulty.

Sherry rushed on. "You're soaked to the skin! What happened? Where's Ms. Townsend's car?"

Sasha was aware that Sherry did not address her directly.

"It was swept away in the flood," Cay replied.

"In the flood! My God! You could have been killed." Sherry stroked his wet head.

"What's going on down there?" a man's voice called from the top of the stairs.

"Everything's fine, Father. There's been some flooding near the main entrance. There's nothing for you to worry about."

"Well, if there isn't, why is Sherry yelling like a banshee?"

"Cay almost drowned out there," Sherry called up to her father-in-law.

"Why are you out of bed?" Olive Knowles scolded Mr. Ellis as she mounted the stairs.

"You know the doctor said to get plenty of rest over the next few days."

"I was resting until I heard the banshee down there."

Sasha looked up and saw Cay Ellis Jr. pointing a shaky finger toward Sherry.

"Oh, Papa. Don't call me that. Cay's half dead and all you can do is call me names."

Cay looked at Sasha. "We do have a guest," he reminded the household. "She's been through quite an ordeal. Olive, I want you to put Sasha in the guest bedroom on the second floor."

"She's going to be staying?" Sherry asked point-blank.

"Are you suggesting she leave in this weather?" Cay's voice was low.

"No, I wasn't suggesting that." She pouted a little. "I just thought that she would be able to go home before the night was over. That's all." She looked at Sasha.

"Well, the way it's looking out there it's going to be a lo-ong night," Olive said as she began to descend the stairs.

"We've got to get the hurricane shutters in place," Cay advised.

"We started on that a short while ago," Olive told him. "Baltron and I were in the middle of putting them up when you came in."

"There are only a few left to do, Mr. Cay," Baltron added.

"I'll help you," Mr. Ellis volunteered.

"You won't do any such thing," Olive reprimanded him. "You need to go back to bed."

"I'm going to help them, Father," Cay said.

"I think you should do as the doctor said and get some rest." He turned to Sasha. "Will you be okay?"

"I'll be fine." Sasha gave him a weak smile.

"Yes, she'll be fine, Cay. We'll take good care of her," Sherry interjected, her smile too sweet. "I would offer you one of my outfits but I think you're too big to fit my clothes. By the way, what size do you wear?"

Sasha thought it was one of the most insincere offers she'd ever had. "That's okay." Sasha shook her head. "I'll—"

"Olive, find Sasha something to wear from the clothes in the Blue Room," Cay announced.

"Sir?" Olive's eyes widened.

"You heard me. I'm sure there's something she can wear in there. There are some brand-new clothes in the cedar closet."

Sherry lowered stiffened arms to her sides as she listened.

"All right, Mr. Cay," Olive responded. "From what I *recall* she is about the right size. Would you like to come with me, Ms. Townsend?"

"Sure." Sasha could feel the woman's resistance, but she followed the housekeeper up the stairs. The entire household's eyes were on her.

"So you're the woman who is staying in the Bethel House now," Cay Ellis Jr. commented as Sasha advanced.

"Yes, I am."

He leaned forward and examined her. "You're a Bethel, all right. You sort of favor

Hazel, but she was a dark-skinned woman. Did you know you favored her?"

"No. No, I didn't." Sasha was uncomfortable beneath his gray-ringed stare. "I didn't know her, or any of the Bethels. You could say our relationship was very distant."

"That may be. But I hear it was close enough for you to think you inherited that land," Mr. Ellis said, peering at her. "And you do look like Hazel when she was young." He turned his back on her and headed for his bedroom. "She could be relentless, too, just like the Bethel that started this entire mess."

Sasha didn't know how Cay Ellis Jr. figured he knew so much about her. Perhaps he had been listening to the conversation she and Cay had before she went out into the storm. She wasn't certain. But she had drawn one conclusion, Cay Ellis Jr. was a man to speak his mind, for good or for bad.

"Here you are right here, Ms. Townsend." Olive opened the bedroom door. "You should be quite comfortable. I think you will find everything you need. I'll have to bring you another bathrobe since it was *necessary* for you to use the first one earlier."

Sasha ignored Olive Knowles's inference. "That will be fine," she said.

Olive started to leave but stopped midway. "And by the way, please be careful when you use the containers in the bathroom down the hall. Some of those bottles are antiques. My *niece*, Precious"—she emphasized the relationship—"used to collect them. I'm sure Mr. Cay wouldn't want them damaged or broken." Olive's eyes were downcast but her chin had a stubborn tilt.

It was obvious that neither Olive nor Sherry wanted her at Guana Manor. Sasha had news for them: she didn't want to be there, either. "I can assure you that won't be a problem," Sasha replied.

Olive nodded and left the room. Moments later she returned with another bathrobe. "If you are in the bath when I come back I'll lay the clothes on the bed."

"Thank you." Sasha watched Olive close the door.

The bath was refreshing. When Sasha was done she dried off and tightened her hair. Sasha didn't realize how tired she was until she sat on the bed and found herself lying down beside the outfits Olive had brought her. A blue pants set caught her attention as the rain pelted against the window, but Sasha's eyes closed before she could examine it closer.

Chapter 5

Sasha was awakened by a noise near her head. Her vision was fuzzy as she became aware of a yellow haze surrounding the bed. The remainder of the room was pitch-black.

"I thought you might need these." It was Cay's voice reaching out to her from the dark.

"Need what?" Sasha replied groggily.

"Candles. This is an old house. The storm blew out some of the circuits."

"I see," Sasha replied, sitting up.

"You don't have to get up. I was trying to put them down without waking you."

"No. I've probably slept too long as it is. What time is it?"

"About six-thirty," Cay replied from the shadows.

Sasha couldn't see Cay but she could smell his aftershave. "I want to thank you for coming after me." Sasha peered into the darkness. "I don't know—where are you?" she asked, frustrated.

"I'm right here." Cay moved within the circle of light and stood over her.

Everything was out of sorts. Cay seemed so tall. "I've got to admit this is a little awkward."

"Is this better?" He knelt beside the bed.

"I wasn't referring to where you were standing," Sasha said nervously. "I was talking about after having bleach poured throughout my house . . . thanking you for anything. You have to admit we are on opposite sides of the fence, so to speak."

"That could be taken literally. The Bethel property is surrounded by trees separating it from the Guana Estate. You've seen the beachfront directly in back of the Bethel House?"

"Yes. Isn't that public property?"

"No, it's part of the estate," he said softly. "The Bethel property sits almost in the middle of my land."

"How can that be?" Sasha squinted.

"Magic Key is essentially Guana Estate. The only part that's public property is the beach near the bridge."

Sasha looked down to gather herself. "So you know what I mean when I say we're on opposite sides of the fence."

"I understand clearly." His eyes remained on her face.

"But I am grateful that you rescued me. I want you to know that, no matter what happens down the road."

"How grateful are you?" Cay inquired softly.

"What?" Sasha looked into his eyes, her senses on edge.

"How grateful are you?" he repeated the question.

Sasha tried to figure out if he was kidding. His eyes were hooded, but she could feel their intensity. Cay Ellis had saved her life. Was he trying to use that as a bargaining tool in the Bethel property dispute? Just when she was beginning to believe there could be a warm heart beneath all his money and power Cay had disappointed her. "Not enough to give you the Bethel property," Sasha declared.

"Is that what you think this is about?" Cay leaned closer.

"Isn't it?" Sasha could feel his breath on her face but she refused to back away.

"No, not now," he said huskily. "It's about this." He pressed his lips against hers.

Neither Cay nor Sasha closed their eyes. He watched her, wondering what her reaction would be. He could sense her body stiffen, but her lips were pliant with a hint of moistness. Cay did not feel her give in to the kiss, but she did not pull away. He believed she was surprised more than anything else. "You didn't foresee that I wanted to kiss you?" he asked, his lips near hers.

"Not really" was Sasha's noncommittal reply. "Should I have?" She turned her face to the side, but their closeness remained. "Why did you kiss me? Did you just want to see what I would do?"

"What do you think?" Cay tried not to show that she had surprised him.

"I think a man who truly wanted to kiss me, and make me feel it, would have closed his eyes." She leaned back on an extended arm and locked into his gaze.

Cay liked the challenge he saw there. Sasha Townsend was a woman with a fighting spirit. In love and in life. "Are you saying that to bait me, so I will do it again?" His eyes sparkled.

A glimpse of a smile touched her lips. "No, I'm saying it so if it happens again you will mean it, and I'll know it."

There was a tap on the door before it opened. Olive stood in the doorway with more candles.

"I'm sorry, Mr. Cay. I didn't expect for you to be in here." She batted her eyes as she tried to think of the proper thing to say. "I thought, with the power out, that Ms. Townsend would need some candles."

"She did"—Cay got up slowly—"but I've met all her needs."

Sasha looked at him and wondered if he was aware of the double entendre. She decided he was and had used it for Olive's benefit.

"Well, I guess she won't need these, will she?" Olive replied.

"No, she couldn't be happier." He looked back at Sasha. "Dinner starts at seven, Sasha," he announced before he slipped past the housekeeper.

Sasha wondered how much larger Olive's eyes could get. She didn't know what Cay Ellis was up to, but she wasn't going to be caught trying to explain her virtue to anyone. Especially not Olive Knowles, who wouldn't think that highly of her no matter what she said.

"Well, I'll be," Sasha heard Olive say as she turned on her heels and closed the door.

Sasha gazed into the candle flame. "I've got to stay the night here at Guana Manor, but I will not be a pawn in the Ellises' affairs," she declared. "I don't know what Cay Ellis's motives are, but if I'm to play the game I will play it my way."

Sasha concluded that her reaction to his kiss wasn't what Cay Ellis had expected. Had she bruised his male ego? The thought made her smile. She had to believe that wasn't done very easily, and something inside of her rejoiced because she had touched him in a unique way. Perhaps that was why he wanted the housekeeper to think something had gone on between them. *But in truth, hadn't there?* a little voice inside her head asked.

Sasha lit two of the candles and the room brightened. She looked at the sky-blue pants set lying across the bed as she thought. Cay Ellis had no idea who he was dealing with. She was certain she could give him whatever he was looking for and more. What Sasha was unclear about was why she would want to.

Sasha could hear the conversation in the dining area before she entered the room. It was a gorgeous setting. The only time she had seen anything like it was on television.

"They say the storm is going to be real bad." The elder Mr. Ellis patted the table with his hand.

"I hope it doesn't uproot the trees I had planted in the east garden." Sherry straightened her napkin. "That garden is nearly perfect."

"You've been working on it long enough and spending more than enough money," Mr. Ellis remarked.

"Well, you know that garden has been my special project, and getting it just right means a lot to me," Sherry replied.

"Speaking of perfect"—Mr. Ellis's mouth widened into a smile—"Sasha Townsend, you look just that." He tossed a side glance at Sherry. "Come in. Come in." Mr. Ellis rose from his chair. "You can sit here to the right of me. If that's all right with you, Cay?"

"Why not?" Cay said with his back to Sasha.

As she walked by him, she could feel his eyes on her. Cay sat at the opposite end of the table from his father, while Sherry sat to Cay's right. There were two other place settings gracing the table.

"My, my, my, isn't that a pretty dress," Mr. Ellis exclaimed as Sasha reached him. He kissed her hand with a loud smack. "We can never have too much beauty in the house, can we, Cay?"

"Never," was Cay's reply.

Sasha glanced at Cay before she sat down. She wondered what kind of relationship the two Ellis men shared.

"Baltron," Mr. Ellis called, "why don't you give Olive some help with the rest of the food.

By the time you both sit down, everything's going to be cold," he complained.

Olive came through the swinging door with a large dish. Baltron was behind her with another. "To be honest with you, Mr. Ellis, I don't feel right eating in here with you all like this."

"And why not? You prefer eating in the hot kitchen when we have a beautiful setup in here?"

"I like eating in the kitchen. I've been doing it for forty years, and—."

"And I've been knowing you for longer than that, so it's not going to hurt a thing for you to sit in here and eat with us," Mr. Ellis declared, shaking his head. "What is it going to take to get you out of that kitchen?"

Baltron gave him a long look before he sat down.

The food smelled wonderful and it looked scrumptious as well. Olive announced each dish as she removed the lids. Sasha could tell this was a part of the housekeeper's work that boosted her pride.

"So is all of the food Bahamian?" Sasha inquired.

"Not all of it. The gumbo, conch fritters, and johnnycakes are, but the rest are my inventions," Olive informed her.

"You should be real hungry, Ms. Townsend," Mr. Ellis chimed in. "I hear you and Cay had it pretty rough out there."

"Yes, we did." She glanced at Cay, who was sitting back in his chair watching in a black silk shirt. There was a handsome broodiness about him. "I have to say, it was kind of scary for a while."

"I'm glad he was there to help you. Because no matter how it might seem with everything that's going on, we're pretty good neighbors. At least, I think we are. I hope you come to believe that." Mr. Ellis shoveled in several spoonfuls of food. "Hey! Wait a minute! Where is the wine?" he boomed.

"The doctor said you shouldn't—" Olive started.

"If you remind me of one more thing that doctor said, I'm really going to be sick," Mr. Ellis warned, leaning across the table with his fork in his hand. "For God's sake, I fell. Anybody can fall."

"I'll get your wine for you, Papa," Sherry offered, pushing back her chair.

"No, I want Sasha to get it. Is it all right for me to call you by your first name?" he asked.

Sasha tilted her head. "Sure."

His smile broadened. "It's good to have a new woman in the house. These blessings are so few and far between." He looked at Cay.

Sasha could feel their eyes on her. "I'll get your wine, Mr. Ellis. Where is it?"

"Over there in the cabinet behind the plate with the Chinese scenery. That's where Olive always hides it."

Olive rolled her eyes.

Sasha got the wine and gave it to Mr. Ellis.

"Yep, it sure is good to have another pretty woman around here," Mr. Ellis repeated as he poured the wine, and Sasha wondered about the real reason behind his praise.

Sherry's utensils clattered as she laid them on her plate. "I'm rather surprised that dress was in the Blue Room," she said, her eyes like wood.

"It was," Olive confirmed, "but there was more of it when I gave it to her," she added in a low voice.

"More of it?" Sherry eyed Sasha.

"I decided I liked it without the pants," Sasha informed her as she ate.

"Oh. Then I was right." Sherry wriggled with satisfaction. "I thought that wasn't Precious's taste. Precious would never do something like that."

"Precious?" Sasha repeated the name.

"Yes, Cay's wife. The one that passed away." Sherry sat up triumphantly. "You didn't know you were wearing her clothes?"

"No, I didn't realize it." Sasha looked at Cay.

"Cay darling, you should have told her," Sherry advised him, doe-eyed. "It seems to have unnerved her a bit."

"I think it would take more than that to unnerve Ms. Townsend. Or am I wrong?" He looked at Sasha as if she were being tested.

"To know I am wearing your dead wife's clothes . . ." Sasha stated straight out. "I must admit, I would consider that a bit unnerving."

"The clothes in the cedar closet were brand-new," Cay advised her. "Precious never wore them. I bought them as a gift to surprise her. She died before I could give them to her."

Silence filled the room.

"See, that's what I'm talking about. We need

some new life in here." Mr. Ellis drained his glass as the lights flickered. He laughed. "Even Precious would agree with me."

"Don't start that mess, Papa." Sherry glanced nervously around the table.

"You say that because you know I'm telling the truth," Mr. Ellis went on. "She wouldn't agree with some other things that have been brewing around here."

"Precious wasn't the kind of person who judged others." Sherry's hand tightened on her glass.

Olive put down her fork abruptly. "I remember a time when we weren't so free when talking about the *sperrids*."

"Well, you might not have talked about them, but you, for one, sure did and do believe in them," Mr. Ellis announced.

"It's one thing to believe something and another thing to make mockery of it," Olive retorted.

"I don't believe any of it," Sherry proclaimed. "It's just the kind of thing that uneducated people embrace. I wouldn't be caught dead upholding that rubbish."

"Dead or alive, it don't matter." Olive hunched her shoulders forward. "Education isn't everything. Sometimes they educate you away from seeing what's always been there. That's how they keep you powerless. They know they can use it against you and you wouldn't even know it. All the time you're thinking, My family comes from the right side of the tracks. I'm educated. I'm better than those of you who aren't like me," she mimicked. "But in truth, you are ignorant and you don't even know it."

Sasha bit into a conch fritter. She could see that Olive and Sherry didn't always get along.

"That's the first time I've been called ignorant." Sherry took a couple of sips of water.

"There's a first time for everything," Olive remarked.

Sherry's face tightened.

"There's a big enough storm brewing outside," Cay said soothingly. "We don't need another one in here. I'd like to hear some music instead." He looked at his father. "How about passing the wine."

"Now, that's a good idea." Just the mention of more alcohol brightened Mr. Ellis's spirit. "Let's all have a little, eh?" He picked up the bottle and passed it to Sasha. "Ye-es, things are brewing everywhere. Maybe now I'll get my son back." He shook a veined finger in the air.

A shadow descended over Cay's face at his father's words.

After the wine had been poured Mr. Ellis proposed a toast: "To resolving the old and creating the new."

Sasha raised her glass along with the others. "To resolving the old and creating the new." Sasha's and Cay's eyes met over their glasses as she took a long sip and he downed the liquid with ease.

Chapter 6

"If I was my old self I'd show all of you how to appreciate music like that." Mr. Ellis patted his heart. "With a good-looking woman like Sasha in your arms, there's no way she wouldn't feel it, too." He extended his arms above the table as if he were dancing with a partner.

"I've had enough for one night," Sherry announced, rising. "I'll see you all in the morning. I hope, after a good night's rest, I'll be more appreciated by some of the members of this family."

"You'll be fine, Sherry," Mr. Ellis quipped. "You have a gift for being resilient." He slurped the last drops of the wine from his glass. "Sweet dreams," he called. "That is, if that's still possible."

Sherry glanced at Cay as she left the room.

Mr. Ellis broke out in his own rendition of "Yesterday When I Was Young" as he poured himself another glass of wine. Olive tried to shame him with her stare but he ignored her.

"You were a little rough on Sherry, Father," Cay remarked as he sipped his wine.

"Somebody's got to pull her coattail. She's clinging so close to yours I don't think you can find it."

"I'll reach it when the time is right."

"Can I count on you to do that?"

"Haven't you always been able to count on me?" Cay replied.

"Yes. But things have changed over the last few years. Changed drastically." Thunder rumbled outside.

"I'm aware of that, probably more than anyone else in this room," Cay said solemnly, "but I can handle this."

Cay Ellis Jr. stared at his son, then sat back and declared, "I believe you can. Yes. Yes, I do." He leaned toward Sasha, placing his hand on top of hers. "Sasha."

"Yes?"

"All good things must come to an end." He patted her hand clumsily. "I know I talk a good game, but, sorry to say, that's all I can deliver at this point in my life. Still there's something everybody needs to remember." He looked at Cay. "From the time we're born, we, human beings, but us Ellises in particular, have our paths cut out for us. It's only when we try to stray off of that path that we find ourselves in trouble." He rose from his chair. "Baltron, come and help an old friend up the stairs."

Silently, Baltron obeyed, and Sasha wondered about the meaning behind Mr. Ellis's statement.

"Now, mind you, Baltron, this is just for tonight." Mr. Ellis looked at him from beneath thick brows. "Maybe tomorrow, because my legs are a little stiff from my arthritis and that damned fall. But after that, I don't want to feel your old arms around me. Hopefully, I'll be ready for some softer ones." They walked out of the dining room together. Olive started clearing the table.

"That leaves you and me, doesn't it?" Cay placed his napkin in the middle of his plate.

"It sure does." Sasha sat back in her chair. She started to ask Cay what his father had meant, but he diverted her attention.

"Have you ever stood in the middle of an oncoming hurricane?"

"No." Sasha looked surprised. "And I don't think I want to."

"I thought you were braver than that, Sasha." His voice caressed her name, and he wondered how brave she was. Brave enough to risk her life for love? His stomach knotted at the unwelcome question.

"Brave?" She seemed to be considering the concept. "I'm brave, but I'm not a fool."

"Neither am I, but I've done it before," he enticed, "and I'm still here to talk about it. Would you like to see me do it again?"

Sasha's eyes narrowed. "Now?"

"Right now."

She stopped and listened to the roaring wind. "I'd like to see you try."

"It's a deal."

"Where are we going?" she asked.

"This way." Cay rose and extended his

hand. Sasha hesitated, then slipped her hand into his as they headed toward a dark hall.

"So you changed your mind?"

"Yes. Things change."

"That's not always true," Cay replied softly.

"It's the only thing I know to be true. I've come to count on it," Sasha stated.

"You don't know how lucky you are to be able to say that. To believe it."

"How so?" She was sincerely puzzled.

He picked up a candelabra and handed it to her. "What if I told you certain things have been put upon this family that have not changed for generations . . . and that I will be dead and gone when they do."

"Sounds rather morbid to me," Sasha replied. "Like your giving me your . . . deceased wife's clothes to wear?"

She watched Cay's face alter in the wavering candlelight. It was obvious he had not come to terms with his wife's death.

"I wasn't trying to be morbid." He unlocked the double doors. "I wanted to honor you."

Startled, Sasha looked into his eyes.

"You are more alive than any woman I know." Cay threw open the doors as a tree of lightning spread across the sky. Sasha was stunned by the sound of thunder that accompanied it. Cay took the candelabra from her and set it on the floor. He walked into the center of the huge hothouse, enclosed in a dome of glass.

"There used to be all sorts of flowering plants in here, but that was a long time ago," he said above the howling wind and rain.

"I can barely hear you." Sasha cupped her hands around her ears.

"Then come closer." Cay beckoned as the lightning continued to light up the sky.

"I'm afraid the glass will break." Sasha examined the myriad of panes as the storm pounded against the unnatural barrier.

"It's specialized Plexiglas. Don't be afraid." He held out his hand again. "Some things are worth bypassing your fear."

The thought of standing in the middle of the storm excited Sasha. She wanted to know how it felt. To feel the power raging all around her To be consumed by it, yet remain intact. Sasha imagined that's how it would be to make love to Cay Ellis.

"Come." He enticed her with both hands, his figure flickering from the sporadic light. "Come and see how it feels."

Tentatively, Sasha started forward. The dome grew darker as the lightning subsided and the sound of the storm intensified. As a result Sasha's ability to see lessened. For insurance, she stretched out her arms to guide her.

Once again lightning lit up the sky, and Cay took hold of her wrists. Sasha's eyes were wide and frightened when he looked into her face. Gently, he turned her loose.

"This, too, is part of living in the Keys," he declared. "It's a part that will either nourish you or break you." He breathed the air as if it were life-giving *prana*. "The stormy side of the people here. The secrets that we hold. It is the price that some of us pay."

"You make it sound ominous. I think it is beautiful." Sasha looked up at the sky.

"It is more than perspective, Sasha. It is reality."

"But isn't that what reality is? *Your* perspective is your reality. *My* perspective is mine."

"Yes, and my reality has made me cautious." He touched her face.

"Are you telling me you're a coward, Cay Ellis?"

"Perhaps." His thumb softly stroked her mouth.

"But I know that's not true," she said, referring to how he rescued her.

"That was uncharacteristic of me. I couldn't help myself." His voice was husky as his face descended.

This time she did not wait to see if he would close his eyes. When his mouth touched hers it was eager, demanding. Sasha wrapped her arms around his neck and molded her body against him. Cay, like the storm outside, let loose the need in him and Sasha had no choice but to reply in kind. She was deeply moved, but there was no way to tell by her verbal response. "So I overpowered you?" She made light of the situation, but Sasha yearned to know how he saw her and what he felt.

"You can say that. And that may not be good," he whispered.

"Not good?" Sasha feigned offense. "This is our second kiss and you don't know if it would be good?"

Cay smirked. "You said the kiss in the bedroom did not count," he reminded her.

"Oh, that's right." Sasha stared into his eyes before she pulled Cay's head toward her. Her kiss was different. It was sweet and caring. Not at all what she had expected to give. She had wanted to inflame, exert her power, but instead she had proclaimed her feelings. Sasha pulled back as a siren sounded in the distance.

"That's a warning," Cay said as he looked at her.

"For who? You or me?" Sasha said softly.

"I don't know, but I plan to find out." His arms tightened about her.

"Cautious, are you?" Sasha placed her finger against his lips. "I believe in change, but not too quickly." She disengaged herself. "Good night," she said, then headed for her bedroom, alone.

Chapter 7

"I thought by now the storm would have been over." Sasha poured herself a cup of coffee the next morning.

"No, this one seems to be hanging around," Olive replied as she cut up fruit for breakfast.

Sasha could tell Olive didn't like her presence in the kitchen. She started to leave but changed her mind. "Why don't you like me, Olive?"

"I-I never said that," Olive stammered, obviously caught off guard.

"You don't have to say it. It's in the way you act. In the things you *don't* say."

"Well, if you don't mind my saying so, it's not my place to like or dislike anyone Mr. Cay invites to Guana Manor." She slipped comfortably into the housekeeper's role.

"I'm not into people's 'places.'" Sasha took a sip of coffee. "Since I've been forced to stay here, it appears for more than one night, I'm just trying to understand."

"In my opinion you haven't been forced into anything. You're the one who appeared on this doorstep." Olive planted her feet and looked Sasha straight in the eye.

"So that's it. You think I'm after something."

"Most of the women that flutter around Mr. Cay are," she said, tilting her chin stubbornly.

"Most of the women?"

"Yes. Before my Precious came, and ever since she passed away, they've come up with every ploy in the book to try to be the next Mrs. Ellis. But I've got to say yours was a little drastic."

Sasha thought, for a woman who said she knew her place, Olive didn't bite her tongue. "I don't know what you're talking about."

"Coming here wet with your clothes clinging to you. A man needs a little bit left to the imagination if you're going to really pique his interest."

"Oh, the see-through poet's shirt. It was peaked all right," Sasha added softly.

"What did you say?" Olive squinted.

"Nothing worth repeating."

The housekeeper glared at her. "That's what's wrong with you young women, you don't know how to make a man feel you're worth waiting and working for. Now, with you, you may have had him for that short period yesterday, but that will be all you'll get. He got what he wanted and he will be gone."

"Is that right?" Olive's audacity knew no bounds.

"Not that Mr. Cay is a whorish man. That he isn't. If he was he would be busy day and night. But he is a man nevertheless."

"I think I need to clear this up before it goes any further." Sasha placed her cup on the counter. "I did not come here to be the next Mrs. Ellis. And"—she wanted to add "if it's any of your business"—"Cay Ellis has not gotten anything from me." She paused for emphasis. "I was drawn into this situation. You should know. Mr. Knowles was the one who brought me here."

"That was early yesterday morning." Olive placed her hand on her hip. "You had your meeting and things were settled. It was you who came back here on your own after you got a real good look at Mr. Cay and Guana Manor."

Now the woman had gone too far. "I came here after my furniture and my belongings were doused with bleach. And I believe your precious Mr. Cay was behind it."

"Bleach had been poured in your house?" Olive's eyes widened.

"Yes." Sasha's anger began to build again. "Everything it touched was ruined."

"Bleach . . . isn't that something. Was there a bottle or bone hanging near your front door?" Olive came a little closer.

"Not that I saw," Sasha answered, confused.

"And there's nobody that you know of that would want to put you through that kind of mischief."

"Nobody that I know of outside of Mr. Cay," Sasha repeated herself. "And I would not call this mischief, I'd call it—"

"Mr. Cay wouldn't do something like that." Olive waved her hand in dismissal. "That's simply out of the question. But I know who would."

"Who?" Sasha was stumped.

"The *chicharney* would."

"*Chicharney*," Sasha repeated. "I've heard Cay use that word before."

"See there." Olive's eyes lit up. "Even Mr. Cay thinks it was the *chicharney*. You poor child." Olive placed her hand on top of Sasha's. "To have actually been a victim of the *chicharney*'s tricks." She shook her head. "But you know, there are a few silk cotton trees on the Bethel land. They were planted by Hazel Bethel a long time ago. The silk cotton trees are where the *chicharney* likes to live."

Sasha was disconcerted by Olive's assessment and her change of heart. "Really?"

"Yes. I can't wait to tell Baltron that the *chicharney* has been up to no good on Magic Key," Olive announced with satisfaction. "And *Sherry* doesn't believe in such things." She turned up her nose.

Sasha decided to remain on Olive's good side. "If you don't mind my asking . . . what does a *chicharney* look like?"

"He is a small three-legged animal." Olive leaned forward. "He sort of resembles a leprechaun."

Sasha tried to smother her smile.

"Now, you laugh if you like." Olive shook her finger.

"No . . . no . . . I think he must be quite comical-looking." Sasha whitewashed the real reason for her mirth.

Olive looked as if she was trying to determine if Sasha was telling the truth. "There are some remarkable things on these Keys and the islands," she said in a dead serious voice. "You just remember that." Olive headed out of the kitchen with a breakfast tray.

Sasha took her coffee into the breakfast room.

"Did you sleep well?" It was Sherry Ellis, sitting at a small table.

"I slept okay. What about you?"

"Not very well," Sherry replied. "I tend to have nightmares." She looked long and hard at Sasha as if she were expecting a reply. When Sasha had none, Sherry asked, "Why don't you sit down and drink your coffee."

"Actually, I was headed back to my room."

"I would like it if you sat down," Sherry insisted. "It's not often that I have a woman near my age to talk to here at Guana Manor." She nudged a chair from underneath the table with her foot.

"Why not?" Sasha sat in a chair on the opposite side.

"Yes. Why not?" Sherry repeated. "Unless you, too, have something against me?"

"I'm just a guest here. Nothing more."

"It seems if Papa has his way you will be more than that." Sherry looked at Sasha meaningfully.

"You would be a better judge of that than I would. I thought he was just having a good time."

"He *was* having a good time. I hear in the old days he was very known for that. Good times and women." Sherry removed a cigarette from the pack beside her plate.

"I don't think Mr. Ellis's past is any of my business," Sasha informed her.

"Don't worry"—Sherry shook her naturally wavy hair—"I'm not revealing any deep dark family secret. It's common knowledge."

"I see."

"Papa doesn't have very high regard for women. He says we're troublemakers."

"I guess he's entitled to his opinion."

Sherry crossed her legs, then lit a cigarette. "Have you noticed all the male portraits on the walls?"

"No, I haven't. I haven't taken it upon myself to explore the place," Sasha replied, seeing that Sherry was intent on giving her view of the Ellises.

"Well, you won't find one painting of a woman other than Papa's mother, Mother Ellis. They say she was very fair skinned, almost white." She paused. "All the other women were obsolete."

"Really." Sasha wondered what Sherry was really driving at.

"Yes, really." Sherry dunked her tea bag before closing the lid on the china teapot. "This is not your normal family." She blew a stream of smoke into the air. "Bizarre things happen around here. Sometimes I wonder if this Florida sun hasn't fried all our brains. Some of these people are so wrapped up in that *obeah* stuff. I heard Mother Ellis banned that kind of talk from Guana Manor. But she believed in the *obeah* all the same. She's the only Ellis woman who commanded any respect. The men were so busy building the businesses and their fortune their women were secondary in their lives."

"Cay's wife didn't seem to be secondary in his life."

"Cay is different." Sherry slid down farther into the padded chair. "Guana Manor and the Ellis fortune mean a lot to him, but human relationships mean more."

"Was Cay's brother, Wally, different?"

"Wally . . ." Sherry contemplated the name. "In the beginning I thought he was, but after a year he turned out to be more and more like Papa." A wistful smile crossed her lips. "Money can be such a seductress. You're entrapped before you know it. You do realize we Ellises are terribly rich, don't you?"

"I can look around and tell you're not hurting financially."

"Hurting financially. That's an understatement." Sherry lit a cigarette and blew the smoke out over her head. "When I was in my late teens my parents brought me to Big Pine Key for a vacation. That was the first time I met the Ellis family. It was at a restaurant. They had a business, and still do, by the way, called Happy Tourists Boat Rental. We ended up renting one of their boats for the weekend. There aren't that many black folks capitalizing on the tourism industry down here in the Keys. Not on the high end, at least." Sherry poured herself a fresh batch of tea. "So my parents, who are into status, and Papa Ellis, who is as well, naturally hit it off. They thought my marrying one of the 'Ellis boys' would be a good idea. Good for my future. Plus Papa wanted to make sure the 'red bone blood,' as he called it, stayed strong in his family tree.'' Sherry ran her hand over her creamy yellow arm. ''And of course, I did think Cay and Wally were good-looking. Any woman would.''

''So you and Wally were married a long time before he died.'' Sherry had piqued Sasha's curiosity.

''No. We had been married two and a half years.'' Sherry's face turned long, then brightened. ''In the beginning I didn't know which one of them I liked. I was young, you know. Thought I was God's gift to man and all that. Plus we lived a long way from here, in Aurora, Colorado.'' She fingered her hair. ''But over the years we managed to keep in touch, and I continued to visit the area.'' Sherry sighed. ''Then one time I came down and found out Cay was getting married. To tell you the truth, I was shocked.''

''Why?''

''Beca-ause, all those years I'd been visiting, he never had a serious girlfriend.'' Her silky brows knitted together. ''Precious popped up out of nowhere, if you ask me. Well, it wasn't long after that they got married, and that kind of helped me make my choice. Wally and I were married a year later. That was five years ago. I was twenty-five.''

''I see,'' Sasha replied.

''You like saying that, don't you?''

''Saying what?''

"I see. Do you really?" She looked Sasha dead in the eyes.

"I don't know what you expect me to say." Sasha shrugged.

"When I married Wally we had the most beautiful wedding down by the water. The sand was white and . . . everything was so beautiful. Even though I had taken my time making up my mind, I believed Wally loved me and our marriage would be beautiful as well. But like I said, Wally turned out to be like Papa, and I had a problem with that, if you know what I mean."

"No, I can't say I do." Sasha frowned at the taste of her now-cold coffee.

"Wally loved women. He'd come home smelling like them. Their scent would be all in his clothes and in his hair." Sherry took a long pull on her cigarette. "Precious never had that kind of problem with Cay. I used to hear laughter coming out of their bedroom window at night, while I was sitting on the veranda waiting for Wally to come home."

"Did Wally know that you knew about the women? That you were unhappy?" It was hard for Sasha to imagine Sherry's husband forcing her to wait for him at night while he pursued other women. Sherry was a beautiful woman herself.

"He knew," Sherry replied. "But he didn't care. It didn't matter that I stopped going to bed with him, either. That just provided him with an excuse to do more of what he was already doing."

"Why are you telling me all this?" Sasha pressed.

"Like I said, it's lonely here. Sometimes I need to bend somebody's ear who is outside of all this. Who isn't biased."

Sasha looked down.

Sherry rested her head in her hand. "One night, after Precious died, I was crying about Wally, and Cay heard me. He came into my bedroom to see what was wrong. He knew what his brother was up to, and he just wanted to comfort me." Sherry paused. "I guess being in the state I was in, I took it the wrong way. I needed to feel love. I wanted to be reassured that my life wasn't just one big mistake. So I turned to Cay. I asked him not to leave my room. I wanted him to stay." Sherry licked her lips and sat back. "That's when Wally came home. He heard me, and saw us on the bed, and jumped to the wrong conclusion. Cay and Wally were kind of distant after that. Papa blamed me."

"That was years ago," Sasha remarked, although she didn't like the feeling that churned in the pit of her stomach.

"It will be two and a half years next month," Sherry informed her.

"I'm sure Mr. Ellis has put most of that behind him."

"Does it seem that way to you?" Sherry didn't wait for Sasha's answer. "The only reason I'm living here today is because of a promise Cay made to me the day after Wally died. He promised I would always have a home at Guana Manor. If it was left up to Papa, I would have been kicked out the day we buried Wally."

"But why do you want to stay here if Mr. Ellis really doesn't want you to?" Sasha knew how it felt to be an outsider. "You're young enough, and definitely attractive enough to start your life somewhere else."

"Because Guana Manor is my home, too." Sherry's features hardened. "I've dreamed of living here since I was a teenager. Of raising a family here, of seeing my portrait go up on these walls and seeing myself buried at Guana Manor in the family cemetery. I'm not going to let anybody or anything cheat me out of that. Not Wally's womanizing during our marriage, not his untimely death." She leaned toward Sasha. "So you can imagine, if I feel this way about my deceased husband, how I would feel about anybody else who might threaten my plans. Now, do you *really* see, Ms. Townsend?"

"I don't think it could be any clearer," Sasha replied.

Sherry's lips spread into a slight smile. "So Papa can hate me all he wants, but as long as I have Cay, I don't have anything to worry about."

"But do you truly have Cay?" Sasha asked, her gaze steady.

"I've always had him. I was just a little slow reeling him in." Sherry looked satisfied. "But I won't be this time, and I won't allow him to get on anybody else's hook, either."

Sasha gave a light chuckle. "So now I know the real purpose behind our little chat. Well, let me put you at ease. I'm not trying to hook Cay, Sherry. So you need not worry about that. But I don't know what Cay's intentions are. He seems to be a man who knows his own mind. If he wasn't, he would have taken you up on your offer in your husband's bedroom a few years ago. But, on second thought, I think most men would shy away from going to bed with their brother's wife."

"Half brother," Sherry informed her.

"Brother nevertheless." Sasha stood up. "And I guess Cay hasn't accepted the offer since then, even though I'm sure you've made it clear to him that it still stands." She pushed her chair away from the table. "So if I were you, Sherry, I might be looking for a burial plot somewhere else." Sasha headed for her bedroom, the only place in Guana Mansion where she could let down her guard.

Chapter 8

"Those new hurricane shutters have paid for themselves over and over again," Cay said as Baltron mopped up a puddle of water near the utility room door.

"Yes, they have been a godsend," Baltron agreed.

"I can't imagine how people made it down here without the aid of technology."

"I don't know about here in the Keys, but in the islands folks managed pretty well. They knew the power of nature and they respected it. They built houses that they knew could be blown away easily, but they could be rebuilt just as easily."

Cay leaned against the wall. "I never thought about it that way. I guess you're right, but there had to be more fatalities."

"Maybe. But nature will always have the right-of-way. If nature chooses, Guana Manor could be gone in a matter of seconds. That's why you should never put your heart into bricks and mortar; you should put your heart into people, family."

"You've told me that over and over again, but people don't live forever, Baltron."

"No, but how they touched your life lasts a lifetime. Be it good or bad."

"It's always puzzled me how you and Father became friends," Cay replied.

"Friends . . . I don't know if I would call us that. As you know, your father is a hard man to get along with. But I've been around for a long time, and things get better between us as the years go by."

"Yes, time can do strange things to you." Cay's eyes clouded. "The older I get, I fear I grow more and more like my old man. I think Wally believed he was like him from the moment he understood the curse. I dealt with it by living from one extreme to the other. Maniacally to barely living at all." Cay sighed. "But then Precious came into my life. She always reassured me that all of life was good. That life itself is a miracle. I couldn't help but love her. She saw nothing but good in everything, and I thought she could help me learn to believe the same."

"Yes, my niece believed in everything. Life's tragedies, its mysteries, and its miracles. Some people are born special that way. Maybe that's what she came to teach us."

"I know that's what led to her early death." Cay's jaw tightened.

"But I can't imagine Precious having it any other way," Baltron countered. "To her, life was magical. All of it. And she sprinkled a bit of it in our lives every day. Have you ever considered that maybe her time had come and she had done all she came to do?"

Cay shook his head. "All I know is she died because she couldn't accept the truth. That the springwater couldn't cure her."

Baltron sat down on an old chair. "It wasn't in her nature not to believe, Cay. She wouldn't have been our Precious if she didn't. Maybe we need more of that in this world today. People don't believe in anything anymore. Precious said belief was the key."

"It didn't open anything for Precious," Cay replied.

"Perhaps it did for you."

"How?" Cay was stunned.

"Take that Ms. Townsend, for instance."

"What about her?" Cay looked at Baltron.

"She's come at a real interesting time. Stirring up all the emotions and memories around the Bethel property. Nobody knew there was anybody left in Hazel Bethel's family to inherit the property. She never got married or had any children, and as far as we knew, her brother, Amos, didn't have any, either. But here she is."

"And so?" Cay stood inordinately still.

"I just think it is kind of interesting, don't you?"

"Should I?" His tone held hope.

"You might not find her timing interesting"—Baltron shuffled his feet—"but you sure do find her interesting."

"I'm like you, Baltron. I still have an eye for a good-looking woman."

"Oh, is that all it is? I've seen plenty of

good-looking women noticing you during these past few years and they didn't do anything for you at all."

"I'll give it to her. Sasha Townsend is different from other women."

"Is she now?" Baltron gave Cay a knowing look.

"But I've learned my lesson, Baltron. I'll never jeopardize another person's life because of what I want. In marrying Precious I thought I had a chance, but I was wrong."

"Why do you say that?"

"Precious was special, and even she couldn't make a difference. So who in the world could?"

"You see Sasha Townsend as different, but you say you can't get involved with her." Baltron leaned back and closed his eyes. "I don't think you'll be able to stifle what she's stirred up in you so easily." He paused and took a deep breath before he spoke again. "You say Precious was special, but Cay, I never saw your eyes light up for Precious the way they light up for this woman."

Cay's face tightened.

"I'm just telling the truth," Baltron declared. "You met Precious when she came here to visit Olive and me. And I know exactly how you felt. It was like having an angel in the house. She was like a light that brought all kinds of warmth to Guana Manor. You'd never known anyone like her before, Cay. Precious charmed us all, and we all loved her." He paused. "And when you married her, you looked so happy. But I never saw passion,

Cay. I don't think you ever knew it with my niece. I believe you thought there was safety in that."

The two men looked at each other.

"There is something between us, Sasha Townsend and me. It's hard to explain," Cay said softly. "Somehow I feel her desire for life. It's like a burning inside of her. It calls to me. You understand what I'm saying?"

Baltron nodded.

"I tell you. It's almost like being out of control." Cay began to pace. "I have never experienced this before, so I've got to be careful. There's a lot at stake here."

"I understand," Baltron assured him.

"Yes"—Cay nodded—"it is passion that I feel for Sasha Townsend, and it is quite different from the love I had for Precious."

"I know you loved Precious. But there's love, Cay, and there's . . . *love*. The kind that makes a man do things he never thought he'd do."

"I'm nearly forty years old. I don't think I want to learn this kind of lesson this late in life."

"What do you mean 'late in life'? You tell me how late thirty-six is when you're seventy-five like me."

Cay managed a smile.

"But listen to this old man." Baltron leaned on the arm of the chair. "If it hits you hard enough, what you feel for this woman, there won't be a thing you can do about it. You'll have to go with it."

"I didn't expect this to happen. I wasn't

looking for it." Cay struggled with the realization.

"Who does? But it's been three years since Precious died. Maybe this is your chance at a real life. A full life. Don't you let your fears mess you out of a real chance at happiness."

"It wasn't my fears that caused Precious's or Wally's death. That was real, and their graves out there in the Guana Estate cemetery prove it."

"They died, Cay. Their deaths may not have had anything to do with the Bethel Curse. But if you believe it, they did."

Cay wanted to accept what Baltron was saying, but what if he was wrong? The curse guaranteed him a life of sorrow. He was doomed to lose anyone he really loved. Could he chance the death of someone else he cared for to find out? The thought was out of the question.

"Precious believed that damned water was what she needed to save her life. Not antibiotics from the hospital or a doctor . . . but that goddamned springwater . . . and she died." Cay trembled. "So don't preach to me about belief." He walked out of the room.

Sasha sprang to her feet. She thought she heard the sound of shattering glass. It had come from one of the rooms down the hall.

She stepped outside her bedroom and bumped into Cay. "I heard glass breaking," she said, following him down the hallway.

"I heard it, too," he replied.

"Oh-h! Goddammit."

"That's my father." They broke into a run. When they opened the door Mr. Ellis was on the floor and rain was pouring into the room.

"What happened?" Cay asked as he helped his father up.

"I don't know. I guess I must have been dreaming." He looked confused. "I thought the storm was over so I opened the shutter, but a gust of wind blew a tree branch against the window and broke it." Mr. Ellis touched his forehead and smeared it with blood. "Then, all of a sudden, the rain started up again."

"The eye of the hurricane just passed over us," Cay informed him. "That's why the rain had stopped."

"Your hand is bleeding." Sasha watched Mr. Ellis's blood dribble onto the floor. "If you want, Cay, I can take your father to my room and bandage his hand while you clean up in here," she offered.

"All right." Cay looked at his father. Sasha could see he was disturbed by the incident.

Passively, Mr. Ellis allowed Cay to pass his arm to Sasha and she led him out into the hall. Once she had settled him in a large chair in her bedroom, Sasha went into the bathroom, where she found some antiseptic and bandages.

"This might hurt a bit," she informed him as she dabbed the injury with peroxide. Mr. Ellis didn't seem to hear her.

"This has never happened before. I felt so confused." He looked at Sasha, his eyes too bright.

"It's understandable, Mr. Ellis. Cay said we had been in the eye of the storm right before you opened the shutter. So you thought the storm was over. It could happen to anyone."

"But not to me. I've been living in the Keys all my life. I'm seventy years old. I've dealt with hurricanes before. I know how these storms work. I should have known better than to open that shutter."

Sasha didn't know what to say. "Cay's got it under control now. He'll get it cleaned up and you'll be able to go back to your room." She started to rise, but Mr. Ellis took hold of her arm.

"Don't send me away, Hazel. You know I want to stay here with you. I know I was wrong—"

"I'm not Hazel, Mr. Ellis," Sasha said softly. "I'm Sasha. Sasha Townsend."

Mr. Ellis looked disconcerted. "I'm sorry. For a moment I thought you were—I don't know what's happening to me."

"Maybe it's the medication the doctor prescribed for you."

"You think so?" Mr. Ellis asked, encouraged.

"It's possible. Especially if you're not accustomed to taking it."

"You're right." He nodded too enthusiastically. "It's probably the medication." He looked down at his shaking hands. "You won't tell anyone, will you?" he asked softly.

"Tell anyone?"

"You won't tell anyone about this."

"Not if you don't think I should. But if I were you I'd want my doctor to know, just in case the medication is too strong. Perhaps he can give you a lighter dosage." Sasha walked toward the bathroom.

"And Sasha," Mr. Ellis called.

"Yes?" She stood in the doorway.

"I don't want you to get the wrong impression. Hazel and I"—his eyes darted to the side—"we were never anything more than neighbors."

"It doesn't matter to me either way, Mr. Ellis."

Suddenly, his face looked tired. "Even if I had cared for her things would never have worked out for us. Mother Ellis would not have allowed it."

"Because of the rift between the families?" Sasha asked.

"No." Mr. Ellis looked at her. "Because her skin was too dark."

To hear the words spoken so bluntly numbed Sasha.

"I've put a couple of boards up to the window and closed the shutter," Cay said as he entered the room. "You can go back to your own bedroom now."

Mr. Ellis sat there nodding his head.

"Father, are you okay?"

"Okay?" Mr. Ellis's voice was shaky. "Of course, I'm okay." He rose from the chair and nearly fell. Cay reached out to catch him. "No, I'm fine." Mr. Ellis moved out of his reach.

Cay stepped aside.

"Thank you, young lady," Mr. Ellis told Sasha. "I hope I'm in better form the next time we meet." He smiled, but there were tension lines around his mouth.

Chapter 9

"Come in," Sasha answered the knock at her bedroom door.

It was Cay. He stepped just inside the doorway. "I wanted to thank you for helping with my father."

"We seem to be forever trading thank-yous, don't we?" Sasha replied, but she wondered if he'd been thinking about last night.

"I guess this kind of situation creates an environment where we have to help one another."

"It seems that way," Sasha replied. She noticed how stiffly Cay stood in the doorway. Almost as if he was making sure he did not enter the room.

"It's an unnatural setup." Cay spoke matter-of-factly. "You put people in situations like this and things are bound to happen. We're not ourselves."

Sasha felt Cay was making an excuse for what had happened between them in the hothouse. "I believe the opposite is true. I think

93

the real person tends to come out under pressure." Their eyes locked.

Cay was the first to look away. "The storm will have passed over in another hour or so. I'm going to go out and check the damage. I'll let you know what I find out."

"You don't have to do me any favors," Sasha replied, becoming annoyed at the barrier he was erecting between them—and at herself for caring.

"I know that. But as you know, I have an interest in the Bethel property. I'm just looking out for my own interest."

"Is that all?"

"Basically."

Sasha got up from the bed and walked over to stand in front of Cay. "I was looking out for my own interest last night, and I see I did the right thing."

"Maybe you did." He paused. "Maybe you didn't." His tone was cool.

"You're so full of double-talk. Just like last night. You're not making any sense at all."

"I know what I'm doing." Cay looked down into her face, his eyes hooded. "You're the one who seems to be confused. Last night you were so clear about what you weren't willing to give, now you appear to be riled because today I'm not interested."

Sasha's eyes glared as he spoke the truth. It stung to hear it. "Is that what you think?" She donned her sexiest smile. "I don't think you could handle me if I offered myself to you." She walked away. Sasha hoped her words needled him as much as his words had affected her. But her satisfaction was cut short by a pair of arms grabbing her from behind.

"Is that what you think?" Cay's voice was hot in her ear as he squeezed his arms around her. "Be careful before you answer, Sasha. Because if I get hold of you now you won't ever doubt my abilities again." He held her for a moment before walking around to face her.

"I-I," Sasha stammered.

"Nothing smart to say?" Cay baited. "Where's that slick little tongue of yours now, huh?" He decided to find out for himself as he captured her mouth with his own. He blazed a trail of kisses from Sasha's mouth to her neck. "Why did you tease me?" he said huskily. "I did not come here for this, but you had to see how far you could push me." His hand roamed down her back and cupped her cheek. He held her against him, kissing her again until Sasha heard herself moan. Hearing the sound of her surrender, Cay wrapped his fingers in her hair and gently pulled her head back. His intense dark eyes pierced her large brown ones. "Do you want to see more?" He placed a succulent kiss on her chin. "Do you?"

Sasha wanted to challenge him, but instead she shook her head no. She was afraid of what it might lead to. Sasha had thought she could control herself when it came to Cay, but from the yearning she felt, Sasha knew she had been wrong.

Slowly, Cay let her go. "I'm going to check for damage once the storm has subsided. I'll let you know what I find out."

Sasha could feel her insides quivering. "Fine," she replied.

He left the room.

Sasha plopped down on the bed, her breath racing. Cay had turned the tables on her. Up to then Sasha had been playing with fire and hadn't known it.

She walked over to the mirror and stared at herself. Sasha knew without a doubt that if Cay had wanted to he could have taken her to a place where she would not have turned back. He could have had her right then and there, and she would have been forced to think about the consequences later. The realization was unnerving.

All of a sudden Sasha felt restless. She had believed she could control her situation with the Ellises. But what was evolving between her and Cay was a whole different matter.

After all, she was a woman with experience. She had believed that if she got involved with Cay Ellis she could have used it to her advantage. But now she was forced to face the fact that, if within those few moments Cay had been able to bring her into full submission . . . *she* was the one who was vulnerable. He had touched her heart. It was the only way he could have swept her away with a kiss.

"This isn't going to work," she said, looking around the room. "I can't get involved with him. I can't afford to. The stakes are too high. If I lose, I will lose everything."

But a small voice inside her whispered, *It is already too late.*

*   *   *

"It goes to show, you can't be mean to people. It doesn't pay off," Olive Knowles said as she walked over to the library window.

"It doesn't show that," Baltron replied. "The way you're talking, Mr. Ellis's having Alzheimer's is some kind of judgment against him."

"You know I don't believe that. There are too many good folks who come down with it. But I can't help it if sometimes I feel it serves Mr. Ellis right. As the years go by I don't know who's worse, him or Mother Ellis. God knows she should have never had chil—" Olive stopped when she spotted Sasha. "Oh. I'm sorry. We didn't know you were in here."

"I haven't been here for long. I needed to get out of my room. I'm worried about my house, if it survived the storm." Sasha volunteered the half-truth.

"I'm sure it did," Olive reassured her. "The Bethel House has done okay all these years. Plus, Cay usually goes out and does a once-over of the land. He'll let you know if there has been any damage to the property."

"I don't feel I should depend on Cay . . . Mr. Ellis." She switched to his surname. "That property is my responsibility now." Sasha looked out the window as Baltron opened the hurricane shutter.

Baltron changed the subject. "I hear you've already had your share of trouble. Olive tells me you were visited by the *chichurney*."

"That's what she tells me."

"What do you think?" He rambled over to Sasha.

"I told Olive I thought Mr. Ellis was behind

it." Sasha looked Baltron straight in the eye before lowering her gaze.

"And I told her that was absurd," Olive jumped in. "So who else could have done it?"

"Why do you think that's so absurd?" Sasha asked. "Mr. Ellis's interest in my property is very clear. Obviously, he didn't expect anyone to inherit it. But here I am."

"It's absurd because he wouldn't do anything to harm the Bethel House," Olive informed her. "Precious used to love that place."

"And he wouldn't harm it because of that?" Sasha wrestled with the emotional implications of Olive's words: to have someone love you so deeply that the house you lived in becomes a shrine. Sasha wondered how it would feel to be loved by a man capable of such depth.

"Yes, but there's a lot more to it than that." Baltron sat on a chair arm and studied Sasha before going on. "Did you know Precious was our niece?"

"Yes, Olive told me."

Baltron nodded. "That's how Cay met her. She came to visit us here at Guana Manor and they married a year or so after that. But Precious couldn't change this house into the kind of place she wanted it to be." Baltron cleared his throat. "Mr. Ellis had his way of seeing things. It was a matter of keeping up the Ellis tradition. They always felt 'old money' style was the best way. The dark woods, antique furniture . . . You know what I mean. Look around in here." He swept the room with his arm. "But Precious liked things that were light and airy with bright colors. That was the way she looked at life." He looked down at his hands. "Mr. Ellis wouldn't allow her to change Guana Manor, but eventually, with Hazel's blessing, she was allowed to turn that house you're living in now into the kind of place she wanted. Actually, it was a happy compromise."

"You mean she and Cay slept and lived there?" The thought was unsettling.

"No, they never slept there. As a matter of fact, they shared the Blue Room, down the hall from your room," Baltron replied. "Your house was a special place for her to do her reading, her dreaming."

"How did she die?" Sasha had to know.

The Knowleses looked at each other.

"She died from an infection," Olive replied.

"An infection?"

"Yes. It was a rare one. Precious used to go out exploring." Olive bit her lip. "She cut her foot and at first the doctors believed the bacteria entered her body through the cut."

"So has anybody else had this infection?" Sasha could tell the Knowleses were uncomfortable.

"It was hard for the doctors to pin down exactly what it was," Baltron replied. "The blood tests said there was no bacteria." His voice dropped. "And the doctors concluded her illness might be psychosomatic."

"You mean they believed there wasn't anything physically wrong with her. She was making herself sick. Sick to the point that she died?" Sasha questioned as she mulled it over.

"You have to understand, Precious was always a little different." Olive sat down across from Sasha. She patted one hand on top of the other. "People loved being around her because of it. She saw life in a way that made it brighter for anyone she talked to. She believed in things that other people wanted to believe in, but were afraid. So when she started fixing up the Bethel House she turned it into a place with crystals and chimes." Olive looked off into space smiling. "With rainbows and sun catchers that reflected on the walls. I'd come in and there would be the smell of frankincense and juniper in the air, and these two beautiful paintings of angels seemed to welcome me as a dolphin fountain trickled near the front door."

"The paintings are still there," Sasha interjected. "I love them. When the sun pours in through the window, they seem to shine. I've never lived in a house that felt like this before," she admitted. She tried to figure out what made the house special. "Even though it's small, because of the archways and the white tiles on the floor, it feels expansive and alive."

"Yes." Olive brightened even more. "So you can imagine how it looked and felt back then." Then she paused. "But still, it wasn't enough for Precious. She wanted more. It wasn't enough for her to believe in the things she did. She wanted other people to believe in them as well. She couldn't understand, if the things she did and talked about brought so much peace and joy to other people, why they didn't believe in them, too." She shook her head. "Precious was determined to find a way to make other people believe. That's when she started doing research. Reading history books about the islands here in the Atlantic Ocean." She paused. "You know, one day she came to see me and she was so happy. She told me that Ponce de León had found the Fountain of Youth near these parts."

Olive laughed and continued. "Precious was determined to find the whereabouts of that fountain and its origins. About a week or so later she discovered Plato's writing about a place called Atlantis that had sunk from a natural disaster. And then she read about a man named Edgar Cayce, and what she read about him proved to Precious that Atlantis was real. That it had been a place where human beings lived who were far more advanced than we are today. And that those people lived for hundreds of years and were never plagued with illness and suffering." Olive looked as if she were in deep thought. "It was a given in Atlantis that human beings never died in the way we believe and that life and death were a perpetual cycle that people consciously chose to ride." Olive leaned toward Sasha in her excitement. "And you see, Precious believed the Fountain of Youth and Atlantis were connected. She thought if she could find proof of their existence, it would be the proof she needed to make other people open up to such wonders, and their lives would be better for it."

"So she discovered the spring?" Sasha looked from Olive to Baltron.

"Yes. She discovered the spring," Baltron replied.

"So did she think it was the Fountain of Youth?" Sasha asked, amazed.

"Precious thought it may have been connected to the fountain, and she believed the water originated from the sunken Atlantis. She was out exploring, trying to find further proof, when she cut her foot."

"But if there wasn't really any bacteria, why did she die from the cut?" Sasha didn't understand.

"That's the part we don't understand." Olive's eyes looked teary. "Precious *told* us bacteria *had* entered her foot, and that it wouldn't be long before she made her transition."

"Transition?" Sasha questioned.

"Before she died," Olive clarified. "And all I know is, after that the illness progressed very rapidly. She was deathly ill in a matter of hours. The doctors couldn't do anything for her."

"How strange." Sasha sat back in her chair.

"So now you see how Mr. Cay couldn't have been behind anything that would damage the Bethel House. He hasn't set foot in it since Precious died three years ago, and it's been sitting there as pretty as you please since Hazel passed away," Olive informed her.

"And that's why Cay doesn't want anyone capitalizing off of the spring." Sasha forgot her attempt to put distance between them. "He doesn't want me to start my bottled water business because of sentimental reasons."

Baltron nodded. "He planted some vines and other things to try and totally conceal it, but they just wouldn't grow. Normally anything will grow on this land, but not there," Baltron told her.

"I had something strange happen to me after I tasted the water." Sasha thought back.

"You did?" Olive's eyes widened.

"Yes. I experienced this euphoric feeling. As a matter of fact, I drifted off. Cay was the one who found me."

"So you and Cay had met before?" Baltron asked. Both of the Knowleses looked surprised.

"We met, but he thought I was a tourist who had wandered off the beaten path. Once he knew I was going to be okay, he left me there. We never introduced ourselves. It was a brief encounter."

"Well, some folks believe—"

"Oh, Olive, hush," Baltron interrupted.

"What do you mean hush? I can talk if I want to," Olive retorted.

Baltron turned his head.

"Like I was saying"—Olive cut her eyes at Baltron—"some folks believe that springwater can cure people."

"What folks, Olive?" Baltron challenged.

"You know what folks," Olive shot back. "And you're one of them."

"Yeah, well . . ." Baltron got up and began to walk away.

"You are." Olive followed behind him.

"Right now we're not talking about my beliefs," Baltron said as he went through the library door.

"I think you just . . ."

Sasha couldn't make out any more of Olive's words.

She sat back and thought about what had transpired. The way the Knowleses described Precious, she had been an unusual individual, and her death seemed to rival her life. But Sasha couldn't help but wonder if Precious had gone insane before she died.

She got up and walked over to the window. Could people really die from illnesses they believe they have? All of it was very strange, and strangest of all was Precious's obsession to prove the existence of Atlantis, a place that most people believe never existed.

It made no sense considering all Precious possessed: Cay, Guana Manor, and the prestige of the Ellis fortune. But perhaps Precious had been searching for something she considered far more important than material gain. And if that was the only kind of woman Cay would ever love, anything meaningful between him and Sasha was impossible. Precious seemed so different from Sasha. For years Sasha could focus only on how she would earn the next dollar to keep herself and her mother going.

These thoughts floated through Sasha's mind as she looked at the rain-soaked landscape. Some of the trees had been blown down, and there were branches and debris everywhere. She didn't like the feeling of inadequacy that rose within her. *I am not here to try to fill Precious's shoes,* she told herself. *I've got more earthly things to be concerned about, like my house and my land.* But Sasha had to admit, some of the things that Olive told her Precious believed about Atlantis intrigued her. Especially the possibility of her mother's soul living forever, and that life and death were parts of an endless cycle chosen freely by all.

Chapter 10

"Where is Olive?" Mr. Ellis looked past Sherry. "I don't want *you* to bring me my pitcher of ice tea."

Sherry noticed that he looked edgy, tired, so she decided to downplay his nasty attitude. "Oh, Papa, relax. Olive is busy. What do you think I'm going to do? Poison you?" She set the morning ritual ice tea on the coffee table.

"Anything's possible," he retorted.

"Well, that's not." She walked over to the draperies and turned the tiebacks just so before she stood back to admire them.

"Since I've known you you've never been the kind of girl to let anything stand in your way. Why should you start now?"

"Who's standing in my way?"

"You know who." Mr. Ellis clinked the inside of his glass with his spoon. "I am."

"You are?" She laughed lightly. "Keeping me from what?"

"From totally showing your claws and going after Cay." He sniffed the pitcher of ice tea, then put it down. "And then becoming the real mistress of Guana Manor."

"Well, aren't you in rare form today. I think your imagination is improving with time."

"No, the passage of time makes me that much more aware of how short my time on earth may be. So I'm determined to call a spade a spade and a snake a snake."

"From some of the things you've said to me in the past, I felt you believed you were doing a pretty good job of that already."

"I've said some things over the years, and from my perspective all of them have been true. Now I'm on a mission. And I intend to accomplish it before I leave here." His voice was serious.

"What's all this talk about dying?" She smiled her widest smile, but it didn't touch her eyes.

"I knew you wanted Cay from the beginning. But what I've realized is that knowing the greedy woman you are, you were probably a greedy girl, too. So you decided to bide your time, see if you could catch a bigger fish, probably in a big city, before you settled on one of my boys down here on Magic Key. I could tell you found both of them attractive, but you had a special spark for Cay. You figured you could plop one of them onto your deck whenever you wanted. But Cay fooled you. He married Precious. And when you couldn't find anyone else who met your and your family's expectations, and who was interested in you, you settled for Wally." He pointed his finger.

"But all the time Wally was the one who really loved you."

Mr. Ellis's account of her life and feelings pressed Sherry's buttons. "I couldn't tell it from the way he treated me while we were married."

A look of anguish crossed Mr. Ellis's face. "Wally had nothing but good intentions when he married you. He went against everything he believed to do it. You were the one who spoiled that. It was all so obvious. If Cay was in a room you couldn't take your eyes off him. You and Wally couldn't do anything alone, you always had to invite Precious and Cay. It was Cay that you wanted to be around." Mr. Ellis looked as if a stench permeated the room. "Precious was oblivious to the whole thing, and Cay just brushed your attentions aside, but it was hurting Wally real bad. He was suffocating knowing his wife wanted his brother in her bed instead of him."

"That's not true," Sherry refuted.

"It's not? Well, why do you think Wally started drinking like he did after he found you trying to bed Cay that night he came home early?"

"Wally was always a drinker," Sherry defended herself.

"Yes, he was a social drinker, but he became an alcoholic after that," Mr. Ellis retorted.

"I am not going to stand here and allow you to blame me for Wally's womanizing and his excessive drinking."

"It doesn't matter if you accept the blame or not. I know it's true. He started going to bed with other women and drinking himself to death when you started withholding your love from him after Cay wouldn't have you."

"How dare you paint me to be such a demon?" Sherry's voice shook with anger. "All the county knows about the countless women you went through and the bastard children you sired during the process. Cay and Wally were just lucky that you cared for their mothers enough to claim them. The truth is you never really cared for anybody but yourself and your mother, who turned you into the heartless old man that you are." She came closer. "Yes, the Ellises have managed to turn Guana Manor into a fine estate with all the right furniture and trappings, but there's one thing it will never have as long as you are the head of the Ellis clan, and that's class. You're trash, Papa. I know it and you know it. And you know what else? Class is something I was born with and will always have." She smirked. "And it's the one thing you've always wanted and will never have."

Mr. Ellis looked down at the coffee table. "You said a mouthful then, didn't you, girl. Most of it is true. But I'm going to tell you something else that's nothing but truth. As long as there is breath in my body I will keep Cay and Guana Manor out of your clutches. Wally died that night because you had refused him." His voice trembled. "He left his own bed at one o'clock in the morning looking for some comfort, some sort of satisfaction. And after he drank himself into a stupor, I hope to God he finally found peace when his car went off the road and hit that tree." The silence was thick. "I will never forgive you for it, Sherry. And I will never forget."

Their gazes met one last time before Sherry hurried from the room.

Mr. Ellis pushed the pitcher farther onto the table. It *was* Sherry's fault that Wally had died, he tried to reassure himself. Nothing else. But he had to fight against remembering the look of devastation in Wally's eyes when he heard about the Bethel Curse.

Unlike Cay, who never gave the curse much credence until Wally and Precious died, Wally believed in it from the very beginning. Maybe it was because he had spent time with family members in the islands who truly believed in the power of the *obeah*. Or maybe it was the way Mr. Ellis lived his life that convinced Wally there was evil in their blood. Mr. Ellis's eyes clouded. Either way, Wally had bought into it, and when he married Sherry he believed he was taking a big risk. A risk that could end in death. And it did. His own.

Mr. Ellis's aging features sagged, and then a steely glint entered his eyes. But if Sherry had just tried to make him happy Wally never would have gone out that night; Mr. Ellis fortified the perspective he chose to believe. Never. He would have stayed safe in his bed, wrapped in the arms of the woman he loved. But Sherry had spurned him. Spurned him for his own brother. And it was because of her that Wally was dead.

*　　*　　*

"Seems like the storm is about over." Sherry had left Mr. Ellis's room and entered Cay's bedroom unannounced.

He looked at her, then continued to take off his shirt. "Don't you knock anymore?" he asked.

"The door was cracked." She walked around the room slowly, calming herself from her confrontation with Mr. Ellis. "You know, I was just serving your father his ice tea and I saw the broken window. What happened?" She picked up a bottle of Lagerfeld, smelled it, and put it down.

"Father opened one of the shutters during the storm and a branch broke one of the windows in his bedroom."

"Why would he do that?"

"He said he thought the storm was over. We were in the middle of the eye. He had been sleeping."

"You know I've been noticing Papa lately. I'm beginning to worry about him." She forced a very concerned look onto her face. "I think old age is beginning to take its toll."

"I didn't know that you cared so much." Cay removed his undershirt. "The two of you haven't gotten along very well through the years."

"I've always felt like a part of this family. Even before Wally and I married. It's impossible not to care." Sherry looked at his bare chest and became silent. Finally, her gaze rose slowly to his face. "You are such a handsome man, Cay." She walked toward him. "Seeing you like this . . . it's hard for me to take my eyes off of you." She touched his pecs. "They're so firm, and such a beautiful rich brown. M-m-m," Sherry sounded in her throat as she leaned her head against him.

Cay's arms remained at his sides. "Aren't you forgetting something, sister-in-law?"

Sherry looked at him with dreamy eyes. "I'm not forgetting anything. I'm simply remembering. It was you I wanted all the time, Cay."

"It wasn't me that you married," he reminded her. "It was my brother. You need to start remembering that."

"But I couldn't marry you, Cay. You had gone off and married Precious. What was I to do?" She pushed out her bottom lip ever so slightly. "But here we are. We've been living in this house together for five years. Two and a half of them we have been single. Two healthy adults with healthy appetites in every way." She lifted onto her toes to be closer to his face. "I'm at the point of starving and I know just what I want." Sherry focused on his lips. But she noticed a hint of cherry-raisin color on them. "What's that on your mouth?"

Cay wiped his mouth with the back of his hand, then looked at the reddish smear.

"You've been kissing Sasha Townsend, haven't you?" Sherry accused.

"If I have, Sherry, it's really none of your concern." He walked away and pulled a clean T-shirt over his head.

"You let me make a fool of myself right after you know you've been kissing that woman," Sherry fumed.

"Careful, if anybody heard you they'd think you were a jealous wife. My wife." He pinned her with his stare. "And that's the problem, Sherry. You're starting to act like you're my wife. But you're not. And you never will be." The bedroom rang with his statement. "You married Wally, and Wally's dead now, just like Precious is dead. We've got to get on with our lives, but it will never be as a couple." He walked away from her. "Like I told you before, you are welcome to live here at Guana Manor until you die, but it will never be as my wife."

Sherry looked down at the floor. "You've made that perfectly clear."

"I hope so," Cay declared. "Because I don't ever want to have to talk to you about this again."

"Don't worry." Sherry's eyes hardened. "You won't."

Chapter 11

"Do me a favor, Sasha," Mr. Ellis called. Sasha approached his room reluctantly. "What is it?"

"Go and get me a fresh pitcher of ice tea. I don't know what's in this stuff Sherry brought in here, and I don't plan to find out." He sat back in his chair.

Sasha walked over and picked up the tray. Silently, she headed for the door.

"Don't let her fool you, Sasha. She's no goody-goody. She's got the airs of one, but I believe she is as low-down as a woman can be."

Sasha wasn't fooled, but she had no intention of getting in the middle of the fray. "I'll see what I can do about the ice tea," she replied as she took the tray down to Olive in the kitchen.

"One storm is over, and the other looks like it's really about to get started," Olive commented.

"I don't know if it's bigger than the one outside, but I think it's been brewing longer."

"It has. I've been watching it coming for years."

"Why do you think it's heating up now?"

Olive thought for a moment. "I think Mr. Ellis is taking a look at his life. Older people tend to do that sometimes when they're afraid the end may not be too far away. Even if they don't believe in the pearly gates, they still tend to want to make things right. It's called fear and getting your affairs in order."

"Mr. Ellis is afraid of Sherry?"

"No, not really. Maybe he's afraid of the part of himself he sees in her." Olive poured the ice tea down the drain, then opened the kitchen window. "I just love the kind of smell you get after a storm, don't you?"

"Now that you've mentioned it, yes," Sasha replied.

Olive continued. "I think Mr. Ellis knew what we all knew, us older folks." She turned to Sasha. "Sherry wasn't in love with Wally; she really wanted Cay. But the truth is she didn't love Cay, either. She loved what the Ellis money could buy, and she loved Guana Manor. But Mr. Ellis wanted a family of Sherry's family's status to merge with his own. He's got some real preferences when it comes to certain things. At least that's what he claims publicly." Olive started preparing a fresh batch of tea. "This family's got all kinds of water under the bridge. To be honest with you, I never thought Wally or Cay would marry. Mother Ellis and Mr. Ellis always talked against it. Said it wouldn't be in their best interest. They encouraged them to play the field, and if there were any children born out of it, claim the ones they wanted, then do like Mr. Ellis did and raise them here at Guana Manor without the mothers."

"I've never heard of such. Usually, it's the mother who raises the child alone," Sasha replied.

"I know." Olive looked as if she knew more but she didn't want to say it. "So that's why I was surprised when Mr. Ellis got involved before Cay and Wally married."

"So you're saying Mr. Ellis did it because he had his own ideas about who his sons should marry and what families they should come from? And because of his objectives he stood silently by, even knowing there could be trouble down the line?"

"I'd say that's pretty much it." Olive poured the fresh tea into the empty pitcher. "Mr. Ellis seemed ill at ease the first year or so, but after that he became comfortable enough. I think he came to believe as long as Cay and Precious were together, there wouldn't be anything to worry about. Sherry would stay in her proper place, and things would work out in the end. But then Precious died, and Wally conveniently died after that."

"Conveniently . . ."

"It might as well have been." She put her hand on her hip. "I never saw Sherry honestly mourn one day for Wally. She tried to act like the bereaved wife, but that didn't last for long. But *truly* mourn him"—Olive shook her head— "it never happened."

"Does Mr. Ellis think Sherry was the cause behind Wally's death?"

"Well, we'll never know for sure. But I do know Sherry has always preferred Cay, and right now he's her full ticket to being the mistress of this household. I think she's spent her youth trying to attain that goal so she's not going to give up on it too easily. I don't think so at all."

"Do you think Cay would ever marry Sherry?" Sasha walked over to the window. She couldn't look at Olive.

"Cay has said over and over again Precious was the only woman he would ever marry," Olive said proudly. "She was like an amulet to him. I guess he believed after God made her he broke the mold. I tell . . ."

Sasha saw Cay walk by the window. He was headed for the SUV. In her head Olive's words taunted her: "Precious was the only woman he would ever marry." Why did the words matter? Why should she care? But there was no doubt that the way Sasha's heart tightened in her chest meant that she did. She had come to Guana Manor to confront the man who was trying to stand in the way of her future, and now she found herself having feelings for him. Real feelings. The kind that could become deep and entangling. Sasha had to pull back.

"I think I'll go with Cay to check on my car and my house." She hurried for the side door. "Can you please bring Mr. Ellis his tea?"

Olive spun around. "Oh, all right," she said, but Sasha was already outside.

She opened the vehicle door and jumped in as Cay started the engine.

"What's going on?"

"I need to know what happened to my car and if my house is okay," Sasha said, looking straight ahead.

"I told you I would—"

"I know what you told me." She looked at him. "But they are my responsibility, not yours. I'd appreciate it if you would just allow me to ride along."

"Your riding along is not the problem," Cay explained. "I don't know if you realize it, but during a storm like the one we just had things are usually torn up pretty bad. Houses get completely destroyed, trees are uprooted, and lots of times there are loose wires. It could be really dangerous."

"Who made you my protector?" Sasha lashed out with misplaced anger. "So if you have some other reason for wanting to pretend you are concerned about me, you can stop right now. Because I don't believe it. Now, if you would just take me to check on my house and help me find my car, that's all I want from you."

"Are you sure about that?" His voice was low.

Sasha knew what he was implying. Although she sat as close to the passenger door as possible she could still feel the electricity between them. She took a deep breath and replied, "Yes, I am. I want to sleep in my own bed tonight."

Cay was silent before replying, "If that's what you want, Sasha."

"It is," she said, staring straight ahead.

They drove off. Cay thought about Sasha's sudden need to leave Guana Manor and he wondered what had triggered it. Sasha was a complicated woman, full of fire. Cay had known that even before he kissed her. He had kissed many women in his lifetime. In his younger days, when he saw women as nothing more than conquests, kissing was a mere tool to manipulate them. He wasn't interested in relationships. Women were easy to get.

It was another reason he'd married Precious so quickly. She possessed a pureness of spirit that he hadn't thought was possible. One that he longed to have. But none of the women he'd ever known, especially Precious, had sparked the desire Sasha had been able to ignite. It baffled and intrigued Cay. In the bedroom, he knew he had Sasha in the palm of his hand and that Sasha wasn't accustomed to that. He had seen surprise and something akin to fear on her face. He had wanted to take it further, to find out just how hot the fires burned . . . but it wasn't that easy. Life was much more complicated than that.

First, he had found out Sasha was not the kind of woman to be toyed with. He felt she knew the games men and women played better than most. Then there was the curse. . . . Years ago, Cay never thought the day would come when he would believe in the curse, but with Wally's and Precious's deaths, that day had surely arrived.

Still, it was hard to ignore the attraction he had for Sasha. Like Precious, Sasha had some quality that he yearned for. Sasha lived and believed in tomorrow. Something he no longer could afford.

To get involved with Sasha Townsend would create other problems as well. There was the issue of the Bethel property. She wanted to sell the water from the spring. But when Precious died Cay had vowed the spring would never cause trouble again. Yet here was Sasha Townsend, wanting to sell that trouble to the world.

"This is where my car was swept away." Sasha's voice invaded his thoughts. "Where do you think it is now?"

"Probably in a small lake about a mile and a half from here."

"You think my car is in a lake?" Sasha asked, dismayed.

"I don't know for sure, but it's highly possible."

Sasha looked over the storm-ravished area in frustration. Suddenly, she pointed. "Look. There's a woman carrying a baby."

Cay followed her line of view.

"They look horrible," Sasha said with compassion. "Where do you think they're going?"

"I have no idea. You know Guana Manor and the Bethel House are the only houses on Magic Key," Cay replied as they watched the woman clutch the baby to her. "Sometimes people use our property for camping. It's illegal, but they do it anyway."

Cay pulled the SUV up beside the pair. The

woman looked disheveled and in shock. The baby, who was about ten months old, was screaming at the top of its lungs.

"Can we help you, ma'am?" Cay asked, descending from the vehicle. Sasha came around to where they stood. The woman looked from Cay to Sasha, her lips trembling and her eyes filled up with tears.

"My husband. I don't know where my husband is."

"When was the last time you saw him?" Sasha inquired.

"We were camping in our RV, and the weather started getting really bad. So Bill decided we should leave the RV, and we found a place to go inside. He went back to get some things for the baby and something for us to eat, but he never came back." Tears ran down her cheeks.

Sasha placed her arm around the woman.

"You found a place to go inside. What kind of place?" Cay asked, puzzled.

"A small shed. A toolshed, back there somewhere." She pointed. "It was nestled between some large pines, and my husband thought it would be safer than the RV. I'm afraid the RV may have been swept up by the storm with my husband in it." She began to tremble.

Sasha looked at Cay.

"I know where she's talking about. We've got a good-size shed on the property. At one point we kept tools for doing work on the west end of the estate in there. But now that Baltron is getting older, we have a maintenance company doing the work." He looked where the woman had pointed. "Come on. Let's see if we can find your husband."

They piled into the SUV. Sasha climbed in first. To make it simpler the woman handed her the baby, who was still squalling. Sasha looked down at the squirming child. "What's wrong?" she cooed. "What's wrong, huh?" Sasha tried to arrange the baby's clothing. It was soaked.

As if he were reading her mind, Cay announced, "Let's turn some heat on in here to dry you two out. And here . . ." He reached across Sasha and the baby to open the glove compartment, where a Happy Tourists magnet gleamed on the door. "There's something in here that might make her feel better." It was a package of Fruit Roll-Ups.

"Fruit Roll-Ups?" Sasha looked at Cay, surprised.

"I'm not supposed to like Fruit Roll-Ups?" he asked.

"Well, Fruit Roll-Ups don't seem to be the kind of thing Cay Ellis the third would dare eat," she added, a nasal quality to her voice.

"See, that goes to show how much you really know about me." His words had a hushed tone as he looked into her eyes. "Practically nothing." Then Cay piped up. "They're convenient, sweet, and nutritious," he rattled off as he tore a package open and handed the slick sheet of purple fruit to the baby. Her chubby hands closed around it gratefully, and into her mouth it went. The crying stopped immediately. "How about you?" He motioned toward Sasha.

She nodded. Because her hands were full, Cay did the honors. Carefully, he placed the treat in Sasha's mouth; her lips softly touched the tip of his finger. Their eyes met before Cay drew his finger away.

"Would you care for one, ma'am?" he inquired.

The woman shook her head as her anxious eyes searched the road ahead of them.

"I guess we're ready then." Cay started the car.

It was a difficult drive. Uprooted trees and branches lay over the road. As Cay had warned, there were loose wires hanging from the utility poles. From time to time he ventured off the road onto the rain-soaked ground to avoid a dangerous situation. There was so much mud and water Sasha feared the SUV might get stuck.

"You had quite a walk, didn't you?" Sasha remarked, looking at the ponds that had formed on the ground from the storm.

"I guess I panicked," the woman told her.

"That's understandable. If I was in your shoes I probably would be worse off than you are. I think you're holding up pretty well," Sasha said, attempting to comfort her.

"It won't be long now," Cay said, driving over a tree branch. "This road is really one big circle, that's probably how you became confused."

Sasha glanced at his concerned features. Ever since he had jeopardized his own life to help her she knew that he wasn't such a bad guy. Still, the situation was so awkward. He was a major threat to her livelihood and her emotional well-being. But Sasha couldn't help but notice how warm Cay felt against her side as she held the baby. His large, muscular frame and the tiny, soft body within her arms felt good. She recalled how her mother had longed for a grandchild, and Sasha had promised her that one day her wish would be fulfilled. Thinking of the things Olive had said, Sasha wondered if she had a baby now, would her mother know it and would she experience joy because of it?

"What's your name?" Sasha asked the woman.

"Nancy." She tried to smile.

"And the baby?"

"Erma."

"My name is Sasha. And this is Cay."

"Are you two a couple?"

"No," Sasha responded, maybe a little too quickly.

"You look like you would make a wonderful couple. People say my husband and I do." Nancy began to search the landscape again.

Sasha could feel the woman's anxiety. She prayed that if they found her husband he would be alive and well. It had to be wonderful having someone in your life that you cared so much about. But Sasha believed, in order for Nancy to care the way she did, her husband had to love her as much as she loved him.

When it came to men, Sasha knew she had been stingy with her affection. Because of her mother's illness there had been no room in her life for a relationship. It wasn't something she was proud of. It was just the way it was.

She looked over at Cay and down at the baby. Her feeling for him frightened her. It was erratic, reactionary, and intense. Sasha's involvement with men was the one area of her life that was easy to control. But when it came to Cay, nothing was further from the truth.

The baby's hands were gooey from the treat, but she was happy and content. "We're going to find your daddy, Erma," Sasha reassured her. "Yes, we are." The baby smiled and dribbled, then continued to chew.

"The toolshed is right over there," Cay announced, rolling down the window. "You can see it from here. What direction were you coming from when you and your husband took refuge there?"

The woman examined the landscape. "I think we were over there. No-o, maybe there." She started to point. "I'm not sure." She was on the verge of tears again.

"Just calm down," Cay advised. "It's going to be all right." Then he took another approach. "When your husband parked the RV, was it near anything special that you can tell me about?"

Nancy put her hand up to her forehead, then looked up excited. "How could I forget. He parked it in the middle of some huge boulders that formed a circle."

Cay's expression darkened. "I know exactly where you parked." He paused. "It's over there." Cay took off again, this time veering off the road. "It's rather difficult to get back up in there with a car, and you say you were driving an RV?"

"That's right." The woman looked rather embarrassed. "Is this your land?"

"Yes."

"Well, we knew that we were trespassing ..." She paused. "And we didn't want anybody to see us from the road," she confessed. "So Bill maneuvered the RV up in here."

"He had to really be maneuvering to do that. The stones are hidden between two sections of forest," Cay remarked as he rolled over a pile of branches.

"I guess that's why I got confused when I came out and I couldn't find him," Nancy replied. "I had been waiting for him to come and get us from the shed, but he never came. So I walked into the woods a little ways, then I got scared." She swallowed. "I didn't want anything to happen to the baby. So I decided to come back to the road and see if I could get some help. I hope you won't file charges against us."

"You've been through enough," Cay replied. "I'm not going to file any charges. But the sign is up there to let people know this is private property. And it's also there to keep people out of trouble. This Key has some places that can really be dangerous if you don't know about them." He stopped the car. "I'm not going to drive any farther. I'll have to get out and look for him by foot. I think the storm did all of this." He looked at the tangled mass of tree limbs and branches. "Either way it's impossible for me to get the SUV up in there without encountering some big problems."

"I'm going with you," Nancy proclaimed.

"I don't know if that's a good idea with the baby," Cay said.

The woman looked at Erma. "Okay, but if we don't find him after a few minutes of walking I'll turn back. I just can't sit here and do nothing."

Cay nodded.

The trees were thick and the ground was covered with soaked pine needles. But the damp air smelled fresh and clean, reminding Sasha that the storm was nature's way of cleansing itself. Although it had stopped raining, drops of water still fell from the branches, exploding in bursts of scented pine.

"I can see part of the clearing ahead," Cay called back to the women, "and the RV is still parked there."

Moments later they stepped into the circle. Sasha realized what the woman had meant when she'd said "How could I forget?" The boulders that surrounded the RV were enormous stones. She couldn't imagine how they had gotten there or who was responsible for the grueling work of moving them.

Nancy rushed over to the small, old RV. "Bill! Bill!" With the baby on her side, she opened the door. "Bi-ill!" She turned to Sasha and Cay, "He's not in there."

"Well, at least you know the RV wasn't swept away by floodwater." Cay tried to comfort her.

"But where could *he* be?" Her eyes searched the clearing.

"I don't know." There was an uncomfortable expression on Cay's face as he examined the landscape. "Maybe we need to get an official search party to look for him. These woods can be pretty treacherous in a storm."

Nancy's eyes widened with apprehension.

"Nancy!" a voice called from the woods.

Nancy turned when she heard her husband call her name. "My God, it's Bill." She ran to him as he entered the clearing.

"Where were you?" Bill asked.

"I waited and waited at the shed, but you never came. So I began to worry and I went to look for you." Nancy didn't get any further. She broke into tears.

"Now, see, you were worried about nothing." Bill put his arms around her. "I had to wait for the water to subside before I could get out of here. Then by the time I came to get you, you weren't there."

"I tried to look for you but I couldn't find you," Nancy said between sniffles, "so I decided to go get some help. Erma and I started walking back up the road and we ran into these people." She looked at Sasha and Cay.

"I guess we had the same idea, but we went opposite ways." Bill gave her a squeeze, then took the baby. "You must have headed south and I went north. I came up on a piece of property that had a little house sitting on it. I thought about going up to it and asking to use the phone, but there was too much water in the front yard. It was impossible to get up to the door. I mean, it was like a tiny lake."

"You must have seen my house," Sasha jumped in.

"Well, if that's your house, I can tell you now, the only reason there isn't water inside of it is because it's built up on those pilings. You were lucky. So what did you use, a rowboat to get across that pond?" he asked, playing with the baby's hand.

"No," Sasha replied. "I didn't stay there during the storm."

"I guess that's one way of handling it. But I think it's going to take a while before the land absorbs all that water."

"Other than the flooding did the house seem okay?" Sasha needed reassurance.

"It looked fine to me, but of course I was standing out on the road. I couldn't get any nearer."

"Bill," Nancy interrupted, "I want to introduce you to Sasha, and this is Cay. We're parked on his land." She looked down.

"Oh, I see." Bill looked at his wife's red face. "I'm sorry, Mr. Cay. I guess I was a little too anxious to get settled. I knew a weather system was moving in, but I never thought it would get as bad as it did. You see, the radio in the RV only works when it wants to. I do apologize for parking on your property."

"I guess no harm was done." Cay put his hands in his pockets. "But you can see how this kind of situation can get a little sticky. If you had encountered any real trouble there wouldn't have been anyone to help you, because we wouldn't have known you were here. So it's for your safety as well."

Bill looked at the sky. "It looks like it's going to be turning dark in a little while. I guess we need to be on our way. Thanks for helping my wife and my baby." He extended his hand.

Cay and Sasha shook it, along with Nancy's outstretched hand.

" 'Bye, Erma." Sasha took a tiny fist in her hand and kissed it. "I hope you have a wonderful, happy life," she said softly.

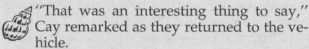 "That was an interesting thing to say," Cay remarked as they returned to the vehicle.

"What?"

"To tell a baby you hope it has a wonderful, happy life," Cay replied, pushing a pine branch aside.

"But I do," Sasha said.

"Have you had a happy life?"

"I've had some happiness." Sasha pressed her hand against a tree trunk to steady herself. "But I think in order to have received my fair share more has to be on the way."

"Has to be?"

"Yes." She glanced at him. "I refuse to believe anything else."

"What does happiness mean to you?" Cay inquired.

"You sure are full of questions," Sasha retorted as she looked at him across the hood of the SUV.

"It's the only way to get answers," Cay said glibly.

They climbed inside.

"I guess happiness means the same thing to me that it means to a lot of people," Sasha continued. "A sense of fulfillment. Believing my life has a purpose. That if I died today I could go satisfied with no regrets."

"I don't think most people look at happiness that deeply," Cay said.

"You don't think so?"

He shook his head. "It's how big their house is, what model car they drive, and how much money they have in the bank."

"That can be easy to do," Sasha replied. "We live in a very materialistic society. But when you equate your identity and self-worth with those kinds of things, what happens if you lose them?" For a moment the SUV was silent. "Nancy and Bill didn't seem to have much, but they seemed like they really loved one another. I think family was the most important thing in their lives. I believe they are happy."

"Sounds like the kind of thing you'd want."

"Maybe." Sasha refused to reveal any more of herself. "Why did you ask me if I felt my life had been happy?"

"Because I wanted to know."

"But why?" she pressed. Cay had not said a family life was what he wanted. He didn't comment about his feelings on family life at all. "Do you have plans to change things for me if my life hasn't been happy?"

"You never know. It's hard for a man like me to make plans," Cay replied in a hushed tone.

Sasha's lips turned a cynical smile. "And see, that's a problem. We may never know. And I for one, at this point in my life, couldn't possibly live like that." She looked off into the woods.

"Sasha." Cay's voice caressed her name. She could feel him gathering his thoughts. "We just met yesterday, and not under the best of circumstances. We don't really know each other. But you know I am attracted to you. It's obvious." He leaned toward her. "I don't know what it is about you"—he studied her face—"but I want you in the worst way."

Sasha controlled the words that were on the tip of her tongue. He wanted her. That was no prize. How many men had said that? "Sometimes wanting someone isn't enough, Cay." Sasha's voice lowered to a whisper before she fortified it. "I've long passed the stage in my life where I allow my feelings to take over and lead me wherever they may. Perhaps if you had caught me in my early twenties I would have been won over by the things you're saying, but not now." She drew a deep breath. "That kind of impetuosity leads to regret. And I don't have time for that."

"Some feelings are hard to ignore." Cay's eyes became hooded as he looked at her lips.

"That's true," Sasha agreed. "But when I think about the consequences, I know I can't afford not to ignore them." Sasha's eyes were downcast.

"What happened to the woman I met yesterday who was challenging me every step of the way?" His mouth lifted in a half smile.

"I told her"—she slowly cast her gaze on his face—"to sit down and shut up before she gets me into a world of trouble."

Cay and Sasha studied one another before Cay sat up in the driver's seat.

"Okay." He drew a deep breath and took the conversation in a different direction. "Thanks to Nancy I've found out Guana Estate suffered very little damage. And, according to her husband, you're not going to be able to get up to the Bethel House tonight. So I guess you'll be under my roof again." He touched her cheek with the back of his hand. "What was it the spider said to the fly?" His hand trailed slowly down her face.

Step into my parlor, Sasha thought, but replied, "I have no idea." She knew she could stay in a hotel off island. It would probably be the smartest and the safest thing to do. But her heart wasn't in it. "Do we still have enough daylight to look for my car?"

Cay focused on the setting sun. "Probably. We can go look for it under one condition."

"And what's that?"

"If it's driveable, that you promise not to drive away when the fear of getting involved with me hits you." His eyes gleamed as he spoke the words he knew so well.

"You're not talking about getting involved," Sasha replied. "What you're talking about is outright sex, and I'm not promising you a thing."

"Well who's going to eat dinner here at the house tonight?" Sasha heard Olive say after she closed Mr. Ellis's door. Then the house went quiet, and Sasha entered the dining room alone. This time there were only two place settings. One at the head of the table, another adjacent to it.

"You can sit wherever you want," Olive said, pushing the swinging door open with her hip. "You'll be dining alone tonight."

"Oh." Disappointment surged. "Where is everyone?" She tried to make the question light.

"Who knows? Some fancy car came and picked up Cay and Sherry, and Mr. Ellis isn't feeling well, so he's in his room. You would think with all the bad weather, getting back over to Big Pine Key would be a little tough. But I guess not."

"So they went to Big Pine Key?" Sasha grappled with the fact that Cay had gone and had not told her, although she knew he wasn't obligated.

"I'm assuming that's where they went. I guess it was a spur-of-the-moment thing. At least I hope it was." Olive's jowls turned heavy. "They knew I was cooking this goose. If they knew they were going out beforehand, one of them should have said something." Olive placed the dishes on the table. "So you'll have your pick of everything."

It was a solemn meal. Although Sasha was accustomed to eating alone, this time she felt lonely. The chandelier seemed too bright and the finery too pristine. She felt like a guest who had outstayed her welcome. She longed for the homeyness of the Bethel House. There was a feeling of peace there. That's why it up-set her all the more to know someone had set out to destroy that peace. She realized she had thought "someone," an unknown, because deep inside Sasha no longer believed Cay was responsible.

After her meal Sasha wandered into the li-brary. The Ellis collection was quite extensive. She leisurely browsed the leather-bound spines, hardbacks, and paperback books. It was an easy system to follow. Each variety had its own section. At least that's what she thought until she came to the bottom corner of one of the shelves. There the books were haphazardly mixed. The titles ranged from *Conversations with God* to *The Last Hours of Ancient Sunlight*, by Thom Hartmann. Heady sub-jects, to say the least.

Sasha browsed through a couple of the books before *Stones of Atlantis* drew her atten-tion. Immediately, she thought of the story At-torney Williams had told her, and of the huge boulders in the clearing. "This could be an in-teresting read." She thumbed through the pages, then placed the book under her arm. Afterward she walked outside.

Sasha sat on the wrought iron furniture that had caught her eye the first time she saw Guana Manor. The moon was high and full, and shone boldly from a sky inundated with stars. It was a breathtaking night, and she closed her eyes to enjoy the night sounds, but instead she heard Baltron and Olive talking from an open window overhead.

"Cay said that couple parked their RV in the middle of the Circle of Stones."

"Yeah, I heard."

"It's a wonder they didn't see her out there." Olive's voice turned excited.

"Obviously, they didn't. Cay didn't say anything about it," Baltron replied.

"You know Cay. He hates to talk about it. He says he doesn't believe it's true, but I think he does. One day that boy is going to get enough of not believing. I hope, once again, it won't be when it's too late."

"It is rather difficult to believe, Olive."

"I don't care how difficult it is. I tell you I saw her, and it was in broad daylight. I know it sounds strange, but we've seen strange things before," she said pointedly. "You were there when she died. You saw that light that billowed out of Precious's body when she crossed over. It was like a camera flash. I'd never seen anything like it."

"Me either."

There was silence.

"And I tell you she was right there in the middle of the stones, looking almost as solid as you are now but with a glow about her body. It nearly scared me to death. But when she smiled, Baltron . . ." Olive paused. "I knew my Precious would never do anything to harm me."

"That would be against her nature," Baltron agreed.

"That's right. And that's why it riles me when Mr. Ellis makes the kind of wisecracks he made last night, talking about the lights flickering. This isn't like a fake séance," she said with heat. "I never should have told him I saw her. But I was so excited when I got back to the house. And Mr. Ellis was the first person I bumped into."

"Never mind. Cay Junior. You know he's got his ways."

"Yes, I know." Olive cleared her throat. "He needs to change some of them."

Sasha remained quiet, and the room upstairs went silent. Had she heard Olive and Baltron correctly? It was hard to fathom what they had been discussing. Olive believed she had seen Precious among the large stones. Seen her after she had died. The thought sent a chill down Sasha's spine. Was it possible? Olive obviously thought it was.

Headlights beaming toward the house sidetracked Sasha's thoughts. She was glad she was in the shadows when the Lincoln pulled up. She watched Cay get out first. Then he assisted Sherry. Without hesitation the silver-gray vehicle pulled off quietly into the night.

"Thank you for a nice evening, Cay."

"You know you don't have to thank me."

"I hope you'll forget the little spat we had earlier." She wrapped her arm through his.

"It's forgotten already, Sherry," he replied.

"I'm glad." She lifted onto her toes and gave him a prolonged kiss before they entered the house.

Sasha felt like a spy. But although it had not been her intention to eavesdrop on anyone's conversation, she was secretly glad she had. It helped to clear her head and put things in perspective. Olive Knowles appeared to be right. Sherry had worked too hard at being the mistress of Guana Manor to give up on that dream now. She would continue to press her affections on Cay, and from where Sasha sat he didn't appear to mind. How long would it be before Sherry convinced him to take her up on her offer? Sasha knew from personal experience that Cay was a passionate man. His brother, Wally, had been dead for over two years. It wasn't inconceivable to think Cay could eventually turn to Sherry. After all, how much could one man resist?

Sasha believed there were no bounds to what Sherry might do to seduce Cay, and that was another reason for her to keep her distance. She did not want to be a casualty of the ongoing saga of the Ellis family.

In that moment Sasha made up her mind. She would leave Guana Manor in the morning. The condition of her property didn't matter. Even if she had to rent a boat, she was going home one way or another.

Chapter 13

"I've been looking for you." Cay stepped out onto the tiled veranda.

"You sure weren't looking very hard." Sasha couldn't suppress the retort.

"Do I detect a hint of anger?" He sat down beside her.

"Not in the least." Sasha got up. She didn't know where she was going, but she wasn't going to sit there and have a pleasant conversation with Cay.

"So I finally caught you in a lie." Cay caught up with her and matched his steps to hers.

"If that's what you've been trying to do . . . congratulations."

"Hey"—Cay stepped in front of her—"won't you let me explain?"

"Like I said before, you don't have to do me any favors." She walked around him.

"Now, *this* is the Sasha I know," he teased.

"And it's the only one you will ever know if this is the way you plan to go about it."

"What if I change my approach?" Cay stepped in front of her again and put his arms around her. "I'm sorry that I wasn't here to eat dinner with you, Sasha. Some unexpected business came up."

"If your sister-in-law is the unexpected business you had to tend to, it's your house, you could have done it here." Sasha tried to walk away but Cay stopped her.

"What are you implying?" His tone turned serious.

"I'm not implying anything. I said what I had to say."

"So you believe I left so I could be with Sherry?" His eyes narrowed. "What kind of man do you take me for?"

"No different from any other. It's obvious Sherry's got the hots for you, so . . ." Sasha looked away.

"But she was my brother's wife. And that is all she ever will be." Cay firmly, but gently, took hold of Sasha's chin to force her to look into his eyes. "Understand?"

"What difference does it make if I understand or not? You can do—"

"I'm growing tired of this game you're playing, Sasha." Cay squeezed her chin. "You were so angry with me that you couldn't stand to sit beside me. Now I tell you what you were thinking was not true, and you try to worm your way out of it. I'm beginning to think you're a coward when it comes to facing your own feelings."

"I don't have to explain my actions to you."

"You don't have to, but I want you to." Cay's thickly lashed eyes pierced Sasha's. "Can't you understand that? You try to act like it's me who's so unreachable, but I think you've played the games you've played for so long you don't know how to do anything else," he accused her.

"You don't know anything about me, about my past. And I can assure you"—she looked into his eyes—"this is not a game."

"Then prove it to me, Sasha." His eyes burned into hers. "Under this beautiful moon. Prove it to me." His words were like silk. "Show me how you really feel."

Sasha looked at Cay's lips as he brought them close to hers. He was offering them to her, but this time he would not be the one to seal the kiss. She would have to meet him halfway.

"Kiss me, Sasha. Right now. Right now." Cay's husky voice droned in Sasha's ears.

Cay's lips were mere inches away from hers, and Sasha could feel herself being drawn in. She wanted to feel his lips against hers again. To experience the pleasure it gave her. She wanted it more than anything and there was no holding back. Hesitantly, her lips touched his. It was a gentle truce, but moments later the heat between them surged.

"No. Wait," Cay said gently, tugging at her arm. "Let's go over here." He led her to another veranda, where he sank down on a chaise with an uncertain Sasha beside him.

"I don't know about this," she protested, her voice trembling.

"I do," Cay confirmed as he wrapped her in his arms. "I've never had a woman affect me the way you do." He kissed Sasha's protesting lips. "I hear myself talking to you and I don't recognize my own words. I have to know if you are all my imagination believes you are." Cay smothered his own words when he pressed his lips firmly against Sasha's. "I want to know you, Sasha." He spoke against her lips. "Know all there is to know, and maybe, just maybe, I will be satisfied."

Cay's kiss was the sweetest kiss Sasha had ever known. She wanted to wallow in his arms. To give him what he wanted because it was also what she wanted. Sasha knew she had never given herself to a man like she could give herself to Cay. It was a wondrous yet devastating realization. Devastating because for him she knew this was just a means to an end. To Sasha, making love to Cay would be only the beginning.

Cay leaned back and tried to pull Sasha closer, but something hard pressed against his back. "Wait a minute. What is this?" He bent forward.

"It's a book." Sasha pulled the book from behind him. "I got it out of the library."

Cay took it out of her hand and started to put it on the table, but the title stopped him. *"Stones of Atlantis."* His expression turned wary. "Where did you get this?"

"I told you, it's a book I got out of your library." Cay's reaction puzzled her. "Should I have checked with you first?"

"No," he said quickly. "I simply thought this book had been thrown away with the others."

"Why would you want to throw it away? I

think the subject is fascinating, especially since you have some of the stones they describe here on Guana Estate. Haven't you ever been curious about them?"

"No," was his monosyllabic reply.

Sasha could feel him withdrawing. "Obviously somebody was, or the book wouldn't be in your home."

"It belonged to Precious."

"So you wanted to throw it away because it was hers." Sasha sat up. "Throwing her books away isn't going to make you forget her, Cay."

"There is nothing that can make me forget her," was his deadpan reply.

For Sasha it was a reality check. Why had she allowed herself to be coerced into this? Before Cay showed up on the veranda, she had convinced herself she wanted no part of the Ellis clan and its problems. Still, she let herself be talked into kissing him. And what did she find out? Not only was she competing with Cay's live-in sister-in-law but his dead wife as well.

"Well, if nothing can make you forget her why are you throwing away her books and trying to bury that spring, the one I want to make a living off of, that reminds you of her? If nothing or nobody can make you forget her, what is the point?" Sasha freed herself from his grip.

"What do you know about that?" Cay's eyes narrowed.

"I know enough"—Sasha moved to the edge of the chaise—"that I should kick myself for even being over here with you. With the way it's going, in the end, people will probably think *I'm* crazy, too, for getting involved with you." As soon as she said it Sasha regretted her impetuous words.

"Crazy, *too*?" Cay's face became a mask.

"I'm sorry, Cay." She touched his arm. "I didn't mean that. I'm so mixed up I don't know if I'm going or coming."

"So who did you think was crazy?" His eyes cut into her. "Precious?"

"I haven't thought about it," Sasha said with a sigh. "I simply heard she had some problems before she died, that's all." She tried to stand up, but Cay took hold of her arm.

"And was I one of her problems?"

"What?"

"You heard me." His voice was harsh. "Was I the reason she died?"

"Now I really don't know what you're talking about." Sasha shook her head.

"You think you know so much." He tightened his grip. "They must have told you that she died because I wouldn't give her what she wanted. That she refused to take the antibiotics the doctors prescribed for her. That she wanted the springwater instead. Precious believed it would cure her. The one damned thing that led to her illness in the first place . . . she believed it could cure her."

"I didn't know that." Sasha tried to extract her arm, but Cay wouldn't let her.

"Oh, you didn't? Well, let me tell you about it, so you'll have all your ducks in a row the next time you judge me." He leaned in closer. "Precious refused to take the medication, so I refused to bring her the water. She was too weak to go get it herself, and I wouldn't allow Olive or any of the others to do it. I was sick and tired of her fantasies that were taking her further and further away from reality. I thought withholding the water would make her take the antibiotics. That she would give in to me so I could give in to her. But she never did. In a way she was headstrong just like you." His eyes searched her face but he didn't seem to see Sasha. "*Her* reality was the *only* reality, and there was no room for anything else. I believed if I could make her see the truth like the rest of us saw it, it would prove the things she believed didn't exist. Atlantis. Healing springwater. Ascension. I thought I could make her face reality and come back to us." Cay turned quiet. "The slash in her foot was a simple cut, but within forty-eight hours her condition turned critical. The doctor never expected such complications or he would have put her in a hospital." His hand dropped to the chaise. "In the end I went to get her the water, even though I never believed it would cure her. She died moments after I returned."

Sasha was at a lost for words. "I-I didn't know that, Cay."

"There's so much you don't know about what has taken place here on Magic Key." His emotionless eyes looked at her before he walked off into the dark. "And that's something you should never forget."

Chapter 14

Early the next morning Sasha returned to the Bethel House. She asked Baltron to give her a lift. She was shocked by the flurry of activity in the front of her house.

"What's going on?"

"You didn't know that Mr. Cay arranged to get this place cleaned up?"

"No, he never said a word to me about it." Sasha looked around her.

"He's like that, you know. Likes to take charge of things," Baltron replied.

"Well, I guess it's okay when it's his things he's taking charge of. But when it's somebody else's, he could at least tell them."

She got out of the Cadillac and walked across the damp grass. She almost collided with two men coming through the front door carrying her bleach-stained couch.

"Wait a minute. Where are you taking that?"

"We're going to give it to the Goodwill." The worker smiled, showing a set of beautiful white teeth. "It smells like hell, but after a

147

good washing and a few days of sitting out in the sun, it can be a nice gift for one of the families that lost their homes during the storm."

Sasha had been on the verge of protesting, but after hearing the man's explanation she didn't know what to say.

"Thanks, ma'am, for your contribution." He continued to talk over the arm of the couch. Then he looked behind her. "Looks like we have good timing. I guess that's your new furniture arriving."

Sasha turned and saw a Beacon's Furniture truck pull up behind the Cadillac.

"Well, I'll be damned." Her mouth dropped open. "He ordered new furniture for the house."

"Looks that way," Baltron replied, walking toward the truck with his arms folded.

Sasha watched the Beacon's driver and a fellow worker hop out of the cab and briskly walk to the back of the truck. The driver threw open the double doors. Sasha and Baltron walked up behind them.

"Good morning. Got your new furniture right here, ma'am," the driver said in a cheery voice. Then he called to his coworker, "Al, let's take the couch off first."

"No, hold it," Sasha said firmly. "I didn't order any furniture."

"I thought you said this was the right address, Al," the man said to his partner.

"It is." He took the pink slip out of his pocket. "Three-forty Bimini Lane. It says so right here."

"This is three-forty Bimini Lane, but I didn't order any furniture. I can't afford this," Sasha tried to explain.

The driver took the slip from Al. "It says it was paid in full." He looked confused.

"I can believe that," Sasha replied. "But I don't want it. You'll have to take it back."

"Take it back?" Al whined.

"That's right," Sasha confirmed. "Take it back."

"Lady, we've got five other deliveries packed behind yours. The only way we're going to be able to deliver them is in the order that they're listed here." The driver fingered his clipboard.

"But you don't understand—"

"No, you don't understand. We're on a tight schedule, and in order to meet it we've got to carry out the instructions we were given from the office." He looked up at the sun that was climbing in the sky. "We're supposed to deliver a living room set and a bedroom set to this address, and that's what we plan to do. You can take it up with the person who bought it for you later." His eyebrows rose meaningfully.

"I'm going to call Cay right now." Sasha turned toward the house.

"It's not going to do you any good, Ms. Sasha. He's gone out of town for two weeks."

"For two weeks!"

"Yes, ma'am," Baltron replied. Sasha could tell he was getting a kick out of this.

"Careful, Al," the driver instructed. "You almost hit the side of the truck."

The two men walked past Sasha. "You need to tell us where to put these, ma'am."

Exasperated, Sasha followed them. "Oh, okay." She had never encountered this kind of situation before. Cay had totally taken over. He had workers coming and going, and men taking furniture out of the house, and new furniture being put in. On top of that, he had left for two weeks without saying a word.

Sasha told the movers where she wanted everything placed. Once they were done she realized the new furniture was nearly a carbon copy of the old. Cay had remembered how the house had been decorated, even though he hadn't been inside for years.

He had said nothing could ever make him forgot Precious. To Sasha, this was proof of how tightly the past still held him.

Baltron closed the door behind the last worker. "Now it looks as good as new in here." He walked down the short hallway and looked in the rooms.

"Yes, exactly the way it looked before Precious died," Sasha said, feeling heavy.

"Not exactly. After that, Hazel made a few changes. You know she let Precious have the run of the house, while she was satisfied with the back room. After Precious died she moved her bed into the room where your bed is now."

"I didn't know that." Sasha saw the room with different eyes as she focused on the rainbow decal stuck on the sliding glass door.

"That door and the patio were put here because this wall faces the east. Precious called the east the place of the rising sun. Of beginnings. You see those little shelves all along the side?"

"Uh-huh."

"All of that was Precious's doing. Hazel used to have all sorts of African violets growing in pots on those shelves. Hazel and Precious thought a lot alike, but Hazel held tight to her African roots. She believed neither plants nor people could flourish without a strong root system."

"Are there any pictures of her?" Sasha walked over to the sliding glass door.

"I think Olive's got some in an old photo album she keeps underneath the bed. Maybe we can show it to you sometime."

"I think I'd like that." Sasha's interest was piqued. "How did Hazel and Precious end up in such a close relationship?"

"It was the strangest thing." Baltron leaned against the wall. "I remember the first time they met. It was like old friends reuniting. If I hadn't known better, I would have sworn they had arranged it."

"Really?" Sasha sat down in a rocker.

"Um-mm. Precious had seen the Bethel House from the road during her first visit to Guana Manor, but she never met Hazel. It wasn't until after she and Cay were married that they met. Precious liked walking, and sometimes she would pass by the Bethel House during her outings. Well, when we were returning home one day, she told me she wanted to go up and introduce herself." He walked over and adjusted the globe of the ceiling fan. "Hazel was standing in the door. We got out of the car, and she held the screen door open until we arrived on the stoop. Now, you've got to understand. Although the feud between the Bethels and the Ellises had been over for generations, there was sort of an understanding that the people from Guana Manor and the folks here on the Bethel property didn't socialize together."

"That was recently?" Sasha looked surprised.

"Yes, pretty recently." Baltron puckered his lips. "Things softened quite a bit after Amos died. For some reason he and Mr. Ellis just couldn't get along. But old ways die hard."

"It's amazing how people can hold grudges for so long. Nurturing ill feelings," Sasha remarked as she rocked. "Nothing good ever comes of it."

"It is amazing," Baltron agreed. "That's why the way Hazel welcomed Precious was so strange. Through the years Olive and I had a few conversations with her, maybe enough to fill up a couple of pages, but we never developed any kind of relationship. So when Hazel looked as if she was waiting for Precious at the door, and welcomed her with almost open arms . . ." He shook his head. "We didn't know what to make of it.

"Hazel gave us a brief tour of the house, her plants and herbs and things, but after that Olive and I sat and waited while the two of them went for a walk. They were gone for a good half hour or more, walking through the key lime orchard on the east side of the property.

From that day on Precious would come and visit Hazel three and four times a week. According to the season they'd gather limes together. Those key limes make some of the best key lime pie I've ever tasted."

"They must have had a lot in common."

Baltron thought for a moment. "In some ways they were alike. Some folks thought of Hazel as an *obeah* woman, and Precious believed in the unseen as well."

"An *obeah* woman?"

"Yes. But I don't think she was. Hazel knew bush medicine, and some say she could hear and see *sperrids*."

"So they were spiritualists?" Sasha attempted to understand.

"Spiritualists?" Now Baltron was confused.

Sasha searched for the right words. "Someone who believes you can communicate with the dead."

For a second Baltron looked undecided. "I guess they were spiritualists. But it was much more than that. At least I know for Precious it was. She believed that seeing *sperrids* was just a little bit of what she called 'the big picture,' To her everything was a manifestation of God, the seen and the unseen. So I think that's why she and Hazel saw eye to eye so well. Precious once said, 'There were two sides to a coin. Good and evil. But there still was only one coin, and that coin was God.' "

"I can see she had a big influence on you." Sasha studied Baltron's face.

"Precious had an influence on everybody. That's just the way it was. But the deeper she followed her beliefs, the more she wanted her surroundings to reflect them. Mr. Ellis didn't like some of the things she was bringing to the house. Said folks would think we were all crazy having that kind of stuff inside Guana Manor." His mouth turned down. "And Precious didn't like discord, so she stopped bringing the things to the mansion. Instead she made gifts of them to Hazel. The two of them kind of fed off each other in a way. Precious's youthful nature was good for Hazel, and Hazel's knowledge of the land and island history was good for Precious."

Sasha hated the tinge of envy she felt toward Precious, but it was real nevertheless. "It seems like Mr. Ellis was one person Precious wasn't able to influence."

"Mr. Ellis is a hard case. His mother, Mother Ellis, wasn't the most loving woman, and she had a big influence on his life, like all mothers do on their children. I think she raised him out of her fears. Maybe, in a way, she was trying to protect him so he would never experience what she had experienced. I sensed she was holding a lot of things inside of her. So I tried to stay out of her way." He showed Sasha his palms. "Around her, everything had to be just so, and Mr. Ellis is the same way. But the truth is, no matter how much people liked Precious, folks thought she was strange. Mr. Ellis didn't like the fact that people were saying he had a daughter-in-law who wasn't quite right in the head."

"Last night I found out Mr. Ellis isn't the

only one who is touchy about the subject,"
Sasha replied.

"What happened?" Baltron looked concerned.

"I took a book from the library and Cay saw
it. It happened to be a book that Precious
bought. Cay said something like he thought all
those books had been thrown away. Then I
came back with something he didn't like . . .
and one thing led to another." Sasha recalled
how Cay had walked off into the dark.

"Uh-huh. Mr. Cay is sensitive about Precious's death. But I think it's time for him to
get over it. Maybe you're the one to help him
do that."

"I don't know if I want to," Sasha said honestly. "It feels like the Bethels and the Ellises
feuding all over again."

"Don't give up too easily," Baltron said,
looking down at his shoes. "He's a good man
with a heavy past." Their eyes met before Baltron went back to talking about the books.
"But I bet he got on Olive this morning about
not throwing those books away. He told her
to get rid of them a long time ago. But Olive
couldn't bring herself to do it. She figured
since Mr. Cay doesn't have time to read like
he used to before his father's health started going bad, the books would be safe in that corner. I bet before he left this morning he
reminded Olive to get rid of them."

"I wouldn't mind taking the books," Sasha
said. "I found some of the subjects rather in-
triguing."

"Is that right?"

She nodded.

"We-ell, it seems sort of right for the books to end up here at the Bethel House, where Precious first kept them." He smiled slightly. "I don't see why we can't get rid of them by giving them to you. I'll be sure to tell Olive."

"Good." Sasha smiled. She wanted to ask him about Olive's belief that she had seen Precious inside the Circle of Stones, but she thought better of it.

"I think I need to get going." Baltron looked out into the hall. "You seem to be settled in pretty well."

"I am." Sasha followed him to the door. "Thank you for everything, and Baltron?"

"Yes?"

"You've lived here on Magic Key all of your life, haven't you?"

"Sure have."

"Have you ever seen any evidence of the things Hazel and Precious believed in?" Sasha hoped he would mention the bright light Olive had claimed burst forth from Precious's body at the moment of her death.

"I can't really say," he said quietly, then he piped up. "But I've heard tell of some things that made me think twice. Precious seemed to think belief was a key that unlocked many doors. I guess I'm a little short on that."

Sasha nodded. "Thanks again, Baltron."

"No need," he said as he stepped out onto the stoop. "I'll bring those books back over to you later."

Chapter 15

"Anybody home?" the voice called through the screen door.

"Just a minute," Sasha said, craning her neck to see who it was with no luck. "I wonder who that is," she mumbled, washing the remnants of onion off her hands.

She walked out of the kitchen and saw Jason Williams standing on the stoop.

"Thought I'd come by and see how you made out during the storm," the attorney said as Sasha approached.

She opened the door. "How kind of you. Would you like to come in?"

"Maybe for a couple of minutes." He brushed past her.

"Have a seat." Sasha motioned toward the couch. "Would you care for something to drink?"

The attorney wiped the beads of perspiration from his forehead with the back of his hand. "Yes, I could use something cold to drink."

"I'll get you some ice tea." Sasha disappeared and came back with a large glass. Then she sat down in the overstuffed chair opposite her guest.

"I have to say I'm rather surprised that you came by."

Attorney Williams lowered the half-empty glass from his mouth. "Well, I thought about this being your first hurricane here in the Keys. And I didn't get the feeling that you had made many friends during the short time you've been living here." He smiled. "The storm really roughed things up."

"I had a close call with some flooding, and that was pretty scary," Sasha said. "But other than having a really soggy front yard to contend with, I'm okay."

"My place fared well, too, but there were some folks on Annette Key whose houses were completely blown away, and a few boats were destroyed in the area."

"I heard about some families' losing their homes. As a matter of fact, my old furniture will be going to them as a donation."

"I thought this was new furniture." He looked at the cardboard taped around the legs of the cocktail table. "You sure move quickly."

"Not really." Sasha leaned back in the chair. "I guess this is something I would have ended up telling you anyway." She watched Attorney Williams finish his tea. Sasha hesitated bringing up the vandalism because it involved Cay. "When I got home the other day from visiting your office, someone had broken in here and poured bleach through my house. They ruined my living room furniture and the mattress and box spring in my bedroom. Along with some of my clothes."

"Really?" Attorney Williams's eyebrows knitted together.

"Yes. It was quite a mess."

"And who do you think did it?"

"Can't you guess?" She put her elbow on the arm of the chair.

"Cay Ellis?" He looked incredulous.

"Well, not him personally, but I thought he had gotten someone else to do it."

"Thought, as in past tense."

"Yes, thought." Sasha looked at him. "Now I'm not sure that he was behind it."

"What made you change your mind?"

"Several things." She didn't know where to start. "First of all, he was the one who paid for the new furniture."

"Is that right?" Attorney Williams gnawed on his bottom lip. "I guess most people wouldn't think the person who was responsible for destroying their old furniture would buy them new furniture to replace it."

"No, you wouldn't."

"Unless he did it to throw you off," Attorney Williams suggested. "Sometimes people with money like playing games." He set the glass on the table. "The Ellises have enough money that buying a couple of rooms of furniture is like buying somebody breakfast. Still, what you're talking about is pretty serious. Breaking and entering is a felony."

"I hadn't thought about that." Sasha's features turned grave.

"I'm not saying that is what happened, but

I've seen it before. Playing God with other people's lives is just a form of entertainment for the truly wealthy." He settled back on the couch. "Have you thought about pressing charges?"

"I've had no proof. And this is the first afternoon I've spent at home since the storm. I really haven't had much time to think about anything."

"What did you do? Go to a hotel to ride it out?"

"No," Sasha sighed. "I spent the past two nights at Guana Manor."

"Wait a minute." Williams moved to the edge of the couch. "You stayed at Guana Manor?"

"Yes, I did. I went over there to confront Cay about the vandalism, but the storm broke loose before I could leave the property. I tried to come back home and my car got caught up in the flooding. It was one thing after another," Sasha tried to explain. She was a little embarrassed when Attorney Williams's eyebrows went up as she used Cay's first name.

"Where's your car now?"

"Baltron Knowles is taking some workers from Guana Manor down to the lake to see if it's in there."

Williams sat back again, rubbing his forehead. "Ms. Townsend, may I give you some professional advice?"

Sasha nodded.

"I really think developing a personal relationship with the Ellises and Guana Manor may not be in your best interest. Unless you have reason to believe otherwise." The statement hung in the air.

Sasha thought about Cay's leaving for two weeks and not telling her. "No. No, I don't."

"Well, let me suggest this. It looks bad enough that you accepted this furniture, though I agree it's too late to return it now. But you should call Mr. Knowles and let him know that you've procured a way to check on your car and that you won't need his help. That will sever that tie. I'll be glad to take you down to the lake to find out if your car is there. That is, if you don't mind?"

Sasha didn't believe Jason Williams was this kind to all of his clients. She got the feeling that he was interested in her in more ways than one. But at the moment it didn't matter. He was right. She was already in a legal battle with the Ellises, and developing personal ties was not a smart thing to do. This was something Sasha had known all along, but her feelings for Cay were affecting her judgment. She had to get a grip on them and admit to herself that there was no future in store for her and Cay Ellis III. Talking to Attorney Williams had been a good reminder.

"I'd appreciate your taking me. I'll give Baltron a call."

"There it is! There's my car." Sasha pointed. The Mazda was lodged against a young pine tree. If not for the pine, the car would have landed in the lake, which was only a few yards away.

"You were really lucky." Attorney Williams

stopped his vehicle before the mud got too deep.

"I wonder if it will start." Sasha began to roll up her pants leg and take off her shoes.

"What are you about to do?" he asked as Sasha got out of the car.

"I'm going to find out."

Williams looked at the six-inch-thick mud. "I'd be careful if I was you. You might catch your death out here."

But Sasha was already on her way. "Don't worry, I'll be fine," she replied, picking her way toward the Mazda.

The car gave a mild grunt the first time Sasha turned the key. After several more tries it chugged until it caught, ran for a few seconds, then cut off again. It was a reassurance that the car wasn't ruined. The interior was pretty bad, Sasha appraised. But the exterior had minimal damage, and Sasha was certain it wouldn't be long before she was driving again. "I need to have it towed, but with a little work she'll be as good as before," she said as she made her way back across the mud.

"You're one brave lady," Williams commented. "Most of the women I know wouldn't dare get in that mud." He looked at Sasha's muddy feet and splattered calves. "I've got a couple of old towels in the trunk of my car that you can use to wipe that stuff off." He glanced at the clean interior of his Acura Legend.

"Thanks, Mr. Williams," Sasha replied. "I

guess I wasn't thinking about how messy this was going to be."

"Look, call me Jason." He smiled at her. "And it's no problem. No problem at all. But I would be careful around here. You know, some people say Cay Ellis's wife died from some kind of infectious bacteria she picked up."

"I've heard," Sasha replied.

"I've got a friend who was one of the doctors who examined her, and he had a different opinion about how she died. So I'm not so sure about the how, but I know she died from something."

"What did he think she died from?" Sasha leaned against the car to wipe off her feet.

"He says it could have been a combination of things." Jason studied the smooth curve of Sasha's calf as he spoke. "But primarily he thinks dehydration started a domino effect of different body functions shutting down."

"Dehydration . . ." Sasha thought about Cay and the springwater.

"Yeah," Jason said. "He said it happened so quick. They'd never seen anything like it."

"Really?"

"That's right. He said when he saw the body it was as if it had been heated at high temperatures from the inside. But not regular heat. Heat that would come from high-intensity light or vibration. Said it was one of the strangest things he had ever seen."

"Did the doctors think there was some kind of foul play or something?" Sasha folded the muddy side of the towel inward as she recalled what Olive had said about the light at the moment of Precious's death.

"No. They felt it was some kind of natural process resulting from the sequence of organs that shut down. That's all they could come up with. And the family was not interested in any kind of autopsy."

"I guess they had been through enough." Sasha's face was solemn.

"Well . . . I think that's enough morbid talk for one afternoon," Jason informed her. "I'm thinking about heading back to Big Pine Key to get something to eat. There's a gas station with a towing service near the restaurant I can recommend. If you want, you can arrange to have your car towed and get something to eat at the same time."

"That sounds like a good idea," Sasha replied as she opened the Acura's door. "I'll also file a vandalism report."

Jason climbed inside the car.

"How well did you know Precious Ellis?" Sasha asked.

"I didn't know her that well." Jason placed his arm across the back of the seat. "I'd seen her a few times at social events, not that I generally get to run in the circles that the Ellises do."

"What did you think of her?"

"She seemed to be a nice woman. Rather quiet, or maybe serene is a better word. Not all that pretty, but she had a special kind of style, I guess." He glanced at Sasha. "Why are you asking about Precious Ellis?"

"Just curious. I heard a few things about her

from her uncle and aunt while I was staying at Guana Manor. She seemed like a rather interesting woman."

"Oh. I thought you were like half of the single women in this area who have their eye on Cay Ellis the third. You know, trying to figure out what kind of woman he likes."

"I don't have any intention to reel in Mr. Ellis," Sasha replied honestly.

"Good. It's guys like him that make it hard for an ordinary fellow like me."

"How's that?"

"He fits that category. You know the type. Tall, dark, and handsome. And he's got money coming out of his ears. A working man like me doesn't hold a chance against him."

"Where I come from attorneys have a better chance than many of their male counterparts," Sasha replied.

"I can hold my own against your average Joe. It's just fellows like Ellis that make it hard." He was silent for a moment. "So, does that mean you would be interested in a guy with a profession like mine?"

Sasha looked at Jason Williams. On a scale of one to ten she would give him a six or six and a half. He seemed to be a nice fellow. "Maybe," she replied.

"Well, maybe isn't no . . . so, as an attorney, I will take that as an opportunity to present my case whenever I'm given the chance."

"That's up to you." Sasha smiled slightly.

"Are you always this noncommittal?" Jason inquired.

"It's been said before." Sasha thought of Cay.

"Well, as long as I know I'm not the only fellow getting the runaround I can deal with it," he remarked before he turned on the radio.

Chapter 16

Sasha had come to love the Bethel House, and spending the early-morning hours watching the sunrise from Hazel's room had become a daily ritual. There was a touch of magic within the tiny structure. The first night she stayed at the house after the storm Sasha had been somewhat wary. Olive's claim that she had seen Precious by the stones had unnerved her, and Sasha wasn't a total disbeliever in the unusual.

There had been days after her mother died that Sasha believed she felt her presence. Once she even thought she smelled her mother's favorite perfume in the middle of the night. Those experiences had compelled Sasha to search for books about people who believed they'd had encounters with deceased loved ones. She was shocked to find there were so many. Shocked, but at the same time comforted.

Yet Olive's experience had been different. She believed she had seen Precious in the stark daylight! In her readings Sasha had not come across a single personal account that mirrored Olive's. But considering Olive's excitement over the *chiccharney*, Sasha wondered if she had an overactive imagination.

Sasha's curiosity was piqued even further the day Baltron returned with Precious's books. He brought the picture album with him.

"Here's a photograph of Precious and Hazel," he said after thumbing through a stack of pictures inside the back cover. "It's not a real good one, though." He peered at the small figures in the middle. "You really can't see their faces. We were on our way to Big Pine Key when Precious jumped out of the car and asked me to take this picture. Hazel happened to be out in the yard that day. You can see the house behind them there. There is another picture that's a good one." Baltron flipped the pages.

"Wait a minute." Sasha stopped him. "Isn't that Cay?"

"Uh-huh. That's Cay and Precious . . . Wally and Sherry." He pointed to the figures as he called the names. "They were going on a trip to Key West when Olive snapped this picture."

"Everyone looks happy except Wally."

"It was kind of hard to tell when Wally was happy or sad," Baltron replied. "I think it was hard for Wally to tell. He had everything going for him but didn't seem to make the right decisions to take advantage of his good fortune."

"And Precious appears to be older than I thought she'd be."

"She had that kind of air about her." Baltron looked at his niece's face. "You've heard folks say someone was 'born an old person'? That's how Precious was. Actually, if she were alive today she'd be thirty-five."

"So young," Sasha commented as Baltron flipped the pages again.

"Now, here's a good picture of Hazel. You can see why Mr. Ellis said you resembled her. Even though she's much older than you, the family resemblance is there."

Sasha *was* surprised by how much she looked like Hazel. She knew, with her pecan-brown skin, she didn't look like her mother—who had been very fair. She had often wondered who she took after, and now she knew. It was her father's side of the family. A side she'd thought she'd never meet.

With her thoughts in the present Sasha looked at the two pictures beside her mother's large one. Precious and Hazel made such an unusual pair. Hazel was sturdy and bent with age, whereas Precious was as tall and thin as a willow.

After Baltron said his goodbye, Sasha settled in to examine the book more closely. When she was through, she rested her hand on its cover. She was amazed by the elaborate history the book painted of earth and humankind. It made her wonder if any of it could possibly be true. Sasha couldn't help but think life would be so different if mankind believed it. The planet would be a more loving place, standing proud in a rich magical history.

A ringing phone jarred her philosophical meanderings. "Hello."

"Hello. It's Jason."

"Hi, Jason. How are you?"

"I'm fine. I'm going to a wine-and-cheese gathering after work today and I wondered if you'd like to come."

"A wine-and-cheese . . . What's the attire? Dressy?"

"Not really," Jason replied. "It sounds more elaborate than it is. Some folks who are interested in making improvements to the downtown area of Big Pine Key are having it, just to butter up all the attorneys around here. They want to make sure we don't oppose anything they want to do. It will be the perfect opportunity for me to tell you what I've found out about the agreement."

"If you've got something, I want to know about it right now," Sasha said, looking at the articles of incorporation she had completed for her bottled water company. "I'd like to file for my incorporation papers as soon as possible."

"I've just made a few contacts, that's all. But it's progress nevertheless."

"Do you know when the property dispute will come up in court?"

"I can tell you all that when I see you, if you're coming."

"I'll come. Where do you want to meet?"

"You don't have to worry about that. I'll pick you up."

"No, that's okay. I don't mind coming over on my own now that I have my car back."

Jason went silent. "I guess you feel if you

come on your own, this will be less of a date."

"I didn't think this was a date," Sasha replied. "Must our getting together have a label?"

"I think that's your nice way of telling me you're not ready to go out on a date with me but you wouldn't mind coming to the wine-and-cheese party. Is that right?"

"Pretty much."

"Okay, date or no date, meet me at the Big Pine Library in the conference room at seven o'clock. Okay?"

"I'll see you then."

"I'm looking for the conference room," she told the ponytailed librarian. The library, located next to a supermarket, was small but modern.

"If you look straight ahead, there it is right back there." The woman pointed.

Sasha followed the woman's instructions and ended up in a room containing about thirty people talking, eating, and drinking. It was a mixed crowd, but the majority of the attendees were men. Jason was nowhere in sight, so Sasha made her way to the nearest cheese tray. After choosing an array of cheddar, Colby, and Swiss, Sasha heard a friendly "Hello. I've never seen you around here." A good-looking guy with a toothy smile spoke as he reached for the tray.

"That's probably because I'm new in the area," Sasha replied.

"I thought so, my name is Edward Johnson, and I'm—"

"He's the biggest flirt in these parts as well as a city attorney," Jason broke in.

At first Edward looked surprised, but he recovered quickly and asked, "You two know each other?"

"Even if we don't, she's under my protection." Jason put his arm around Sasha's shoulders. "You have more than your fair share of women as it is."

"I can't believe you said that," Edward replied.

"I've learned when I'm around you I've got to speak up quickly before it's too late," Jason ribbed him.

"So, I see you've got a new friend," a familiar female voice commented. Surprisingly, Sherry appeared from behind a large man who held two hors d'ouevre plates filled to the brim.

"Actually," Sasha began.

"I believe you could say that," Jason replied.

"I was talking to Sasha." Sherry gave Jason a syrupy smile.

"And you two know each other?" Edward pointed from Sherry to Sasha.

Sasha nodded.

"I'm going to leave you to it, man." Edward made a face and a hasty retreat.

"What did he mean by that?" Sasha asked.

"Edward always thinks he's got everything figured out. It's a prerequisite for being a politician," Jason replied, then he turned to Sherry. "What brings you to this kind of function? I didn't think it was your kind of gathering."

"Maybe I'm not as predictable as you think I am." Sherry sipped her glass of wine.

"I don't think that's the case." Jason smiled, but the smile didn't light his eyes. "You know that agreement you Ellises claim proves you own the Bethel land?"

"Yes."

"You might as well know I'm going to slaughter it in court."

Sasha's eyebrow rose. Jason had not discussed the issue with her, but here he was challenging Sherry with the legalities of it.

"Don't speak too quickly, Jason. You better make sure you've done your homework." Sherry swirled the sparkling liquid around in her glass. "You know, sometimes you like to jump the gun with unfounded conclusions."

Sasha saw Jason's jaw tighten. "I can assure you that is not the case this time."

Silence swelled between them.

"I've got a great idea." Sherry placed her index finger against her fuchsia lips. "Why don't you and Sasha come to dinner tomorrow night so we can discuss this as old friends?" Her voice softened on the last two words.

Jason studied Sherry's face before he replied. "I don't mind coming over and discussing the matter, although settling this thing out of court might be the best thing for the Ellises. But it's definitely up to Sasha whether she'd like to pursue this or not."

Up to me, Sasha thought. She was certain there was an undercurrent flowing between

Jason and Sherry that had nothing to do with her. "If you think it can be settled out of court, I'm open to that. I just want to get it done." Sasha took a sip of wine and asked, "Is Cay back?"

Sherry's pupils appeared to darken. "So you didn't know. He's been back for days. I wouldn't dream of discussing this without him."

"Really?" Sasha replied. She knew Sherry was playing up that Cay had returned but hadn't bothered to contact her. It was a decent jab, and it stung.

"Really." Sherry smiled prettily. "It's settled, then. Let's make it cocktails at seven and dinner at seven-thirty."

"That sounds fine," Sasha replied, but she wondered if Sherry was telling the truth about when Cay had returned. She had concluded Sherry was not a woman to be trusted.

"We'll be there," Jason agreed.

Sherry placed her empty glass on the table. "I better mill around and make the best of this. It's not often that I come out to this kind of function." Sherry looked at Jason, then disappeared into the crowd.

"I wonder why she had such a change of heart?" Sasha bit off some cheese.

Jason downed the remainder of his wine. "Perhaps she's heard from some of the people I've been talking to. Or perhaps seeing that you've got an attorney did it."

"Does my hiring *you* as an attorney have anything to do with it?"

"I wouldn't think so."

"I'm not blind, Jason. There was definitely something going on between you two that didn't have anything to do with me and the Bethel property."

"As I told you before," Jason replied, "I know the Ellises, and I know them well. Some of the things I know about them, and the kind of influence their money has had on people, I don't like."

"This sore spot you have for the Ellises' money isn't going to be a problem for me in the long run, is it?" Sasha said, putting him on the spot.

"Absolutely not. If anything"—he smiled devilishly—"it might help."

Chapter 17

The next day Sasha slowly opened her eyes and looked at the sun through the sliding glass door. She was startled to see how far it had climbed into the sky. "How long was I meditating?" she asked herself. She looked at the clock on the decorators table. Thirty minutes had passed, much longer than her usual session.

Slowly, the memory of what she had experienced impressed itself on her conscious mind. She gazed at the sky as the images renewed themselves. She recalled standing in the clearing outside the Circle of Stones on Guana Estate. Precious and Hazel were there, but they were inside the circle. Where they stood, the light was bright and beautiful. It was unlike anything she had ever seen. It gave her a warm, secure feeling just to be near it. Sasha tried to recapture the sensation. Their faces shone with joy. She wanted to know what could make them feel that way. What was the source of their happiness? That's when they beckoned to her. Sasha clasped her hands together and realized it was only within the Circle of Stones that the light shone. Outside of it there were varying degrees of darkness. Then, suddenly, she understood that light meant truth and darkness stood for ignorance.

Sasha got up and began to walk around the room. This was a new experience for her. She had been meditating on and off for the last year, but had become more dedicated to the practice once her mother died. She was in need of the peace and solace the silence gave her.

"There had to have been a reason behind all that. Everything was so real," she said to herself as she stood in front of the photographs. "I have to go back to the Circle of Stones," she determined. "I'll go there tonight after the dinner meeting at Guana Manor."

"What would you like to drink?" Sherry posed in her smooth black dress.

"A screwdriver," Jason said, leaning against the bar.

"And you, Sasha?" Sherry twirled her hand graciously. It was obvious she loved playing the hostess.

"Grand Marnier," Sasha replied. She felt nervous. She wanted to get seeing Cay again over with right away, but it hadn't happened. Olive was the one who'd opened the door, and later it was Sherry who'd welcomed them, alone. Part of Sasha felt good about that. It made Cay and Sherry less the man and woman of Guana Manor, but the other part of her was less enthusiastic. She didn't want to be caught off guard by anything Cay said or did. Her feelings were too unstable for that.

Sasha heard footsteps approaching as she reached for her drink, then she heard his voice.

"Attorney Williams."

"Hello, Mr. Ellis," Jason replied.

She turned to see them shaking hands. Cay was inches taller than Jason, and he looked lean and appealing in his Italian shirt and pants. "Sasha." He nodded toward her from across the room.

"Hello, Cay." Her voice was resonant.

"And will you be having cognac, Cay darling?" Sherry called.

"Yes," he replied.

"I thought so," Sherry sang. "It's always been your favorite." She poured for Cay and herself before crossing the floor. "There." She passed Cay his snifter.

"I haven't been seeing you around." Cay directed the comment to Jason.

"I've been here. Been keeping busy." He adjusted his tie.

There was a somewhat uncomfortable silence.

"Were you out of town for long?" Jason asked.

"I was gone for about two weeks. I thought perhaps I would be able to return early"—he looked at Sasha—"but it wasn't possible."

"Would anybody care to sit down?" Sherry jumped in to try to detract from Cay's uncovering her lie.

"That's okay." Sasha held Sherry's gaze long enough to let her know she'd heard Cay's comment. "I like standing."

"Speaking of standing, do you like your new furniture?" Cay turned to Sasha and looked so deeply into her eyes she felt as if he were mere inches away.

"New furniture?" Sherry repeated, surprised.

"Yes, I do. It worked out fine. But I would have preferred to have been told about it before you bought it," Sasha admonished him.

"Cay, I didn't know you were so prone to keeping secrets." Sherry attempted to keep her voice at an even keel.

"Yes, Mr. Ellis. I also found it rather unusual that you bought my client furniture."

"I can't see why my buying Sasha furniture has anything to do with anyone except for Sasha and me." His voice was silky. "The furniture was a gift from one friend to another."

"You never know," Sherry chimed in. "You might be stepping on Jason's toes in other ways as well. The two of them looked rather cozy at a wine-and-cheese party I attended yesterday." Sherry sidled up to Cay.

"That's right, Mr. Ellis, you never know, so perhaps you should ask a woman if she is open to receiving such a gift, especially when she suspects you of being the reason she was in need of new furniture in the first place."

Cay looked at Sasha, but before she could comment Sherry had taken him by the arm. "I think we can go in to dinner now." She began to move with him across the room.

Sasha and Jason fell in behind Cay and Sherry. Olive had prepared a delicious meal of turtle steaks, pigeon peas and rice, cabbage, and johnnycakes. Two candle arrangements made the china and silverware twinkle, providing an air of elegance to the meal.

"Everything looks wonderful, Olive," Sherry said as she placed her napkin in her lap.

Olive's thank-you was perfunctory. Afterward she rolled her eyes toward the ceiling.

Sasha and the others ate their food in silence. From time to time she could feel Cay's brooding eyes on her. Sasha could tell Sherry was pleased that her innuendo about Jason was taking root. But Sasha wasn't averse to planting seeds of her own.

"Sherry, I just want you to know Jason and I met when I hired him as my attorney, and so far that's the extent of our relationship."

Jason glanced up from his plate, but he continued to eat. Sasha felt he was somewhat ill at ease. In light of his being fairly eager to attend the dinner, she didn't understand why.

"I see." Sherry's face lengthened.

"That's in case you're interested." Then Sasha employed some dramatics of her own. "But I nearly forgot, at the wine-and-cheese party you called Jason an old friend. How long have you known each another?" Sasha cut into her turtle steak, looking from Sherry to Jason.

"We've known each other for quite a while," Sherry replied.

Jason continued to look at his plate.

"As I told Jason, I hope there is no conflict

of interest here." Sasha dug in even further.

"Why, none at all." Sherry appeared affronted.

"There's no need to become riled, Sherry. No one would dare think you've ever been involved with the likes of me," Jason retorted.

"Now, Jason, you're being unfair. That's not what I meant." She straightened her wine and water glasses. "I guess I'm a little flabbergasted because from the very first time I visited Magic Key I have always been involved with the Ellis family, and then, of course, I married Wally. So it just seems a little disrespectful to imply I may have been involved with anyone else."

Jason turned stone-faced before he took a long sip of wine.

"So what have we here?" Mr. Ellis walked in looking healthier than Sasha had ever seen him.

"Oh, hi, Papa," Sherry said nervously. "We're having dinner."

"I can see that for myself." He walked over to the table. "I mean, what's the occasion? I don't believe I've ever met this young man before."

"I've seen you around town, sir." Jason stood up. "I'm Attorney Jason Williams. Sasha Townsend hired me to look out for her interest concerning the Bethel Agreement."

"So is this dinner for business or pleasure?" Mr. Ellis continued his interrogation.

"Primarily business, sir." Jason remained standing.

"Why wasn't I told about this, Cay? It's one

thing to take over while I'm sick, but to completely overlook me when I'm feeling fit is another."

"I just got back in town at noon today. That's when Sherry told me about the dinner. I assumed you would be attending," Cay said, leaning on the chair arm.

"Is that right? So this is another one of your back door plots, is it, Sherry?"

"Papa, please." Sherry looked embarrassed. "Certainly not. I was told that you would be busy all day today, and I assumed that meant you wouldn't be available for dinner," she tried to explain.

"Who told you that?" Mr. Ellis challenged.

"Baltron said you had business to attend to outside the house—"

"Who made Baltron my keeper? And you could have called me on the cell phone at any time; that's why I got the goddamned bothersome thing."

The room went silent.

"I'm sure it won't be a problem for Olive to put another place setting on the table," Sherry said lamely. "I'll go ask her."

"Don't bother. I've already had something to eat. And that's not the point." He banged on the table with his fist. "I want to know everything that goes on around here, Ms. Sherry. Can you understand that?"

"Yes, Papa," Sherry replied stiffly.

"Cay can make these kinds of decisions. But I want to know if and when attorneys are being invited to Guana Manor. No matter what the circumstance might be. Nothing personal, son''—Mr. Ellis gestured in Jason's direction—''but I don't trust the sons-a-bitches. They've done enough dirt on my behalf for me to know they can't be trusted.'' Mr. Ellis placed both fists on the table and leaned toward Sherry. ''And, Miss Ma'am, you're going to keep stirring up stuff here until one day you're going to have a big pot of shit, and the stench is going to be all over you. Mark my words.'' Mr. Ellis tugged at his pants. ''And with that I'll say good night all.'' He tilted his head and left the dining room.

''Well,'' Sherry said breathlessly, ''I don't know if I can finish my meal after that. I've never been so embarrassed in my life.''

''By now you should know how Papa is, Sherry.'' Cay looked around the table. ''He wants to make sure everybody knows who the head honcho is. That's all. He feels any business that involves Guana Manor is his business, and he's right.''

''I understand that, but sometimes he can be so crude.'' Sherry sniffed.

''I know,'' Cay agreed. ''But we've all got our faults and our reasons for doing things the way we do. So don't let him upset you.''

''You've always been so kind to me, Cay.'' Sherry turned adoring eyes on her brother-in-law.

''And what is your motive, Mr. Ellis, for being kind to my client, then trying to enforce an agreement that is as old as dirt?'' Jason's tone was aggressive.

Cay sat back in his chair, studying Jason, who appeared to be agitated.

"I don't know if the Bethel Agreement is as old as that," Cay said calmly. "But yes, I acknowledge that it was drawn up a long time ago between my ancestors and Sasha's. However, what is the point of an agreement if it can be tossed out because of its age?"

"It just makes no sense," Jason argued. "It's not a deed. And I believe if you had one you would have produced it by now. Yet you're going through all of this over that little piece of land that couldn't possibly mean that much to you. The Ellises own practically all of Magic Key and all sorts of property on Big Pine Key. Personally, I don't think it's about the land. I believe it's all about power. The rich versus the poor," Jason summed it up.

"Personally?" Cay's tone held an icy chill. "How did this become a personal matter for you, Attorney Williams? Not too long ago Sasha made it clear that she hired you as her attorney, nothing more. I think you need to remember that."

"I thought we came here to try and come to some kind of agreement," Sasha said, muscling her way into the conversation. "That's what I'm interested in. Any other interests I might have outside of this is not the issue. Is there a way, Cay, that we can put this agreement to rest with both of us being mutually satisfied?"

"I believe there is." Cay looked directly at Sasha. "I'm willing to consider the agreement null and void as long as everything on the property remains as it is."

"Meaning?" Sasha wanted to make sure she understood.

"You must abandon your idea of starting a bottled water business."

"And that's supposed to be a compromise?" Sasha was incredulous.

"It is. All of the Bethel property would be yours."

"Technically, the Bethel property is already mine," she retorted. "How am I supposed to support myself while I live there? Have you ever thought about that?"

"No, he hasn't," Jason interjected. "And you know why?" He paused dramatically. "Because money isn't an issue for him. Figuring out how he's going to live until he turns old and gray is a moot point for the Ellises."

"I don't think we're going to get anywhere this way." Sherry placed both her hands on the table. "I have another idea. One that Cay had seriously considered while Hazel was alive, long before Sasha came to Magic Key." She turned to Cay. "I know you've been very busy these last few weeks; perhaps you simply forgot. What if Guana Manor wanted to buy out Sasha's interest in the Bethel property?"

"Buy me out?" Sasha was taken aback.

"Yes. Pay you whatever the house and the surrounding area are worth." Sherry's eyes gleamed, but Cay's countenance became unreadable.

"How much money are you talking about?" Sasha looked at Cay. She couldn't help it.

"We'd have to get back to you with the particulars, but it would be a substantial sum,"

Sherry announced. "This could be a perfect solution to the situation, might it not, Cay?"
Sherry was excited.

"Maybe," was all he would say.

"Would the payoff include a reasonable per-
centage of the money Sasha believed she could
have made from her bottled water business?"
Jason pressed.

Sherry looked at Cay. "Yes, that would be
taken into consideration."

"What do you think, Sasha?" Jason asked.

"I don't know what to think." Sasha was
stunned. If she was paid off, the money could
be substantial, but it would also mean she
would no longer live on Magic Key. "Of
course, I'd have to see what kind of money we
are talking about."

"Of course," Sherry chimed in.

"Since this is something you have discussed
in the past . . ." Jason waited for Cay's ac-
knowledgment.

"Yes, it had been discussed." Cay's tone
was flat.

"Then it sounds like we could have a possible solution," Jason announced. "We will
wait for your offer."

Chapter 18

~

Cay held the flashlight high above his head. It was difficult to walk in the attic. The last time he had been there was after Precious's funeral. He had tossed the trunks containing her clothes and her belongings onto the creaky planks. He could not bring himself to completely part with the memories.

Cay looked around him, then glanced out of the window. As a child this had been his lookout point. From here he could see the entire road leading up to the property, and if he strained enough, he could see the little house beyond. The Bethel House. Here, in secret, Cay had watched the comings and goings of the adults. Especially his father.

Cay switched off the light and walked over to the window. He could see Attorney Williams's car turning onto the Bethel property driveway. It stopped mere yards away from the stoop, causing the motion lights to pop on. Cay waited to see the two figures get out of the car and enter the cottage. But it never happened. Seconds later the car turned and headed back toward the road. To his surprise, another set of headlights came on. He could feel his stomach churn. "She's going to spend the night at his place." His harsh whisper settled amid the boxes and items from the past.

Cay watched Sasha's car leave the Bethel House. He clenched the flashlight tightly in his hand, assuming she would catch up with Jason Williams's taillights, but the Mazda turned back toward Guana Manor. Stunned, Cay continued to watch. "Where in the world is she going?" He shined the flashlight on his watch. He knew how much time it took for a car to return to Guana Manor from the Bethel House, but the seconds continued to tick away. Sasha was headed farther into the Key.

Cay was more than curious. Where could Sasha be going on Magic Key at this time of night? He was determined to find out.   .

The SUV headed down the foggy road, but there was no sign of Sasha's car. Then the road headed eastward and he caught sight of her tiny red lights in the distance. "Is she headed toward the lake?" he pondered, keeping his distance; then he saw the lights pull off the road. "She's headed toward those stones." A dawning sense of déjà vu crept over him. One that chilled his spine. It wasn't the first time that a woman he cared for had ventured off into the night in search of God only knows what. And those searches had culminated in an unhappy ending. "What in the hell has gotten into her? Why is she headed toward the Circle of Stones?"

* * *

Sasha's heart was beating fast as she entered the woods. She thought, *I don't know why I convinced myself to come out here at this time of night. This was the stupidest idea I've ever had. Coming during the day would have been a much brighter idea.*

But the image of Precious and Hazel calling to her was very vivid in her mind. Very powerful. And, Sasha thought, if Precious and Hazel had found happiness on the other side, maybe her mother had as well. But it was the joy they exuded that had really captured her. If the living could possess that kind of joy . . . Sasha jumped when she heard an animal scurrying to the right of her. "I've come this far, so there's no need to turn back now," she told herself. "It can't be but a little farther. Just a little farther."

When Sasha emerged in the clearing she breathed a sigh of relief. But the sound caught in her throat as the majesty of the megaliths descended around her. "This is unbelievable," she uttered as she turned slowly in the middle of the circle.

Impossible as it seemed, in the moonlight the stones appeared even larger than before. The soft light altered the color of the surfaces, turning them into a shimmery silver. Sasha walked over and placed her hand on one of the boulders. It was smooth and warm, and maybe it was the excitement of the moment, but Sasha also sensed a quiet strength within it. "If I only knew why I'm here," she spoke softly into the night.

"I'd like to know that as well," Cay proclaimed.

"What are you doing here?" Sasha spun around.

"That's my question." Cay stood inches away from her.

"I-I wasn't ready to settle down for the night," she lied, "so—"

"You decided to do a little trespassing."

"To be honest, I wasn't thinking about the trespassing," Sasha replied.

"Then what were you thinking?"

"I wasn't." She continued to evade the truth, not knowing how Cay would react to it. "I just wanted to get out and think." She took several steps back. Sasha could feel the monolith against her back.

"Well, it was a stupid thing to do, coming out here in the middle of the night alone." His tone was harsh.

Sasha couldn't stomach Cay's chastising her. "Who made you my bodyguard?"

"Make jokes if you want, but you put yourself in jeopardy coming out here like this."

"In jeopardy from what? Or should I say who?" Sasha refused to back down. "The only person I need protection from is you, because you're playing Monopoly with my life."

"That's not what I'm doing."

"Well, what would you call it?"

"I've told you before, but you're so hardheaded you can't hear me. There are things you don't understand. Things here on Magic Key beyond what you've experienced." He stood as still as the stones behind them. "You shouldn't play with it. You'll only get hurt. I care about you, Sasha. I don't want that to happen."

Sasha wanted to believe him but she couldn't. "That is total BS and you know it. How can you stand there and say you care about me, when it would be so easy for you to tear up that Bethel Agreement and just let me be. But you care for me so much"—her expression mirrored the irony—"that you would prefer to pay me off and send me packing over my digging up memories of your precious Precious."

Cay's mouth clamped into a stubborn line.

"See there? That's what I mean. I can't compete with a dead woman, Cay."

"It's not just Precious."

"It's not?" Sasha tried to understand. "Then what is it? Are you afraid of something?" Sasha looked deep into his eyes. "What are you afraid of?"

"Do you really want to know?" He grabbed her shoulders. "I'm afraid of losing you, of never seeing you again." He squeezed until her arms smarted. "Of never seeing the light of life shine in your eyes like it does tonight. In the beginning you were right. I wanted to keep you from flaunting my painful memories to the world. That's what selling that water represented to me. Your selling, to the masses, the one thing that Precious wanted before she died. Selling it as a life-giving substance, something good and wholesome . . . and I couldn't stand the thought of it." His voice implored her to understand.

"But then I began to care for you." He brought his face closer to Sasha's. "To really care for you, Sasha. To want to feel you in my arms, feel the heat of life that coursed through your veins." Cay looked down. He seemed to be searching for the right words to say. "But there is something that stops me. Something that has nothing to do with you and everything to do with me—and my family."

"So I'm not good enough for you Ellises, is that it?"

"No, it's much deeper than that." His gaze raced over her face.

"Then what?" Cay's zeal was frightening Sasha.

"Can't you see it? You inherited the Bethel property from family members you've never met before. And that experience you had at the spring. Wasn't that enough to warn you away? But no, you were being drawn in even then. Drawn to a family that is linked to the past and not the future. Why do you think this island is called Magic Key, Sasha? Do you think everything that is happening here is just happenstance? Coincidence?"

"What else am I supposed to think?" Sasha searched the depths of Cay's blazing eyes.

"I've lived here all my life, and although I've tried to ignore it, I have learned there is more to life than the average person ever imagined. This is a world of duality, Sasha. Not one way, but two."

Sasha's face reflected her uncertainty.

"There is more than good on this Key, Sasha. There is evil as well. They both reside on Magic Key. And sometimes it is hard to tell one from another. Where the line of delineation lies. So tell me, was it good or evil that compelled you to come into the woods, alone, in the middle of the night? Was it good or evil that drove Precious to believe in something so much that she would not give up on it, even though it cost her her life?"

Sasha could feel his anxiety. She knew he was speaking from his heart, reaching out to her from the depths of his life. There was something there he believed to be so horrible that he couldn't even put it into words. Suddenly, Sasha thought about the meditation that had led her to the Circle of Stones. Could Cay be right? Was it evil disguising itself as good that had led her to the woods? She looked into his intense, dark eyes and saw a gnawing hopelessness tinged with pain. But as Sasha continued to search their depths for the truth, the image of Hazel and Precious beckoning to her arose in her memory, along with the joy that had filled their faces. A joy that filled her with hope.

"No, I don't know much about Magic Key, Cay. We both know that. And maybe, here on this Key, there are things beyond human knowing, understanding. But that isn't necessarily all bad." Sasha strove to express how she felt. "Do you want to know what I think is our greatest enemy?"

Cay nodded slowly.

"Not wanting to know the truth, and allowing fear to keep us from finding out. Fear is our greatest enemy, Cay, because once you become its prisoner, it's hard to break free. Fear could keep you from discovering that life is more beautiful and fulfilling than you could have ever imagined. From discovering that love and goodness do triumph over evil. Wouldn't that make it worth reaching for?"

"You sound like Precious." Cay inhaled deeply. "She believed that goodness could prevail over evil. But look at where she is now. I don't want to lose you before I've ever had you, Sasha." He wrapped her in his arms.

Sasha could feel Cay's fear as he laid his face against her hair. "Oh, Cay," she replied, hugging him back. "You are such a strange man." She could feel the rapid beat of his heart. "You know, at this moment, we are the ones who are wading in dangerous territory. You and I, standing here in the moonlight, holding one another like this. The way I see it, this is the greatest danger."

"You don't know how true that is," Cay said softly. "In each other's arms we should be safe." He looked down into her face. "There should be refuge here."

Sasha felt as if she would drown in the liquid softness of Cay's eyes. She lifted her face and placed a soft kiss on his lips. That precious moment turned into an eternity as Cay drew her closer, kissing her forehead and then her cheek.

"Sasha." He planted small kisses on her face and neck until he reached the hollow at the base of her throat. "How I've wanted to do this. You are so beautiful to me, so desirable.

There has never been a woman who could hold a candle to you."

Sasha held her breath. "Never?" She waited for the answer.

"Never," Cay replied solemnly.

Their mouths met again, celebrating the barrier they had broken. It was a deep, drunken kiss full of understanding and surrender.

"I've never met a man who made me feel the way you do," Sasha confessed. "It frightens me. I'm afraid if I give myself to you, I will want to give so much there will be nothing left."

"Don't worry." Cay sank down onto the grass, pulling Sasha toward him. "I will replenish you."

Sasha hesitated, but in the end she tumbled, gently, on top of him. "And how will you do that?" she asked breathlessly.

"Like this, my Sasha. Like this."

Cay enfolded her in his arms, but this time when he kissed her she could feel the urgency of his desire. She shivered inside and rode the wave of electricity that bolted through them. Cay's hands roamed over her back, and their bodies sought intimacy through their clothing. Sasha could feel Cay's ropelike muscles underneath the material he wore and the hardness that formed between his legs. The feeling of his body coupled with Sasha's imagination made her moan.

"How long I have waited to hear such sounds," he whispered in her ear. "Your sounds, Sasha. But I'm not going to spoil this by being too eager. I want to remember everything tonight. Every single thing."

Sasha had no idea what Cay would do next. She seemed to float on a cloud of anticipation and desire. Through the pleasurable fog she watched Cay stand up, his body forming a shadow against the monolith. Cay's eyes never left hers as he began to undress.

"I cannot wait to have you, but I force myself to wait," he mouthed, his eyes becoming cloudy.

Sasha thought her heart would explode as she watched him become nude in the moonlight. He was a mass of muscles and tendons, a gorgeous specimen of masculinity, and every aspect of him was exaggerated by his shadow. "And now it is your turn."

Slowly, Sasha reached to unzip her dress.

"No," Cay said, "the pleasure must be mine."

He helped her to her feet, and with a grace akin to reverence Cay undressed her, then formed a pallet from their clothes. When Sasha finally stood completely nude, she did not know what was brighter, the celestial light or the passion in Cay's eyes.

"I don't know how I ever let my fear keep me away from you." His gaze drank of her body. "If I die tomorrow it will not matter, for in taking you I will have taken a ride to heaven."

"Oh, my God. What are you doing to me?" Sasha trembled. "I feel as if everything in me could just explode from your words alone." Her eyes were clenched tightly. "This is my fear. I am afraid of totally losing myself to you," she confessed softly.

He kissed her trembling lips. "Remember your own words, Sasha." His desire for her had made him bold. "Fear is our enemy, and out of love I dare it to touch us now."

The word *love* rang in Sasha's mind. Did Cay realize what he'd said? Or were his words the reflection of an opportune moment? Sasha did not know, and it was only for a second that she cared as their embraces turned from tentative to a fiery passion, building up to the actual moment when they would be one.

"There can be only one first time," Sasha whispered in his ear. "I want you to remember this moment, Cay, and I want to treasure it for the rest of my life."

Cay tightened his arms around her. "I will remember it, Sasha. There is no doubt in my mind that it will be branded on my spirit."

His entry was smooth and yet earthy, and their bodies moved like the rhythmic beating of a heart. It did not take long for Cay's and Sasha's pleasure to become unbearable, and they both yearned for, but tried to hold off, the ultimate release.

"This is heaven, Sasha," Cay breathed into Sasha's ears. "You are my heaven." He moaned as he reached his peak.

"And you are my . . . undoing," Sasha cried as she went over the edge.

Chapter 19

Sasha opened her eyes and felt the tickle of grass against her skin. She laughed softly. "I'll probably be calling you later on, asking you to scratch the mosquito bites I undoubtedly possess by now."

"I'll scratch your itch any time you want," Cay said huskily, sitting up.

"You'll probably be too busy scratching your own."

"Never." He planted a smack on her lips. "Never too busy."

They studied each other's faces.

"What if someone walks up and finds us lying out here in the open like this?" Sasha asked.

"You didn't seem concerned about that a few minutes ago." A devilish smile touched Cay's lips.

"No, I was too busy then," Sasha said impishly.

"If they come right now"—playfully, he pulled Sasha on top of him—"they'll get a good look at you."

"Now, see here. Already you're using this situation to your advantage." She squirmed, giggling. "It isn't fair," she said, looking up at the monolith, only inches away. Sasha stopped moving when an image began to emerge on the gray surface. She wondered if her eyes were deceiving her or if it was the slant of the moonlight that had caused the colors to appear. But she continued to watch as they evolved from faded shades into the intense hues of a perfect rainbow.

"What is it?" Cay asked, aware of a change in her body language.

"There's a rainbow on the stone."

"A rainbow?" Cay turned over to see for himself as Sasha watched the colors fade.

"I don't see anything."

Sasha couldn't speak, she was so stunned by the incident.

Cay looked up at the moon. "Perhaps it was an illusion created by the moonlight."

Sasha continued to stare at the monolith. Those were *not* shades of gray, she thought. There had been a rainbow, arch and all, on the stone. It had been as clear as day. Was this the reason Precious and Hazel had summoned her to the Circle of Stones?

"Sasha, are you okay?" Concern etched Cay's features.

"Yes." She looked at him. "Yes, I'm fine."

"Are you certain?"

"Absolutely." She gave a slight smile, then looked away. "I guess we should get dressed before every mosquito out here discovers us."

"Sounds like a good idea to me." Cay

reached for his pants, but he continued to watch Sasha.

"Do you want to come to the Be— . . . my house?" Sasha offered, feeling uncomfortable using the term "the Bethel House" with Cay. "I could fix us something to drink. I have some wine and some coffee."

"I haven't been inside the Bethel House for a long time," Cay replied with his shirt in his hand. "I don't know. . . ."

"It's okay." Sasha looked down, feeling a tinge of hurt. "If you're not ready to come into the house because of Precious, you're not ready."

"Just give me a little more time, Sasha." He lifted her chin to make her look at him. "I'm sure I'll be able to work through this."

Sasha nodded, but regret for what she had done emerged.

"We could go to Guana Manor," he suggested.

Sasha shook her head. "I don't think so. We were just battling it out at dinner, remember? I think it would look rather strange if you brought me home so soon. Everybody would probably figure I was trying to win you over using the oldest way known to man."

"If it's true, I must say I like this methodology," he teased.

They walked toward the woods.

"What about breakfast tomorrow?" Cay offered.

"Where?"

"On Big Pine Key."

"I don't know." Sasha looked torn. "I can

just see me having breakfast with you and my attorney walks in. That's after he's already warned me against fraternizing with the enemy, let alone making love to him."

Cay pulled Sasha to him. "I like that term, 'making love.' "

"You know, I kind of like it, too." Sasha felt uncomfortable under his intense scrutiny.

"I tell you what. Let's have breakfast in the Bahamas."

"What?" A large smile spread over Sasha's face.

"You heard me. I've got a seaplane, even though I've been too busy to fly it lately. It'll give me an excuse to do something I love to do."

"You know how to fly a plane?"

"I sure do." He beamed. "So I'll be by to get you early in the morning. Say . . . seven?"

"All right." Sasha looked at Cay with admiration. "Well, aren't you all that and a bag of chips."

"I didn't realize that Cay had left the house," Sherry said, looking out the window.

"Yep. He left about an hour ago," Baltron replied from the stairs.

"Did he say where he was going?"

"No." Baltron shook his head.

"I don't understand it. I told him I wanted to talk to him after dinner." She paced across the foyer.

"Mr. Cay's a grown man, Ms. Sherry. I don't keep up with his comings and goings." Baltron continued on his way.

"I know that," Sherry snapped. " I don't—" She stopped when Cay opened the front door.

"Oh, there you are." Sherry smiled sweetly. "I was wondering where you were."

"I went out." Cay started for the stairs.

"You must have forgotten." Sherry fell in behind him. "I told you I wanted to talk to you after dinner about buying Sasha out of the Bethel property."

"I'm sorry. I did forget." Cay turned to face her. "But let's not do it tonight. Let's save it for later."

"Later." Sherry looked crestfallen. "I thought this was something we could wrap up very quickly. It's not like you've never considered the idea before. It's just a matter of your giving me the go-ahead. I'll dig up the figures we discussed a while back and forward them to Jason Williams."

"Like I said, I'm not ready to do that at this time, Sherry."

Sherry was irritated, but she tried not to show it. She wanted to resolve the Bethel House issue, and buying out Sasha Townsend was the perfect thing to do. Sasha would be off of Magic Island and out of their lives.

Sherry watched Cay climb the stairs. She looked at the back of his head in frustration. "Wait a minute, Cay. There's something in your hair." She hurried behind him, grateful for the opportunity to touch him.

Cay moved away.

"They're pine needles," she announced, surprised. "And you smell like grass." She looked up into Cay's blank face. "Don't tell me you've been rolling around on the ground with that woman."

"It's none of your business, Sherry."

Sherry wanted to tell him that it *was* her business, that he was her business because he was the future of Guana Manor, but she restrained herself, recalling their earlier conversation. "She's not worthy of you, Cay," Sherry said haughtily.

"I'll be the judge of that." He turned his back and walked up the stairs.

Chapter 20

🐚 "Oh, no-o. I don't think I like landing on water." Sasha could see the silver promotional magnet through her half-shut eyes as the seaplane made its descent.

"There's nothing to it, Sasha," Cay assured her. "Just relax. I've got it under control."

"Did you tell the water that?" She clenched her eyes. "Planes weren't meant to land on water. They were meant to land on concrete." Her voice went up.

Cay chuckled, and Sasha felt a slight thud. She opened her eyes as water sprayed against the windows. The seaplane glided a short distance on the Northwest Providence Channel, then onto the sandy beach.

"Now, that wasn't so bad, was it?" Cay turned bright eyes in her direction.

"Ask me after I get my heart out of my throat," Sasha retorted.

"It's got to come out or you won't be able to eat breakfast." Cay took the keys out of the ignition and got out of the plane. He came around to the other side, opened the door, and helped Sasha down.

"Out of all the Bahama Islands, why do you think we came to Freeport, on Grand Bahama Island?" he asked.

Sasha looked around. The landscape looked familiar. It reminded her of the Keys. "Because it was the closest?"

"No. Bimini was closer," he replied. "I chose Freeport because of the Ruby Swiss Restaurant. The last time I was here they had a gourmet breakfast that was wonderful."

"How long ago was that?" Sasha noticed a customs and immigration sign.

"A long time."

"What? Six months? A year?" Sasha pressed.

"Try two to three years." Cay nodded to a customs officer.

"Ca-ay. By now they may be closed."

"What can I say? We'll just have to take that chance."

They stood behind the yellow line. Sasha watched Cay go through customs. Once he was done she presented her papers and crossed to the other side. "That was easy," she remarked as she joined him.

"You've never been to the islands before?"

"Nope. This is my first time out of the States," Sasha confessed.

"Stick with me." Cay bent over and whispered in her ear. "We'll have one big adventure after another."

One of Sasha's eyebrows went up. "The jury is still out on whether those adventures will be good or bad. I'll save the verdict for later."

She smiled. "So, how much time do you have, Mr. Cay?"

"How much do I need?"

"It's according to what you plan to accomplish," Sasha replied, giving him the eye.

"Oh, I see." Cay's lips turned a sexy smile. "In that case, I've got all the time in the world."

"You're going to need it. That quick tumble in the grass was just an appetizer. You have no idea what the full-course meal is like," she continued to tease.

Cay laughed long and hard as they walked over to the curb and hailed a taxi.

Breakfast was more than Sasha had expected, and as they emerged from the upscale restaurant it was hard for her to believe that she was actually in the Bahamas with Cay. Sitting across from him at the breakfast table had brought the entire morning into perspective, and Sasha was on a roller coaster of emotions. The flirtatious woman she had been no more than an hour before had become reticent. Eruptions of feelings surfaced intermittently. Every time Sasha looked at Cay, she was forced to face the fact that she was falling in love with him.

"You sure have gotten quiet," he remarked.

"Have I?" Sasha didn't want to focus on herself, so she zoomed in on a large straw market across the street. "Hey, look at that. Let's check out the purses and hats," she exclaimed. "I've got to have a closer look. Come on."

Sasha dashed across the street in the middle

of flowing traffic. She made it to the other side with ease and dug into her purse for her sunglasses. Quickly, she placed them over her eyes. They would serve as a barrier. She did not want Cay to know the depth of her feelings. She was having a difficult time dealing with them.

"My goodness." Cay caught up to her. "You took off across that street like the Road Runner."

"Did I?" She threw a smile in his direction, then continued to look at a table piled high with hats.

"Didn't your mother teach you to look both ways before crossing the street?"

"Yes, and that's why I'm standing here safe and sound," Sasha tossed back. "How do you like this one?" She pulled a wide-brim hat with a colorful band down on her head.

"Looks great," Cay replied, a little confused by Sasha's actions.

"This bag should go with it." She pulled the straw straps up on her shoulder. "This will be perfect. So if I buy lots of touristy stuff I'll have someplace to put it."

"Sounds like a good idea," Cay replied.

"I'll take them," Sasha told the woman sitting under the blue-and-white umbrella. She took out her wallet.

"I've got it," Cay remarked.

"No," Sasha said emphatically, then softened her tone. "There's no need. I've got it."

Cay's eyes narrowed before he replied, "If you insist."

Sasha could feel him watching her as she

took her change from the vendor. "So, what do we do now?" Sasha asked in her most matter-of-fact voice.

"I thought perhaps we'd walk around the island." Cay looked down the street. "Do some sight-seeing before we take off and do some island-hopping."

"Oh, so we're going to go to some of the other islands as well?" Sasha was truly surprised.

"Why not? We've got the transportation." Cay studied her face.

"Sounds exciting."

"Does it really? You seem a little nervous."

"I'm not nervous," Sasha lied. "It sounds great to me."

"Good. We'll go to Nassau for lunch, and then have dinner and spend the night on Abacos. We'll return to Magic Key in the morning."

"My, my, my, you sure know how to impress a girl," Sasha quipped.

"You'll love Abacos," Cay continued. "It's got a little of everything. Atmosphere, fine dining . . ." He tried to see Sasha's eyes behind her sunglasses. "Perhaps you can get a massage and be pampered a bit before coming to bed tonight. Would you like that?"

"What woman wouldn't?"

"I want to know if you would like it, Sasha. Not any woman. You." Cay made his feelings plain.

"I'm awestruck," Sasha replied softly.

"Don't be." Cay pulled her close to him on the heavily trafficked street. "I want you to enjoy yourself. To look forward to it."

"I'm looking very forward to all of it," Sasha replied huskily.

"So am I," Cay said.

Sasha's knees felt as if they would give way, so she disengaged herself from his arms. "Is this the kind of life that the rich and famous live?"

"I'm not famous," he replied.

They began to walk down the street.

"Okay then, the filthy rich."

"Why must I be filthy? Why can't I just be rich?" Cay asked.

"I don't know. Somehow it just seems a little obscene. You have enough money that you can take a mini-vacation at the flick of an eyebrow, while there are other people who are trying to figure out what they're going to eat tomorrow." She thought about the very tough days she and her mother had shared.

"I didn't choose to be rich, Sasha. My family was already wealthy when I was born. But to tell you the truth, if I had to make a choice, I would be born rich again. Are you holding a grudge against me because of it?"

Sasha thought for a moment before replying, "I don't think so."

"Do you feel I should apologize for it? That I shouldn't"—he looked up at the sky, as if searching for the right words—"do or buy the things that are accessible to me because of my money?"

"No," Sasha replied softly.

"Then what is it?"

"Maybe it's because your money is the same

money that might be used to buy me out of the Bethel property."

"That decision hasn't been made," Cay replied. "But it's not like you wouldn't have a choice in the matter."

"What sort of choice?" she challenged. "There's only a certain amount of turning down of money I'm capable of doing. The thing that bothers me about it is that I would consider selling my dream of a different kind of future for money. The very same thing that makes you believe you can do, say, or have anything you want."

A group of schoolgirls in uniforms walked by laughing and talking.

"I don't believe I can do, say, or have anything I want, and I don't think this is the place to discuss this," Cay said as a woman with a bag of fruit bumped into him. "As a matter of fact, I don't think we should discuss it at all while we are in the Bahamas. We came here to get away from all that," he reminded her.

Sasha looked to the side.

"How about it? Let's call a truce until we return," Cay prodded.

Sasha looked at Cay's outstretched hand. She wondered if she wanted to fight with him to put some distance between them. She wasn't sure. All Sasha knew was that she was being sucked into Cay Ellis's world of wealth and privilege, being swallowed up whole. She could envision herself residing there happily ever after. But in real life it didn't go that way. In real life he would simply chew her up and spit her out. Sasha feared she would end up being "something to do" in Cay's life, and that was something she could not take.

Sasha wanted to relax and embrace what Cay offered. She knew it was the only way to get what she wanted: a bona fide relationship. Not a month of tolerating a man for what he could do for her, but a relationship with a future. And Sasha knew if she wanted a future she had to take a chance on chance. She had to believe in something or someone outside of herself. Sabotage was not an option. She pulled the hat down on her head. "An Ellis-Bethel truce?" Sasha asked.

Cay nodded.

"All right," she replied. "I'll give it a try."

Chapter 21

"The office is closed, ma'am." The young woman hiked the purse strap up on her shoulder. "We close at five o'clock."

Sherry ignored what the secretary was telling her. "Is Attorney Williams here?"

"Yes, ma'am, but like I said we—"

"Tell him Ms. Ellis would like to see him."

"Ma'am, we are clo—"

"Just do what I said, please."

The secretary leaned over the desk and picked up the telephone. "Attorney Williams, there's a Ms. Ellis here to see you." She waited. "I tried to tell her, but she insisted. Ma'am, what's your first name?" She looked at her watch.

"Sherry. Sherry Ellis."

"Her name is Sherry Ellis." She paused, listening. "I'll tell her. And Attorney Williams, the day-care center is closing early today, so I need to leave now. That's if it's all right?" She nodded, "Thank you. I'll see you in the morning." She hung up the telephone. "Just have a seat over there, Ms. Ellis. Attorney Williams has another appointment, but he said he'll see you on his way out."

"Thank you," Sherry replied.

The secretary headed out the door, and Sherry left the outer office and entered the hallway. She walked past the first empty office, then stopped in front of Jason's door. He was gathering up papers from his desk and placing them in his briefcase. He looked startled to see Sherry in his office.

"Hello, Jason."

"Hello," he replied. "You should have called before you came by. I've got another appointment." He threw a couple of files inside the case. "I told the secretary to tell you to wait in the outer office."

"She told me, but I've never been good at following instructions."

Jason glanced up from packing, then looked down again. "I assume you have the buyout offer with you."

"As a matter of fact, I don't," Sherry replied.

"Why not?" Jason stopped packing. "Cay hasn't changed his mind, has he?" There was a distinct nervous edge to Jason's voice.

"So you *do* really want to settle this out of court," Sherry observed with satisfaction.

"I just want to settle it," Jason replied. "And that brings us back to the offer."

"I don't have an offer because, after you left last night, Cay wasn't in the mood to discuss it. And today he up and left without telling anybody anything. Left a note saying he'd be back tomorrow morning."

"Well"—Jason snapped the briefcase shut—

"I guess you will come up with a figure when he gets back. Another day won't make that big of a difference from our perspective. But I will seek a court date before Friday if we can't settle this thing."

"How do you know that?" Sherry walked languorously over to the window. "You haven't asked your client." She turned around and faced him. "Have you talked to her today?"

"I don't see how my talking to my client is any of your affair," Jason replied. "So let's get down to it, Sherry. If you don't have the buyout agreement, why did you come here?"

"I just happened to be in town"—she put on a doe-eyed look—"and I knew you were expecting me to contact you, so I decided to drop in."

"I know you better than that." Jason straightened the remaining papers and folders on his desk. "You're not that generous with yourself, or your time, unless there's something in it for you."

"Shame on you, Jason." Sherry sauntered over and stood in front of him. "I'm not that bad, am I?"

"Worse," he replied, eyeing her suspiciously.

"I can't help it if, back then, you weren't in a position to offer me all the things that were important for my future. What you had to offer"—she gently squeezed his genitals—"was wonderful. It just wasn't enough."

Jason held his breath, releasing it only when he began to speak. "What do you want from me, Sherry? Are you finally getting bored at Guana Manor? Is Cay not paying you the attention you thought he wouldn't be able to hold back once Wally died?" His eyes turned dark. "That's one thing I have to give to him; he wasn't like the rest of us silly fools, Wally and I, who couldn't see past what you had between your legs. Even though that's the only thing I'll give to Cay Ellis. I'll be glad to help Sasha get some of the Ellis money. They've got too much of it anyway."

Sherry's cheeks heightened in color, but she kept her cool. "After last night she may not want any of *our* money."

"What?"

"It's possible." Sherry sat back on the desk. "After that big display of the Ellises against the Bethels, she and Cay found some secluded spot on the Guana Estate grounds to roll around on last night."

"I don't believe you," Jason retorted.

"You don't." Sherry laughed slyly. "I don't know why not. Cay's always been able to beat you to the punch."

"Except with you," Jason said, sticking in a barb. "Oh, but I forgot, that's because he didn't want you."

"When did you become Cay's ally?" Sherry's temper flared. "Ever since I've known you, you've despised him. But, of course"— she paused for emphasis—"I know jealousy when I see it."

Jason's jaw tightened. "I don't have time for this." He picked up his briefcase. "I've got some real business to take care of, and I don't have time to rehash the past with you."

Sherry thought quickly. The conversation was not turning out the way she'd thought it would. She had planned to bring Jason into her corner, not make an enemy of him. "Look ... I'm sorry, Jason. I didn't come here to argue with you." She hoped her eyes looked softly sincere.

Jason studied Sherry's face. She was such a beautiful woman. He remembered a time when he would have done anything to be able to call her his, and it wasn't for the sex, as he had implied, it was because he'd loved her. But that was years ago. "What is it, Sherry? Why have you paid me this special visit?"

"I'm concerned about this whole Bethel property thing," she informed him.

"I don't think I'm the person you need to be discussing your concerns with. I represent Sasha Townsend, remember?"

"I know that." Sherry placed her hands in her lap. "But we *both* hope to benefit from this."

Jason believed he had more to lose than Sherry ever imagined. "Talk about jealousy ..." A cynical smile crossed his face. "So you must see Sasha as a threat to your becoming the permanent mistress of the Guana Estate."

"You give her too much credit, Jason. Just because she's been able to turn your head."

"From what you told me she's done more than that for your man Cay."

"Sasha Townsend is just another passing ship in the night." She made a dismissive gesture in the air. "Cay Ellis Junior is my major concern."

"Cay Ellis Junior? I heard him give you and Cay the power to settle the Bethel property issue."

"Yes, you did. But as of late"—she gazed off to the side—"he's been real vindictive towards me." Sherry got off the desk. "He blames me for Wally's death."

"So he found out?"

Sherry's eyes turned serious. "Found out what?"

"Come on, Sherry." Jason shook his head. "You know what. Are you still in denial about that?"

"But I don't believe—"

"You don't believe, huh? That's why you wanted my mother to put a fix on Wally, because you didn't believe."

"I was upset." Sherry looked distraught. "And I didn't really believe it would work."

"Yes, you did. You believed every word of it."

Sherry was silent. "Papa doesn't know about that. He accuses me of withholding sex from Wally and driving him to drink. He thinks Wally left that night because he was in need of a certain kind of satisfaction that I wasn't willing to supply."

"So he's only got a part of the picture." Jason put his briefcase back on top of the desk. "You know, I started to blow that innocent act you put on last night, but it wouldn't have been in my best interest."

"What are you talking about?"

"Your undying loyalty to the Ellis family. It's about as pitiful as your claim not to believe in the *obeah*." He shook his head and laughed. "So Mr. Ellis only suspects you of being an unloving wife. He didn't know you *wanted* Wally to roam the streets at night and drink himself into oblivion."

"Maybe all by his little self Wally turned into a class-one alcoholic," she continued. "It happens all the time."

"You don't fool me, Sherry," Jason said cynically. "You're such a hypocrite. I remember that was one of the first things you asked me the night I met you: 'I heard your mother is an *obeah* woman, is it true?' " Jason looked off. "Hell, I didn't know what to say. Nobody had ever come up to me and directly asked me about my mother. I'd heard rumors, had been teased as a kid, but no one had ever had the nerve to ask me that. But not you, Ms. Sherry." He looked her up and down.

"The first time I saw you, we were hanging out at Alligator Alley, and I thought you were the most beautiful woman I had ever seen. So when you came over to me and asked about my mother, I was shocked, didn't know what to say." A wistful look crossed his features. "I assumed Wally had told you about her. He was deep into that sort of thing." He paced. "But after Wally came over and got you, and took you back where all the folks of his caliber were sitting, I didn't run into you again for years. It was only after Cay married Precious that I saw you again. I guess seeing him actually get married compelled you to go slumming that night, and you found me. I felt like I was living a dream, and that night I told you anything I thought you wanted to hear. I told you my mother had put a curse on Cay Ellis Junior. That she was the reason one woman couldn't satisfy him and he was acting like a rabbit all over the county. I told you she did it because he pulled a one-night stand on her." He shook his head.

"Boy, I wanted to impress you. Show you that even though my family didn't have the Ellis fortune, we had the power of the *obeah* on our side. And that seemed to hit you in all the right spots. I guess power is the button a man needs to push to get next to you." He looked down at the cleavage peeking out of the top of Sherry's dress.

"I don't think I ever wanted anything or anybody that bad before"—he paused—"or since, I said and did whatever I thought I had to in order to keep you, and you played me every step of the way. You let me go on planning and dreaming, when you knew all the time that you were married to one of the Ellises." Jason watched Sherry turn her old wedding ring around on her finger. "And all that time, I never realized you just wanted to be close to me because of my mother. Because of her power. That's why you wanted me around."

"That wasn't totally true, Jason." For the first time, her voice was sincere. "I came to care for you."

Jason studied her, and a spark of hope sputtered, but he dowsed it. "You may have," he acknowledged, "but being near me in your mind was like being near the power of the *obeah*. Something powerful enough to control the mighty Ellises. You didn't want to get to know my mother directly because you were afraid she would be able to see right through you, see the truth." Jason nodded with understanding. "And you know what?"

Sherry remained silent.

"She still knew the truth, and she tried to warn me, but I wouldn't hear anything from anybody against you. Then you married Wally, and it nearly killed me."

"Jason, I don't want to talk about this. That's all in the past." Sherry sliced her hand through the air.

But Jason persisted. "Even after you married Wally I still loved you, and you knew it. That's why you came to me that night crying and saying Wally was abusing you. You said you were afraid to do anything about it because of the Ellises' influence in these parts, and of course, I believed you. So when you asked me if my mother could help, I told you yes. I would have done anything to remain in your life."

"I was much younger then, Jason. I didn't know what happiness was." Sherry's eyes were sad as she tried to explain. "You have to understand where I came from. I had been taught, from the time I was a little girl, to marry into a family with money and a good reputation. I finally decided the Big Pine Key area was the perfect place. It was the kind of place where I could build my own personal empire. By marrying into the Ellis family I became a kind of royalty around here, above reproach, beyond criticism." Sherry lifted her chin. "I liked that."

"Well . . . you made your decision, and now you're a part of the Ellis family and their fortune. It's up to you to stay in good standing with the power structure there." Jason put his hand on his briefcase again. "You know there's no love lost between me and that family."

"But you're the only person I have any kind of real relationship with outside of the family. If I can't come to you, who can I take my burdens to?" Sherry hoped she looked vulnerable as she approached him.

"There's not much I can do for you now, Sherry. I surely can't ask my mother to put a fix on anyone else for you. It's impossible. She's been dead now for a couple of years. And even if I could I wouldn't. And there's something I've been wanting to tell you for a long time."

"What?"

"The things I told you about my mother and the Ellises, most of them were lies."

"What do you mean?" She looked surprised.

"They never happened. I made them up."

"But you told me she put a curse on them. You had me bring a lock of Wally's hair, some of his fingernails . . . the things you said she used to curse Mr. Ellis."

"I know what I did and said, but in the end my mother never used them. She wouldn't do it because she said you were no good for me."

"So you lied to me?"

"No more than you lied to me."

Sherry's face puffed up with indignation. "What did she do with the things I gave you?"

"She kept them. They're probably in the trunk with the rest of the tools of her trade. After she died I couldn't bring myself to throw them away. *Obeah* woman or not, she was the only family I've ever known."

Sherry's mind was turning. "I wouldn't mind seeing her things."

"What for?" Jason looked stunned.

"I'm curious. That's all."

"Curious?" Jason studied Sherry's face. "I think this goes beyond curiosity. I think you're still seeking power. You'd try to use that stuff yourself, wouldn't you?" He squinted his eyes. "You planning to put a fix on somebody, Sherry? Let me guess. Is it Cay, to make him want you? Or is it Mr. Ellis and Sasha Townsend, so they can get out of your way?"

"I haven't said I was going to do anything. I simply—"

"You simply don't know what in the world you're fooling with. You've lived in these parts for a while, but you really have never accepted the culture of people like myself. You think it's something like a faucet that you can turn on and off. It's not like that, Sherry. It can backfire on you. The *obeah* . . . it's real."

"That's crap. Anybody can mumble a few words and throw some bones on the floor."

"That's not all." Jason shook his head.

"There's a lot more. This is powerful stuff, Sherry."

"Are you worried about little ol' me, Jason?" Sherry stood so close to him he could see the glittery sheen of the expensive, scented powder on the tops of her breasts.

"I think you need to go home and throw those silly ideas out of your head. That's what I think."

Sherry slowly wet her bottom lip with the tip of her tongue. She put her arms around Jason's neck and brought his mouth down to hers. It was a kiss meant to tantalize. "It's been a long time since I had a man, Jason." She rubbed her body against his. "Is what I'm doing now another silly idea of mine?" she crooned. "Do you think so, huh?"

Jason's eyes were hungry when he looked down into her face. "Don't start with me, Sherry, unless you plan to end up with me."

"Anything's possible," she encouraged him. "A lot of things have changed. You're no longer a young man striving to go to law school. You're a powerful attorney now, and I can see myself as the wife of a powerful attorney."

Jason gazed into Sherry's eyes. They were misty with desire. He could feel his need for her swelling, and it didn't take long before he devoured her mouth as he leaned her against the desk.

Chapter 22

"Baltron, have you ever wanted to change the past?" Mr. Ellis asked.

Baltron thought about it for a second. "Right now I can't think of a time when I wanted to, but I'm sure there had to be times."

"I guess my old age is showing," Mr. Ellis replied. "Seems like I'm constantly thinking of how I might have done things differently."

"Well, you're not dead yet, so it seems to me you still have plenty of time."

"Maybe." Mr. Ellis leaned back and put his feet on a footstool. "Through the years I earned myself quite a reputation, didn't I?"

"I would say you did."

"Did you ever wonder what drove me to do the things that I was doing? Things that were making the people I claimed I loved unhappy."

"It wasn't my place to question you, Mr. Ellis," Baltron replied.

"I'm so sick of—" He smacked his fist against the palm of his hand. "We're not talking about places now. I need you to talk to me,

Baltron." He made a face. "I know during the early years I made you feel more like a servant than a friend. But as time goes by, when I look around, you're the only friend I have." He went silent. "Although at one time I did have someone else."

"You did?"

"Yes." Mr. Ellis paused. "Hazel."

Baltron was surprised by Mr. Ellis's candidness. "To be honest, Olive and I kind of figured that," he replied.

"Yes?" Mr. Ellis wound his thumbs slowly around one another.

"Yeah. We'd see you coming from the Bethel House late at night. Only visiting when Amos wasn't there. So we figured it was something you and Hazel wanted to keep quiet about."

"Ye-es, there was something." He smiled to himself. "And we had our reasons for wanting to keep it quiet. Amos and I didn't get along at all. We still had our own private feud going. He would have pitched a fit if he had known I was coming to the Bethel House. He would have thought I was simply trying to take advantage of his sister."

"Yes, he would have," Baltron said.

"You know . . . I'd never had a female friend like Hazel before," Mr. Ellis confessed.

"She was an extraordinary woman."

Mr. Ellis puffed up his jowls. "Yes, she was extraordinary. But that's not what I mean. I mean we were just friends. Nothing else."

"You mean to tell me you and she never . . ."

Mr. Ellis shook his head. "Not once."

"I've got to tell you"—Baltron leaned forward in his seat—"I'm surprised. You know, Hazel was a very attractive woman in her younger days."

"And I was very aware of that. But maybe it was the way our friendship began that kept our relationship strictly platonic."

Baltron's brow furrowed. "And how was that?"

"Believe it or not, I ended up going to her for help."

"Is that right?" Baltron looked truly surprised. "Was Mother Ellis still alive then?"

Mr. Ellis rubbed his chin. "Yes, she was. This was back when I was a young man. And you know my mother was something else. She was the other reason Hazel and I decided we should keep our friendship a secret."

"No disrespect to Mother Ellis, but I can't imagine what she would have said or done had she known. That was one tough woman. I don't think I've known anyone who had their lines drawn and their boxes closed as tightly as Mother Ellis."

"She was strict about certain things. Being paper bag brown wasn't good enough for her. You had to be at least a shade lighter. If you didn't have as much money as we had, your family had to have 'old respectable' money in its history. You know, my mother was a major influence on my claiming Cay and Wally as mine." He looked peevish. "My oats had been sown in many a field. The reason Mother Ellis said I should claim them was their mamas were light-skinned women. Nothing more. And at the time, women and children weren't important to me anyway, so I let her direct that part of my life. It probably wasn't the smartest or the best thing to do, but I let her do it."

Baltron grunted. "So what made you go to Hazel?"

Mr. Ellis leaned on the chair arm. "I'd gotten drunk one night, hanging out with some men on Big Pine Key, and we started talking about *obeah*. I told them it was an issue of mind over matter. Because that's what I believed. You know Mother wouldn't allow talk of it in our house. Later I came to understand it was the one thing she was afraid of."

"I know," Baltron said. "It was more than once that I had to hush Olive up when we first started working here. She would be telling stories about things that happened on Cat Island when her grandmother was still alive, and Mother Ellis would come walking through. One time she overheard Olive and threatened to fire her if it ever happened again. She didn't like that stuff one bit. Not one bit," Baltron concurred.

"Yes, I know. And because she didn't talk about it while I was growing up, it worked just the opposite on me. I didn't believe a word of it. And I made a bet with those men that night that I could get with any *obeah* woman, lay with her and leave her high and dry, and nothing would come of it."

"No, you didn't?"

"Yes, I did. I guess it was the alcohol talking," Mr. Ellis surmised.

"Did they take you up on the bet?"

"Yes, they took me up on it. And after I realized what I had said, you know I couldn't back down. So I told them I needed two weeks to carry it out. They gave me one."

"The ways of the young," Baltron contemplated. "As young men we can be foolish and heartless, can't we?"

"Yes, we can, and I was one of the worst," Mr. Ellis confessed. "I thought I knew everything, and I knew no more than what I could stick in my pocket."

Baltron nodded his head in agreement.

"I had gone to bed with many women around here, but I had never bedded a so-called *obeah* woman, and I thought it was high time I did. So the men chose the woman who lived on the east side of Big Pine Key. She dealt in white and black *obeah*."

"Yes. I had heard of her," Baltron told him.

"I got with her all right, on the deadline day of the deal. It was probably the biggest mistake I ever made in my life," Mr. Ellis said.

"Sure enough?"

"Yes." Mr. Ellis took a deep breath. "I laid with Mabel, and I never went back to see her, not one time, after that. But one day I bumped into her when I was out. At least at the time I thought I had bumped into her. But I've thought about it over the years, and I now believe she might have planned it. She had given me just enough time where the memory of the bet and that night I spent with her had almost faded. That woman looked me in the eye and told me she didn't need to put a curse on me because I was already cursed. That all the Ellises were. That I would never want more out of life than to satisfy my body, and that true satisfaction would be the one thing I would never find." He paused. "She said I wouldn't find it with a woman or a friend." Mr. Ellis looked Baltron directly in the eyes. "She told me my life was living proof of the curse."

"Well, I'll be." Baltron hung his head.

"It's the truth," Mr. Ellis declared. "It's the God truth."

"So you believed her?"

"I didn't know what to believe in the beginning, but after that I started thinking. I went with a few women, and I never seemed to reach what I was reaching for. And that made me wonder, because it had always been that way. But I decided to bide my time. And after a few months I was certain something wasn't right."

Baltron listened, slowly shaking his head.

"I tried to talk to Mother about it, but she threw a hissy fit that day like I'd never seen. Do you remember?"

"I sure do. Her health started going downhill after that. I don't think she ever recovered."

"No, she didn't." Mr. Ellis closed his eyes. "And I knew she knew something she wasn't telling me, so I decided to get some help. I remember one of the men, a fellow named Bob, talked about a woman named Hazel. He said she was a bush woman and that she helped a lot of folks around here. When I realized he was talking about Hazel Bethel, I thought it was a strange kind of justice indeed. Out of all the people who could possibly help me, the one who had a reputation of doing good was an enemy of my family."

"I guess that would have been a tough call," Baltron confirmed.

"I felt it was, but I was a young man back then. Thirty years old. That's young. And there hadn't been any children that I knew of. Up to then my mother had been happy being the only woman of Guana Manor, but after she got sick she began to complain about getting old and wanting grandchildren who would live at Guana Estate. She didn't necessarily want their mothers here, but she wanted the children."

"So you started to fear there weren't going to be any children?" Baltron approached the matter delicately.

"To be honest, I wasn't worried about children. I started to fear for my manhood. That word would get around that I was inadequate and that I wasn't able to satisfy a woman. That was my biggest fear."

"I can imagine that would be pretty scary for any man," Baltron verified.

"Goddamn frightening," Mr. Ellis assured him. "So I went to see Hazel. I remember it just as if it were yesterday. Back then Amos was living with his wife and child, the one that died when he was a teenager—" Mr. Ellis paused to see if Baltron was with him. Baltron nodded, so Mr. Ellis continued. "They were living in Homestead, Florida. Amos made regular visits to the Bethel House, saying he was checking on his sister, but through the years I heard a couple of rumors that he had another woman on Big Pine Key who eventually had a child that he never claimed. I believe that other woman was Sasha Townsend's mother."

"Sure enough?"

"Don't pin me on it. But that's what I think."

"What makes you remember your first visit with Hazel so well?" Baltron leaned his elbow on the table.

"It was the way she looked. There was a special air about her, Baltron. Although she was a slight woman back then, she seemed to dominate the doorway. I remember she had on a white dress. It was made out of an eyelet material. You know what I'm talking about? Eyelet?"

"I think so." Baltron's brows furrowed. "That's that material where the edges of the little holes are kind of crocheted and the patterns form flowers and things."

"That's about right," Mr. Ellis agreed. "Well . . . she had on a free-flowing dress made from that, and it had big bell sleeves. The sleeves and the hem of the dress were trimmed in eyelet." Mr. Ellis's eyes turned cloudy. "And when I first saw her I thought she had a neat afro crowning her head, but that wasn't what it was. She was wearing her hair off of her face and it tumbled down her back in locks."

"Is that right?" Baltron looked puzzled. "Come to think of it, I never saw Hazel's hair.

She always wore it covered when she was out."

"I know. That's why I was so surprised. And these locks were fluid and shiny. They were beautiful, and so was she," Mr. Ellis proclaimed. "She recognized me right away and immediately became suspicious as to why I had come to her house. She asked me what I wanted. And I tell you, I was so dumbfounded by the sight and presence of her that I didn't know what to say." His mouth turned a slight smile.

"I never really paid attention to her before. It's amazing when you think about it, as close as the Bethel House is to Guana Manor. We're sitting on the same land. But for generations the barrier between the Ellises and the Bethels remained so strong that I, for one, had practically dehumanized them." His eyes softened into the past. "Then Hazel had the nerve to show compassion for me. She said in the most soothing voice, 'What is it, Mr. Ellis?' She sounded so kind," he said, struck by the irony of the situation, "so what else could come out of me but the truth. I told her, 'I'm afraid, and I thought you might be able to help me.' And you know what she said?"

Baltron shook his head.

"She said, 'I'll do my best.' "

"Just like that?"

"Just like that. As if the Ellises and the Bethels had never known a fight."

"That's something," Baltron declared. "And was she able to help you?"

"Being around Hazel started me on a road

to finding some peace and worth within my-self. Mind you, I said *some* peace. But even to get that far meant telling her my story, and that was most difficult to do because I felt as if I was talking to someone who wouldn't think about doing anybody harm. And for me to confess that I hadn't cared how my actions hurt others . . . it was a hard thing to do."

"Ye-es, I can imagine," Baltron agreed again.

"Even then, with all that, the value of family still didn't dawn on me for years. Cay and Wally were here growing up under my nose, and I just didn't realize what I had."

"It's kind of interesting how things worked out the way Mother Ellis wanted. With Cay's mother dying in childbirth and all," Baltron said hesitantly."

"I'll say." The thought of the curse hung in silence between them. "And Wally's mother didn't want to be tied down with a child. She wasn't from these parts and got hooked up with me while she was traveling the country. I would have married her, just because of Wally. But I could sense a restlessness about her. And sure enough, after she had the baby she told me Guana Estate would be nothing but a beautiful prison for her. She needed the big-city life, and that was something I wasn't able to give her, but I was able to give her enough money to go and leave us in peace."

"I thought something like that had happened. But you know, she never really seemed to fit in around here," Baltron said.

"No, she didn't." Mr. Ellis tapped his fingers on an end table. "And I guess I'm no different from anybody else who starts getting old and sick, and thinks the end may be near. I just want to right some of the wrongs I've done. Encouraging Wally to marry Sherry was one of them."

"Don't be taking on things that you can't change," Baltron advised him.

"I can't change it now, but I *knew* from the very beginning she really wanted Cay. Even though we know that's not true, either. She really wanted the power of the Ellis name and Guana Estate. But like my mother, I decided to exert my will about what kind of blood my grandchildren would have." Mr. Ellis sat back again. "I knew there was no real fire between Cay and Precious, and there wasn't much going on in the bedroom. So I never thought there would be grandchildren out of their union. What a sacrifice. I believe Cay was trying to escape his fate with that marriage."

"Perhaps," Baltron replied.

Mr. Ellis sighed. "So I figured with Sherry being the hot-blooded creature that she was, I'd get grandsons through her. But that woman had her own plans. The more ill Precious became the more she turned her sights on Cay again."

Baltron remained quiet.

"See"—he pointed—"you know I'm telling the truth. I wrecked my own son's life to fulfill Mother's obsession of having old money and red bone blood in this family. And that Sherry's a cunning one, yes she is. But I vow she will not ruin Cay's life like she ruined

Wally's—or become the mistress of Guana Manor."

"There's no need to get all worked up," Baltron said, attempting to calm Mr. Ellis.

"I'm not worked up. I'm just certain. Cay has been the kind of young man that I wish I had been. He's tried to live a decent life despite the burdens of this family. And I'm not going to sit back and allow Sherry to take advantage of him."

"Don't you think that Cay can also see his way past Sherry?"

"Maybe. But I don't put it past her to go after him in ways that most women wouldn't think of."

"What are you talking about?" Baltron leaned closer. "All the *obeah* men and women in these parts are dead now."

"Yes, I know that, and I don't know that Sherry would go that route," Mr. Ellis admitted. "All I know is she wants Cay and Guana Manor, and she will do anything she needs to do to get them. And anybody and anything that is standing in her way needs to watch out."

"Are you thinking about Sasha Townsend?" Baltron asked.

"Maybe." He paused. "But I know I'm thinking about myself," Mr. Ellis declared.

Sasha puffed as she climbed the stairs of the candy-striped lighthouse of Hope Town. It had been her idea to look out over the ocean from the top, but she had been wrong in assuming the lighthouse would have an elevator. "I thought we'd never make it up here," she said breathlessly.

"But take a look at this," Cay replied as he walked over to a window, "and you will know every step was worth it."

"Oh, my God, it's unbelievable." She gazed out at the vast Atlantic Ocean. "There's no end to it."

"It does seem that way, doesn't it? Something right here on earth that's endless." Cay contemplated the view for a while, then he said softly, "Unlike life and relationships, the Atlantic Ocean goes on forever."

"What a discouraging thing to say," Sasha replied.

"Is it?" Cay looked at Sasha, then out over the water. "I guess it is, but at this point in my life it's what I know to be true. I know of so few relationships that have stood the test of time, and death for certain is the end to life."

"I don't agree," Sasha replied stubbornly. "Yes, the relationships I've known haven't survived, but that doesn't mean I have to dwell on them. There will be others. And as far as death goes, there are many people from different religious and spiritual paths who would not agree that death is the end of life. Some actually say it is the beginning."

"Sasha, I'm beginning to think you are one of those fanciful believers." One side of his mouth lifted. "If there's good and there's bad, let's only see the good. If there is either reality or dreams, you'd choose the dreams."

"What's wrong with that? What's wrong with, if you have a choice, choosing what is beautiful and uplifting, a way that brings hope?" Sasha reached out to him. "If we don't believe in a better world, Cay, we might as well die and give in to the thing we fear so much."

"It all sounds good. But it's not the way it is." Cay's features turned hard. "Life is what it is. And it's not all beautiful. We as human beings are plopped down here in the middle of it. We are born and then we die. All the belief in the world is not going to change that. And because I don't know that death will be any better than life . . . I'll stick with what I know."

"It surely won't change if you can't even imagine that it will." Sasha felt restricted. "Nothing will ever be if you can't imagine it first."

"I can imagine some things." Cay stepped over and put his arms around her waist. "I can imagine us having a wonderful dinner with entertainment on Green Turtle Cay and settling down there for the night. I can also imagine what we would do after we settle in." He drew Sasha close.

"You've impressed me with your vivid, expansive imagination," she said wryly. "I was talking about imagining a better world, and the only place your mind can conjure up is a bedroom." Sasha stiffened within his arms.

"That's not true." Cay's dark eyes searched hers. "I can imagine far more than that, but what good would it do me? I don't have a crystal ball and I don't intend to buy one. What I do have is a beautiful, sexy woman in my arms." He closed his eyes and stroked Sasha's back, letting his hand slide down to the curve of her hip. "One who smells of perfume." Cay inhaled, and rubbed his face against her hair before trailing the tip of his nose down her earlobe. "And one I can taste." His lips brushed a portion of her neck. "This is the kind of reality I choose to believe in, Sasha. The things I can see and feel. They are real. Your being here is real."

Sasha loved the feeling of Cay's arms around her and the feeling of love within her. She knew it wouldn't go away after tonight or tomorrow. For Sasha, it had the potential to go on forever.

Cay gave a slight smile. "Are you getting hungry?"

"Not yet," Sasha replied. Food was the last thing on her mind.

"Well, let's head over to Green Turtle Cay anyway, and maybe you can buy an outfit for tonight and get that massage I talked about earlier. I'll get on the phone and make our reservations and take care of some other business. Sound good?"

"That sounds real good," Sasha replied, feeling a need to flee.

Sasha stood looking at the shiny room numbers on the hotel door. Before today, she had never known a concierge or an executive floor existed. It was the floor where the businessmen and the well-to-do stayed, she thought wryly, but tonight she would be staying there.

Sasha had always known that the gap between the haves and the have-nots was enormous. Just like the gap between Cay Ellis III's life and her own.

She looked at the plastic bag draped over her arm. Inside was her new black cocktail dress. It was a prize. The shoes, bag, and jewelry she'd bought with Cay's credit card set it off to a tee. She was going to be gorgeous tonight, probably more gorgeous than she had ever been, so why wasn't she giddy with anticipation? It was because she was in love with Cay. *In love,* and not just a mellow and smooth love, but a volatile, unpredictable, and overpowering love.

Sasha thought, perhaps if she wasn't, she would get through the night with little thought. She would be distant but enjoy herself, chalking up the entire Bahama Islands experience as one hell of a good time. But that was impossible, because she was in love with Cay and she could feel all the hopes and dreams that came with that emotion.

The hotel door opened suddenly, and Sasha found herself staring at a tight-faced Cay. "Where in the world have you been?" he asked. "I was about to go looking for you."

"I'm not late, am I?" Sasha feigned a calm that she did not feel as she walked toward him. "I thought you said you were going to set dinner for seven-thirty."

"That is what I said." Cay closed the door behind them. "But you left here at two, and I assumed we would relax together before we headed over to the restaurant. It is now six-twenty."

"I guess it took longer than you anticipated, didn't it?" Sasha replied, knowing all along she had planned it that way.

Sasha had had plenty of time to think while shopping and being pampered at the spa. She had fallen for a man who wasn't emotionally in her league, and that wasn't smart. "I guess I better hurry," she said, entering the bathroom and quickly closing the door behind her.

Cay stared at the bathroom door before he went and sat down on the bed. Something was wrong. He listened to the sound of running water. "Damn her." He looked at the clock. "Why did she do that?"

Cay thought about what Sasha had said moments before: "I guess it took longer than *you* anticipated, didn't it?" One of his eyebrows arched high. Sasha had known he was waiting for her, and she knew what he wanted, but she had made it her business to stay away.

Cay was peeved. Sasha hadn't thought about what he might be feeling. He had begun to worry, thinking something might have happened to her. All kinds of images had crowded his mind, and in the end he had asked himself the question he feared the most: *Has she been taken from me already?* The uncertainty forced Cay to realize how much he cared for Sasha. He cared a hell of a lot for her, and her insensitivity angered him.

Was he someone for her to play with? She appeared to take his feelings so lightly. Or was she holding his fortune, or the issue with the Bethel property, against him? He did not know. All Cay knew was he had never been so full for a woman.

He looked at the king-size bed. Here they were in a hotel room together, but he wasn't able to show her how he felt. Why? He answered the question himself . . . because she had planned it that way.

"I'll be out in a minute," Sasha called. "All I have to do is put on my clothes."

Cay began to visualize a nude Sasha dressing in front of the bathroom mirror. It was more than he could take. He found himself opening the bathroom door.

"What *are* you doing?" Sasha asked, her eyes wide.

"Like you, I'm doing just what I want to do. Since you deliberately avoided giving me the pleasure of being with you, I'll gain my pleasure another way." His eyes gleamed as he looked at Sasha standing nude in front of the mirror, her new lace lingerie in her hands. "I want to watch you dress."

"You must be kidding," she retorted.

"Do I look like I'm kidding?" His voice was as cool as steel. "You knew I was waiting for you. I made that quite plain before you left, but you decided to stay away to tease me. So tease me, Sasha. I give you my permission."

"Give me permission? I don't think I like this," Sasha said cautiously.

"No one said you had to like it. Believe me, I'll enjoy it enough for the two of us. The way I see it, it shouldn't be a problem for you. You forgot I was here waiting for you so now all you have to do is forget that I am here watching you."

Sasha felt goose bumps rising all over her body as she looked down at the tiny, lacy articles in her hands. Cay knew she had avoided making love to him. This was his way of letting her know he didn't appreciate it and that he wanted something in exchange for what he did not get.

Sasha's heartbeat accelerated along with her anger. "I am not going along with this." She went to close the door.

"I wouldn't close that door if I were you, Sasha." Cay's voice was low. "Not unless you want me to dress you. And believe me, in the end, if I have to be the one to do it, we will be late for dinner, if we make it there at all."

Their gazes met as Sasha held the door. She

could see an ember in Cay's eyes that could quickly turn into a blaze.

"So, what's it going to be?" He gazed at her breasts before he stopped at the curly triangle between her legs.

Sasha gave him a defiant look before she let go of the door and walked back inside the bathroom. Stiffly, she looked in the mirror and laid the lingerie on the counter. The face that gazed back at her was made up to perfection. The stylist had piled her natural, twisted hair on top of her head, creating a full crown of tiny, spongy coils. It did not look like the face of a woman who could be subdued. The cosmetologist had turned it into the face of a seductress.

Sasha could feel obstinacy rising within her. *So he wants to watch me dress, does he?* Sexily, she cut her eyes at him. *I'm accustomed to giving a man what he wants. I can do the same for you, Cay,* Sasha thought vengefully. *And I dare you to touch me afterward.*

Sasha reached for one of the plush towels and slowly spread it out on the large bathroom counter. She willed herself not to look at Cay, cutting him out of her world and entering one of fantasy. Sasha willed herself to be the ultimate enchantress, beguiling to all men, and her body reflected her thoughts.

He had wanted Sasha to feel shamed by his request. Actually, he'd wanted her to feel ashamed for discounting his feelings, but shamed was not what she appeared to be. It was as if she had erected an invisible barrier between them, a one-way mirror. Sasha appeared empowered as she turned her back toward it.

Gracefully, she lifted herself onto the counter and sat back with her back pressed against the mirror, her eyes closed. With style, Sasha lifted her arms and smelled the perfume on her wrists, then held herself, creating a deep cleavage between her breasts. She sighed. *I will give him what he wants, but I will do it my way.*

Cay's dark eyes turned into slits as he watched her. Sasha was not trembling with meekness and submission. She was glowing with a pure female energy, in a place that he could peer into but had not been invited to share.

Cay had not expected such a display of feminine sensuousness. He had told her to tease him, but he had not known how adeptly she could carry out the task.

Sasha placed her palms on the counter and slid one pointed foot, and then the other, into the tiny underwear. She leaned against the mirror and arched her back, again closing her eyes, before slowly pulling the garment up around her body and settling it about her hips. Sighing, Sasha reached for her bra, but it wasn't there. Her eyes flew open, and there was Cay standing a couple of feet away with it dangling from his fingertips.

"Are you looking for this?"

"Yes, I am." Sasha took the lacy object.

Cay did not move.

"You said as long as I dressed myself in front of you, I'd have no trouble out of you."

She managed to fasten the garment and pull the straps up on her shoulders.

"That was before I knew how skillful you were at dressing yourself," he replied.

"So now that you do know"—Sasha climbed off the counter—"you also know I don't need your help."

"No, you don't." He leaned over and sniffed her perfume before he drew back slowly and looked at his watch.

"I assume we can make it on time, that is, if I finish dressing now," Sasha said, her eyes steady.

"Yes." Cay appeared to be trying to size her up. "Yes, we can." Then he said, "You know, I'm beginning to realize how much I don't know about you."

"Are you?" Sasha picked up her hose. "You know we all come with a past. And I'm discovering things about you that I never imagined," she replied.

"Well, this will be a night of great explorations, won't it?"

Fear and excitement erupted inside Sasha, but on the outside she remained calm. "Are you planning to go on a safari?"

A slight smile touched Cay's lips. "It could be as wild as that since I don't know my game as well as I thought I did. It could be a real wild time."

Sasha stepped into her strapless, thigh-high dress. "Would you zip me up, please?" She offered him her back.

Cay studied the expanse of brown skin before he eased the zipper upward. The dress tightened around Sasha's waist and hips. His fingers lingered on the metallic object before he brushed them lightly across the width of her back.

"Un-un-un." Sasha turned and looked into his eyes. "No touching unless you're invited."

Sasha recognized a hint of a smile. "We'll see about that," Cay replied.

Chapter 24

"Right this way." The host bowed slightly, then proceeded before Sasha and Cay. They maneuvered between a number of tables covered with white linen. "This is the table we reserved for you, Mr. Ellis. Is it satisfactory?"

Cay looked through the window at the lights across the water. "Sasha, do you like the view?"

Sasha admired the twinkling lights that appeared to be suspended in the darkness. "It's beautiful," she replied.

"That's what I wanted to hear. This will do just fine," he told the host.

"I'm glad you like it, ma'am," the host said, pulling out a chair for Sasha. "I'll have your waiter bring you a wine list right away." He bowed again and left.

Sasha glanced around the restaurant, then settled her gaze on the table. There was an array of dishes and silverware, and a floating candle glowed in the middle of a small floral arrangement. Everything was simply beautiful, and she felt good as a result. Tentatively, she looked up at Cay. He had been very silent on the way to the restaurant. She noticed how handsome he appeared in a shimmering gold summer-knit sweater beneath a black sports coat. She wanted to tell him, but he was watching her like a hawk, as he had done during the horse and buggy ride over to the restaurant.

"Why are you looking at me like that?" Sasha asked, exasperated.

"You are some kind of woman. Do you know that? I can never tell what you will do. One moment you're shy and coy, the next you're an enticing woman who knows exactly what she's doing. I just want to be prepared for whoever shows up next."

"I've been a single woman for a long time, Cay. I'm far from innocent. If that's what you are looking for, you're definitely barking up the wrong tree." She glanced at two couples being led through the room by the maître d'.

One of the men did a double take. "Cay Ellis. Well, hello-o. Fancy meeting you here."

Sasha thought she could see all thirty-two of his teeth.

"Mr. Ashford. Nice to see you again," Cay replied, distracted by the greeting.

"Why, honey," Mr. Ashford said, pulling his wife forward by her waist, "this is Mr. Ellis, the gentleman you've heard so much about."

"Hello, Mr. Ellis." She offered her hand.

Cay stood up. "Mrs. Ashford."

"It is truly a pleasure meeting you." She

clasped his hand in both of hers. "I want to take this opportunity to thank you for what you did."

Sasha noticed that Cay looked a bit uncomfortable. She had never seen him embarrassed before.

"It's not necessary, Mrs. Ashford."

Mr. Ashford was beaming by now, and Sasha could tell he had been drinking. "These are our friends, Randy Davis and Cynthia Barnes."

They all shook hands.

"This is my ... friend, Sasha Townsend," Cay introduced her.

"Mr. Ashford." Sasha stood up for convenience's sake. After Cay's introduction she felt a little awkward. His hesitation about her status had been obvious to her, if not to anyone else.

"Nice to meet you, Ms. Townsend." Mr. Ashford shook her hand vigorously.

"Is this our table?" Mrs. Ashford turned to the host and motioned to the table directly across from Cay and Sasha.

"Yes, it is, ma'am."

"I'd say this is some coincidence." Mr. Ashford looked from Sasha and Cay's table to his own, his face flushed with alcohol. "And I'm not the kind of man to let an opportunity like this pass me by. Waiter, I'd like for you to pull our table over here." He pointed to the side of Cay and Sasha's table. "And the entire bill will be on me."

Everyone seemed stunned.

"You don't have to do this, Mr. Ashford," Cay protested.

"I know I don't have to, but you've been one of the most caring businessmen I've ever known. You knew I was in trouble, and even though you didn't need the inventory, you helped me liquidate those goods in a time that was crucial for my wife and me. It would be my pleasure to buy you and Ms. Townsend dinner."

Sasha was intrigued by Mr. Ashford's candidness—and by what he said about Cay.

"Stanley"—his wife tugged gently at his arm—"maybe Mr. Ellis and Ms. Townsend want to spend a quiet evening alone."

"I just want to show Mr. Ellis my appreciation, sugar. Can't I do that?" he insisted, a bit too loudly.

Some people at adjacent tables turned around to look. Mrs. Ashford was clearly embarrassed. She glanced at Randy and Cynthia.

"That will be fine, Mr. Ashford." Cay smiled graciously. "By all means join us." He nodded for the host to move the table.

"See there, Leslie, I told you Mr. Ellis is a great fellow." Mr. Ashford insisted on helping the waiter move the table and the chairs. "Now, how should we sit?" He looked befuddled.

"I'll sit right here," Cynthia said, slipping into the chair next to Cay. "I want a seat next to the man who's being held in such high esteem tonight."

Sasha felt as if her forced smile would crack at any moment. She realized she had been looking forward to a private evening, and now she was facing an intoxicated woman sitting beside Cay. He seemed aware of her sentiments, and was clearly amused as he leaned back comfortably in his chair.

"All righty then, that gets us rolling." Mr. Ashford smiled again. "So, Randy, why don't you sit next to Ms. Townsend, and Leslie, darlin', you sit next to Randy. I'll sit next to Cynthia. This is great. Just great." He beamed, easing his big body into the medium-size chair. "So are you here on Green Turtle Cay for business or pleasure, Mr. Ellis?"

"Pleasure," Cay said softly without hesitation.

Everyone at the table looked at Sasha. Mrs. Ashford's cheeks turned red; Mr. Ashford's smile broadened, if that was possible; and Randy began to look at Sasha as if she were a part of the dessert menu. Cynthia was the only one who didn't seem very interested.

"You did say you were just friends." Cynthia looked from Cay to Sasha. "I don't see any rings on any fingers."

Sasha couldn't believe it. Was Cynthia with this fellow Randy or not? First she had made it her business to sit down beside Cay, and now she was inquiring about the status of their relationship.

"Cynthia can be a little pushy sometimes," Randy volunteered. "Keep your dress down, babe," he told her. Sasha could see signs of irritation on his boyish features. "Nobody has told you it's a go yet."

"See, that shows how much you pay attention to me. I'm not wearing a dress," Cynthia retorted, eyes gleaming.

Mrs. Ashford looked down at the table, and even Mr. Ashford looked a bit embarrassed.

"Pleasure, that's what brought me and my wife here," Mr. Ashford spoke up rather quickly. "Leslie and I are just looking to have a good time now that we've gotten past that trouble. We met Randy over on Abacos. He lives there, and we spent the night in his hotel. Cynthia"—he motioned to the pixieish female—"is a friend of his."

Cay nodded.

"So what about you, Ms. Townsend, where are you from?" Mr. Ashford continued.

"I'm originally from Gary, Indiana. I lived there all of my life before I went off to college, then I returned to take care of my mother, who was ill. After she died I moved to the Keys."

"That must have been rather difficult," Mrs. Ashford said, "taking care of your mother like that. I know how it was for me when my mother became ill. We ended up putting her in a nursing home. It got to be an impossible situation."

"I wasn't in a position to do that, so I did what I had to do." She paused. "And if I had to do it again I would."

Cay's features softened as he leaned across the table toward Sasha. "I didn't know your mother was ill and you took care of her until she passed away."

"Well," Sasha replied softly, "it's not the kind of information you volunteer unless someone is interested enough to ask." She gazed into his compassionate eyes.

"All right. Break it up. Break it up," Cynthia said, patting the table. "I'm jealous." She pouted. "Randy, you used to use that tone when you spoke to me. But you don't anymore."

"Maybe you don't give me cause to," Randy replied.

The table got quiet.

"Stanley and I live in Fort Lauderdale," Mrs. Ashford said to Sasha. "How do you like living in the Keys?"

Sasha could tell Mrs. Ashford felt obligated to keep the conversation going. "I love it," she replied. "I hope to make the Keys my long-term home." She did not look at Cay.

"And what do you do, Mr. Ellis, that has Stanley so fired up about you?" Cynthia leaned on Cay's chair arm.

"A little of everything," he said diplomatically. "But my family has been in the tourism industry in the Keys for a couple of generations."

"Wow. Tourism in the Keys. Sounds lucrative," Cynthia chimed in.

Cay simply smiled.

"Here's the wine list, sir," the waiter said to Mr. Ashford.

"Give it to Mr. Ellis." He pointed to Cay. "I'll trust his judgment any day."

The waiter went around the table, gave Cay the menu, then stood silently by.

"Let's see what we have here." Cay glanced over the list, then asked, "Are we going to be eating seafood tonight?"

"We're in the islands; we've got to have sea-food," Cynthia said, forcing Cay to share the menu with her. Everyone agreed.

"Then I suggest we go with a white wine," Cay announced.

"Sounds good, but make it kind of sweet," Mr. Ashford advised. "Leslie hasn't developed the taste buds for really dry wine."

Mrs. Ashford looked down. "Stanley, you didn't have to tell them that," she chastised him.

"Don't worry about it, Mrs. Ashford." Sasha smiled at the woman. "I haven't developed my taste buds, either."

Mrs. Ashford's eyes lit up with appreciation.

Cay looked at the two women before looking back at the menu. "We'll start with a couple of bottles of Robert Mondavi's Moscato d'Oro," he instructed, handing the list back to the waiter.

"Thank you," the man said, then walked away.

"I've never heard of that wine before," Mr. Ashford said, glancing at the ceiling.

"I like it," Cay said. "It's semidry with a fruity taste. I think it's an excellent California wine. I hope you like it, Sasha," he said, pulling her into the conversation.

"I'm sure I will." She felt pleased by his attentiveness.

After the wine arrived conversation eventually got easier. Sasha discovered she sincerely liked Leslie Ashford, a quiet woman with a calm demeanor. But her curiosity about Cynthia and Randy's relationship increased.

She guessed that either Cynthia was starving for Randy's attention or they were competing to see who could make the other the most jealous.

Everyone was eating dessert when the entertainment started. A team of jugglers went first, spinning and tossing objects from the islands. A female contortionist with amazing abilities followed. She kept everyone's eyes on the stage except for Cynthia's.

"Believe it not, I can do that," Cynthia professed to Cay while the performer was in a very accessible position.

"Impressive," Cay replied, looking down into her inviting features.

"Isn't it?" She set her empty wineglass down. "Perhaps I can show you sometime."

Sasha glanced at Randy, who let go of an "Oo-wee" as he ogled the contortionist. She looked at Cay and gave him a fake smile. It was proving to be an interesting night indeed.

Chapter 25

~2~

"I went by the Bethel House." Sherry pinched a piece off a johnnycake, then placed the morsel in her mouth. "Sasha's car was parked out front, but she wasn't there."

Olive looked as if she could blow steam when she eyed the crumbled bread. "Ms. Sherry, the food will be on the table shortly. There's some cut-up fruit over there if you want something to snack on *before* dinner."

Aware of Olive's tight-lipped expression, Sherry moved on to the fruit. "Sorry about that. Your johnnycakes are always so good. One day you've got to teach me how to make them."

"Didn't think you were interested," Olive replied without looking up.

"I guess time is helping me see things in a different light," Sherry said. "Take Papa, for instance."

"What about Mr. Ellis?" Olive cranked up the salad spinner.

"Well, he's getting on in years, and I guess

I've given him just cause to feel the way he does about me."

"You guess," Olive said beneath her breath.

Sherry decided to ignore Olive's quip. "But you have to admit, Olive, he hasn't been the easiest man to live with. You've had some close calls with him yourself."

"I'll admit that. But he is his mother's son, and that's the only reason why I pardon some of the things he does. When you bring a child up with all the prejudices and screwed-up ideas that Mr. Ellis was brought up with, what else can you expect? Thank God, Baltron and I were around to help bring some balance and tenderness into Cay's and Wally's lives."

"And thank God you've been around all these years that I've been here."

Olive raised a discerning eyebrow.

"I mean that, Olive. I realize there are a lot of things I could learn from you." Sherry munched a grape. "For so long I acted as if I was above you and your beliefs, and now I know that isn't true, and it never has been."

Despite herself, Olive stopped what she was doing and gave Sherry her full attention. "Is this coming from your heart, Ms. Sherry? Or is this another one of your performances?"

Sherry walked over to Olive. "I know I haven't been an ideal person, and I deserve anything you might say against me. But I'm tired of being on the outside, Olive."

"Or do you mean you're tired of not being able to really get next to Mr. Cay?"

Sherry drew a breath and held back the retort that tingled her tongue.

"There's no need to try and deny it, Ms. Sherry." Olive's head took on a stubborn tilt. "If we're talking honestly that's what you were doing."

Sherry looked down at the marble island counter. "I've always made it known that I wanted to be a part of this family," Sherry began quietly. "Maybe I shouldn't have married Wally, but at the time I thought we would make a good couple."

"And at the time Mr. Cay had already married Precious."

"Yes, Cay had already married Precious," Sherry admitted doggedly. "But it wasn't like I had rigged this great plot for Precious and Wally to die," she defended herself. "It just seemed to me after they did, Cay and I getting together was the most natural thing to do."

"There are other folks who don't hold the same opinion." Olive gave Sherry a deadpan look. "But let's forget about everybody else but Mr. Cay. His opinion is the only one that really matters. And I don't think he feels the way you do."

Sherry remained quiet.

"So, if you're really tired of the problems you've been having here at Guana Manor," Olive continued, "that's one of the truths you got to face. You're Mr. Cay's sister-in-law, and you need to start looking elsewhere for a man."

"Things here at Guana have gotten to be pretty rough. All these horrible arguments and confrontations drain me so. Life's so complicated. I just want to get on with it. I'm tired of fighting with everyone in this house. It's hard for me to admit it, but I realize I must be causing some of the problems, and I'm truly sorry."

Olive looked dumbfounded. "Ms. Sherry, I've got to tell you, I never expected to hear you say that."

"Well, I've got to admit I never thought I would."

They looked at one another. Tentative smiles passed between them.

"Now, you must tell me, how do you make those johnnycakes." Sherry took a spatula and began to remove the bread from the paper towel–lined pan.

"Oh, there's nothing to it. It's just a mixture of cornmeal, self-rising flour, coconut milk, and egg. I add a little ginger, to give it my own special flavor, before frying them in a little oil."

"How can something so simple be so good?" Sherry was confident she had broken down Olive's defenses.

"My mother taught me how to fix them when I was a little girl. My father loved them."

An odd expression crossed Sherry's face. "You know, when I think about it, the reason I acted the way I did was because I was jealous."

"Say what?" Olive put her hands on her hips.

"I was jealous of your sense of family." Sherry's lip quaked before she collected herself. "I mean, you seem to know so much about where you come from and your history. There's a natural kind of pride and strength in that. Your ancestors were never slaves, were they, Olive?"

"Not really. The slave-trading boat my great-greatgrandfather was being transported on was shipwrecked. He and some others were able to swim to Cat Island. A free life began for them there."

"So you can trace your ancestral roots back for generations." Sherry sighed. "I walked around here acting uppity, proud of who I am, but the truth is, I felt inadequate around you. I like to brag on my family tree, but the truth is I can only take it back so far."

Olive was won over by the admission. "Yes, I do know a lot about my family history, but like any history, it wasn't all good. Some of the things folks on the islands have done I'm not so proud of. My ancestors may have profited from the slave trade that was going on here in the States."

This time Sherry was surprised. "I didn't realize that."

"It's true. It was all about money, as it is today." Olive dumped the salad into a large bowl. "No matter what race he is, man seems always to have profited from the misfortunes of other men. Even bring it about if he could."

Sherry looked down when she heard the timely truism.

Olive continued. "I remember some of the stories my grandmother used to tell me. Some of them were pretty hard to believe. Fascinating, actually." Her eyes widened.

"What was your grandmother's name?" Sherry pushed to show her interest.

"Ruth," Olive said with retrospection. "Ruth Owens."

"Ruth," Sherry repeated the name. "I bet she did have some tales to tell. I bet she knew a lot about your ancestors in Africa. The things they did. The way they believed and lived."

"Yes, she did, and of course they brought their culture with them to the islands. What else would they do?" Olive gave one strong nod. "Back in her day, my grandmother said, the *obeah* was really strong. That's where it came from. The *obeah* started in Africa." Then Olive turned her back. "Although I know you say you don't believe in any of it."

Sherry's eyes brightened with interest. "I just couldn't imagine it, that's all. And I guess I was a little afraid. I mean, how can something like that really work?" Sherry had worked her way around to the point of the entire exchange.

"All I know is Grandma Ruth said the *obeah* men and women knew how to work with the *sperrids*."

"They did? How did they manage that?"

"They respected the *sperrids* and were respected in return. Said they had some *sperrids* that were very loyal to them." Olive wiped her hands on a dish towel. "And the *sperrids* could tell when a dabbler was even looking their way."

"A dabbler?" Olive's lingo confused Sherry.

"A dabbler is somebody who was just playing with the power," Olive explained. "Said sometimes they'd zap their life force or their mind from them before they even got started."

Sherry looked uneasy. "But you said the spirits were loyal to them."

"Yes. Loyal. They could call on the dead when they wanted to."

Skeptical, Sherry looked up at the ceiling. "And that's how they did it? By calling on the dead? They didn't use any special tools or words . . ."

"Of course, they used them. I remember folks saying the tools they used were alive with the *obeah*'s spirit." Olive took to talking about one of her favorite subjects. "I've heard tell of them using pieces of clothing, photographs, and other things belonging to folks to put a fix on them. And herbs, too. Herbs that could kill or cure. But it was because they knew how." She pointed her finger. "Grandma Ruth told me it's a real power that they tap into. The power of good and evil—or God and the devil, as I like to say."

"But *you* never really saw an *obeah* perform this kind of thing."

"I didn't say that," Olive quickly disputed her.

"So you have seen it?" Sherry used Olive's desire to show how much she knew about the *obeah* to manipulate her.

"Yes. Long time ago, when I was just a little girl. The *obeah* man put a photograph and something that looked like hair on a table. There was also a candle with some pins stuck in it nearby. But like I said, I was really small at the time, and none of the adults knew I saw them. I was peeking through a window." Olive made sure she had Sherry's full attention. "The *obeah* man called some names and said a few other things I don't quite remember. Then he lit the candle. All the grown folks in there looked scared. I don't think he was calling on good when he put the mouth on that person. No, I don't think he was. Later on, I came to understand that particular *obeah* man chose to call on the evil. He didn't have to. He could have called on good just as easily. The *obeah* is not the way of evil; a person chooses evil or good in using it. The *obeah* is simply a way of power."

Simply a way of power. Sherry focused on Olive's words. Jason would show her his mother's tools tonight, and she was certain she would be able to convince him to give them to her. Jason had been right when he'd said she was drawn to power. What other way was there? Life had taught Sherry she had to have control. She had been a victim before, and that was something she would never be again.

Chapter 26

The jugglers and the contortionist left the floor, and a band in bright suits took their place. They played a lively set of Bahamian tunes, incorporating cowbells and conch shells. A few couples, all tourists, got on the dance floor and did their thing. Although Mr. Ashford let out a few alcohol-induced yelps, no one from their table joined the crowd.

Professional dancers were the next performers to take over the limelight. They showed the crowd how it was really done. Sasha was impressed, and she grooved to the music. Cay appeared to be content, watching quietly. But Cynthia was the live wire of the group. She shimmied her shoulders, her breasts shaking like molds of golden Jell-O above her strapless jumpsuit.

"And now we're going to have a limbo contest," the bandleader announced as the music ended. "We want everybody to participate, so we're going to start the limbo stick out real high, make it easy for you." He gave a big smile. "A shot of rum for half price will be available to everyone. It will give you the boost you need to get up here." He waved his arm generously, then applauded until the crowd joined in. "This is how it goes," the announcer explained. "Each table will be considered as a team. All it takes is for one of your team members to win the contest, and that table will receive a bottle of Dom Pérignon as their prize. So I want to know what table will *not* be winning that bottle of champagne tonight?"

Hands shot up around the room but were snatched down when their owners realized what he'd asked.

"Tricked you, didn't I?" The bandleader grinned.

"You sure did," Stanley Ashford shouted back. "But you can count my table in the contest, and we're going to win that champagne."

"Say what?" The announcer played off Mr. Ashford's claim. "Folks, we've got a challenge to the other tables from the gentleman right here. So what are we waiting for? Let the contest begin."

"This is going to be a riot." Cynthia swayed her hips from side to side as she rose from her chair.

"You can say that again." Mr. Ashford weaved as he pushed his chair back.

A lopsided grin appeared on Cay's face as he rose from his seat and removed his black jacket. "After you." He motioned toward Sasha.

Sasha's eyebrows rose at the spontaneity of the moment. "So you're going to do it?" She couldn't imagine the dignified Cay Ellis going under a limbo stick.

"Oh, you don't think I can?" he challenged.

"I just can't imagine you doing it." She grinned.

"Well, watch this," he said as they left the table.

The music started, and people from all the tables lined up. Two waiters held the limbo stick about five feet from the floor, and the first round was a breeze. Everybody went under the stick with virtually no problem. Leslie Ashford grinned like a schoolgirl once she emerged on the other side.

"I can't remember the last time I had so much fun," Leslie told Sasha.

"I can't either." Sasha laughed as she watched a very large man walk like a duck beneath the stick.

The mike crackled as the announcer picked it up again. "Now we're going to get serious," he announced as the stick was lowered to about three and a half feet. "We'll see who really knows how to limbo."

A wave of gleeful protestation bounced through the crowd. Many of the older people went back to their seats.

Cay moved close to Sasha. "I want to make sure I'm standing out there"—he pointed to a place that had a good view of the action— "when you go beneath that one." He clandestinely tugged at the hem of her short, tight dress.

"I believe you have a one-track mind, Mr.

Ellis," Sasha replied softly. The evening had lightened her mood.

"Let's just say I haven't forgotten last night. That was some discovery." He blew softly in her ear. "I want to make sure that my memory didn't exaggerate the experience."

Sasha moved forward with the crowd, but her body tingled. "I don't think this is the place to talk about it." She looked over at Cynthia, who was eyeing them with an envious look on her face.

"I can't think of a better place." He moved along with her. "This is the first opportunity I've had this evening to say what I really want to say. I'm like Mr. Ashford, taking full advantage of the situation."

An "Oh-h!" rose from the crowd as Mr. Ashford nearly fell. Instinctively, Sasha grabbed Cay, then clapped when Mr. Ashford recovered.

"That's what I want," Cay told her.

"What?" She glanced at him from beneath curly lashes.

"I want you to let go of all your reservations, do what you really want to do. I want you to come out of that head of yours. Do you think that's possible?"

Sasha could feel the heat rising within her. "Anything's possible," she replied.

"Come on, Sasha," Cynthia said, injecting herself into the exchange. She grabbed Sasha's hand and gave Cay a pouty look. "Let's show them how to really do it." She led Sasha to the front of the crowd.

It took all Sasha had not to pull away. She

looked back at Cay as Cynthia dragged her forward.

"I'm next." Cynthia raised her arms over her head and wriggled her fingers. The crowd increased the volume of their clapping as Cynthia cried "Oh, yeah!" She leaned back and began to hop forward with her knees bent, contracting her midriff with jerky motions. She took her time going beneath the limbo stick, but she made it to the other side like a pro. "He-ey," she sang out, popping her fingers and looking at Cay and Randy.

"Come on, girl," she called to Sasha as she stood between the two men. "I know you can do it."

It was an obvious setup. Cynthia wanted to either show Sasha up or get her to embarrass herself. Sasha wasn't falling for either one. She smiled at Cay and began to move to the music as she approached the limbo stick, but instead of leaning backward Sasha squatted daintily and shuffled her way underneath. On the other side, she broke into a series of dance steps that made the crowd whoop and holler. Again she smiled at Cay, who feigned extreme disappointment, but he clapped for her anyway.

"You wriggled out of that one, didn't you?" he chided.

"Did you think I wouldn't?" she enjoined.

Randy tried the stick and fell, Leslie passed, and Cay was successful but refused to go again when they lowered it another foot. Three people lined up to compete. Cynthia was the only woman.

"That's going to be really difficult," Sasha told Leslie.

"I'd say. I wouldn't think of trying, but of course, I'm not Cynthia." The two women laughed.

Cynthia shouldn't have tried, either. She ended up on her back right away, her legs flailing in the air.

"That's all right, baby," Randy called out to her. "I'll buy you a bottle of Dom Pérignon."

"Will you, sweetie?" Cynthia pouted, got up off the floor, and walked to where Randy was waiting with a big hug.

Still the contest continued, and another man fell, but the last one was as flexible as cooked spaghetti. He went beneath the stick with ease, and a drumroll heightened the excitement when the stick was lowered again.

"I can't believe this," Sasha said. "He's going to try it again. He's got to be part of the show."

"Probably," Leslie replied, mesmerized.

"But how in the world can he fold up his body like that?" Sasha had to ask. "It's nearly impossible."

"He's got to get into some kind of altered state." Leslie watched with her arms folded. "I've read something about this kind of thing. People like fire walkers and others who stick objects through their tongues without pain or blood."

"Yes, I've seen some of that on television," Sasha said as she watched the man lean farther and farther back.

Mrs. Ashford's mouth remained open as the

man folded his body like a bend in an accor-dion. "There's no way he could do that unless his mind is in an altered state." She leaned toward Sasha. "Nothing but pure mind. The body is just a vehicle. We are so much more," she declared.

Applause exploded in the restaurant after the performer successfully maneuvered him-self beneath the two-and-a-half-foot-high stick, and the bandleader appeared at the mike again.

"You didn't know the contest was rigged, did you?" He stretched out his arm toward the male contortionist. "But I'll tell you what we're going to do. We're going to provide everyone at the young woman's table and the gentleman's table"—he pointed to Cynthia and the other finalist—"with a glass of Dom Pérignon. How's that?" The announcer backed away from the mike, clapping.

"Why not?" Mr. Ashford said in a slurred voice. "I never turn down free drinks."

Chapter 27

The evening was finally over, and the couples bade one another good-night.

Cay placed his hand in the small of Sasha's back as they walked to the horse and buggy and climbed aboard.

Sasha laid her head against the cushioned seat of the carriage and closed her eyes. The breeze was soft and warm against her face, and her head was light because of the champagne.

"This is heaven," Sasha proclaimed.

"Is it? I didn't realize you were so easy to please," Cay replied, looking at her relaxed features.

"Sometimes I am. Like right now, I'm very easy. Very easy." Sasha's eyes were moist and welcoming when she opened them again.

"Now you're talking," Cay replied.

They studied one another.

"You are an interesting man, Cay Ellis," Sasha finally said.

"Am I?" His dark eyes sparkled with light from the passing street lamps.

"Absolutely." Sasha's brow furrowed. "The Ashfords believe you were their guardian angel. That you went out of your way to help them in their time of greatest need." She twisted her head from side to side. "It's difficult to think of you that way."

"How have you thought of me?" Cay asked softly.

Sasha took a deep breath. "As this rich so-and-so who gets what he wants no matter how it affects other people."

"Whoa." Cay squeezed his eyes shut as if he had been slapped. "That was a quick answer. You didn't have to think about that at all, did you?

"Nope." Sasha smiled slightly. "Not at all."

"Do you want to know how I see you?"

Sasha looked a little puzzled. She had never considered Cay's perspective. "How do you see me?"

"As this fanatically independent woman who pushes for what she wants no matter if it is in her best interest or not." He rolled the sentence off his tongue and then took a deep breath.

"Fanatically independent." Sasha sat up straight. "There is no such thing."

"I think there is," Cay said in a self-assured, soft tone.

"Give me an example," Sasha demanded defensively.

"When a person refuses help just for the sake of refusing it. When she just wants to be able to prove she can do it alone." He looked down at the match cover in his hand. "I think it's a person who doesn't believe she can count on anyone but herself."

"But isn't that the way it really is?" Sasha argued. "I mean, if people offer to help you, normally they want something in return. So when you're truly down and out, and you need someone to give you a helping hand, there's never a soul within shouting distance. But if they're like you"—she pointed at Cay— "have everything, don't need anything, people just come running. They can't offer you enough. They can't do enough. But let some poor wretch whose life depends on their donation ask for one, they'll be refused," she declared.

"You seem to feel pretty strongly about that," Cay said, looking at Sasha's tight features.

"I do have strong feelings about it. I've been there. My mother and I both have been there."

"What happened?" Cay asked softly.

"Just what I said. We were in dire straits, and no matter who we asked or how much we pleaded no one would help us without a price." Sasha looked away. She could feel the tears welling up in her eyes. She hadn't realized how much emotional charge she still held about the ordeal.

"How long did you take care of your mother, Sasha?"

"She started getting sick eight years ago, but it was during the last four years that I actually took care of her," she said softly. "Four years of trying to get her the best medical treatment I could with virtually no money." A tear escaped down her cheek. Sasha swiped it away. "You don't know how helpless you feel when someone you love is slipping away from you before your very eyes and there's nothing you can really do about it. To know that if you had a better job, or knew how to be more creative about bringing in money, the person's burden would be lessened considerably." She looked at him with eyes that were too bright. "But when you don't have the money or the creativity to provide what it takes, you can only do things to buy them a little more time. Anything." Sasha looked at her hands, in her lap.

The carriage stopped in front of the hotel. Cay paid the driver and they entered the building in silence. Sasha couldn't look at Cay while they rode the elevator. She felt extremely exposed standing beside him. She had shared her deepest pain with him. The words had simply tumbled out. It wasn't what she had intended.

Once they were in the suite Cay found a jazz station on the radio. The soothing sound eased into every corner of the room. He hoped it would help Sasha feel more at ease. She had turned silent. Cay realized it didn't take much for Sasha to retreat into herself.

"Want some wine?" he asked standing in front of the mini-bar.

Sasha paused for a moment. "Yes, please."

He poured two glasses of wine and joined Sasha on the couch. Cay sat close, but not too close.

"It sounds like a horrible thing to have gone

through, Sasha. I'd do anything to be able to change it, but I can't."

"I'm not asking you to change anyth—" Sasha revealed the chip on her shoulder.

"Sh-sh-sh." Cay gently put his finger up to his mouth. "I know you aren't. I just wanted you to know that I wish I could."

Sasha looked down at her glass.

"I wish that for two reasons," Cay continued. "I wish that I had been there in *your* greatest time of need, and I must admit the other reason is a selfish one."

Sasha looked up at him, puzzled.

"I wish that you had never experienced it, so that you would not see me as your enemy."

"But Cay, it's rather hard to see you any other way. You and Guana Manor are the main things standing between me and my financial independence."

"Not really. It's not over yet."

"So, you mean you're not going to—"

"I mean it's not over yet." Sasha started to interrupt. Cay stopped her. "Remember, we called a truce."

"But it's very difficult not to talk about this," Sasha insisted.

"I understand. But maybe if we try seeing each other as two human beings who aren't bad people, but just people who are trying to live their lives the best way they can, taking into consideration our histories and our flaws, maybe then we can find some common ground."

Sasha folded her arms across her chest. "I'll

give us that, but honestly, what other common ground do we have?'' Her eyes sought an answer.

''You're not the only one who has suffered in the past. I lost people I loved as well. They slipped away from me right before my eyes.''

Sasha knew one of the people he was talking about was Precious. Somehow she did not want to be reminded of Precious on this of all nights.

Cay continued. ''My brother, Wally, suffered tremendously. I knew he was hurting, but there was nothing I was able to do. As a matter of fact, I seemed to be a part of his dilemma.''

''I had forgotten about your brother,'' Sasha admitted.

''And, of course, there was Precious,'' Cay added softly. ''And there was also my father.''

''Your father? But Mr. Ellis is still alive.''

''Yes, he is. But a person doesn't have to die to be lost to you. He can be around every day, and you can feel totally outside of his plans, his thoughts, and what appears to be important to him. At this point in my life it doesn't matter that much to me anymore, but when I was a child it mattered an awful lot.''

''Where was your mother?''

''My mother died right after I was born, and although I never heard anyone blame me for her death, I grew up with a sense of guilt, as if it were my fault.'' Cay's eyes became hooded. ''There was this empty place in my life that hurt, but I blamed myself for it being empty. It's kind of funny, but through the years no one ever mentioned her name. Do you know I've never seen a picture of my mother?"

Sasha couldn't believe it. "Never?"

"Never. But I remember the time when Wally's mother was at Guana Manor. I was so happy." His lips turned a slight smile. "I believed somehow God had given me a mother despite my not deserving one." Cay shook his head. "And then, shortly after Wally was born, she left."

"I can't imagine growing up without my mother," Sasha sympathized. "So even though you had Mr. Ellis you must have felt very alone."

"I did feel alone." He tried to smile. "I had Baltron and Olive, but it's not quite the same." His eyes turned distant. "Yes. One by one I've seen the people that I care about die or leave, and there was nothing I could do about it. My money didn't help me. There was no amount of money in the world that could have kept them here. And there is no amount that can bring them back. If there was, and I had it, I would give every cent. Can you imagine living in a world where, since you were a child, the special people in your life were taken away?" He searched her eyes for understanding.

Sasha reached out and touched Cay's hand. "No, I can't."

"So we have more in common than you thought. Our lives haven't been pretty, and we're not always right, but that's a part of being human. I guess some of our burdens are greater to bear than others." His features turned troubled. "But we were never promised that life would be perfect, were we?"

Their gazes held before they kissed. There was no pretense, no overwhelming passion. Cay's and Sasha's lives met in a place of mutual understanding. Afterward Sasha wrapped her arms around Cay and pulled him close.

"Does this mean you are welcoming me?" His voice lowered to a whisper.

"I welcome you with open arms," Sasha replied, her eyes moist with sincerity. "Not only my arms but my heart and my mind are open to you as well."

A rush of love and desire flooded through Cay, and his mouth came down on Sasha's again. He wanted her to know how he felt. "I have never felt like this about any woman," he whispered huskily as he rubbed his face against her hair.

"You can never say that enough," Sasha whispered. It satisfied her need to be special that no one, not even Precious, had touched his life the way she had.

He looked into her eyes. The vulnerable light of love there frightened him. But like a light at the end of a tunnel it beckoned to him as well. Cay knew Sasha had given her heart to him, and it was such a fragile, rare gift. "Then I will never stop saying it. Never."

Cay saw her eyes fill with moisture as she withdrew from his embrace. She stood up and walked over by the bed. Silently, Sasha removed her clothes and lay back on the cotton sheets. "Come to me, Cay," she beckoned softly.

Cay removed his clothes and climbed into bed beside her. They were no youngsters at the game of love, and because of it they knew when something truly special had entered their lives.

"Wouldn't it be wonderful if the world could stop spinning right now?" Sasha said as she held him against her. "And all the horrible things that can happen to two people who dare to give themselves to one another would simply fade away, and the pleasure and joy of this moment would be locked perpetually in time for all lovers to experience. Wouldn't that be wonderful, Cay?"

"You know, you can talk." He stroked her face. "Saving others through love . . . I can't think of anything more powerful."

The next kiss swept them deep into the heart of love. It was hard for Sasha and Cay to believe that one kiss could bind two people so magically, and when he entered her, it was an extension of that love. The depth of that moment sealed what they had come to understand: neither Cay nor Sasha had ever truly been *in love* before.

With the gentleness of a baby being rocked in a cradle they began, until the repetitive motion awakened a tormenting ache within. The sweetest of sensations yearned to be soothed, and soothe them they did, until they cried out each other's names in their most glorious of moments.

Lying across Cay's chest, Sasha could barely keep her eyes open. She was happy and satisfied in a way she had never known before.

She listened to his steady breathing above her head that coincided with the rising and falling of his chest. "I guess he's asleep," Sasha spoke softly. "You sleep, Cay Ellis the third. I think it would be wonderful to share the rest of my nights like this with you."

Cay closed his eyes as if he were in pain. No woman had ever fulfilled him like Sasha had. He knew, this night, they had given all they had to one another. He had never dreamed it could be this way.

Cay's marriage to Precious had yielded nothing of the kind. Precious had reintroduced chastity and purity into his life. He had hoped it would shield him against what he was beginning to fear was true. It had been a bittersweet exchange for the passion he craved. But accepting the Bethel Curse as real was the hardest thing he'd ever had to do.

Cay let go a tremulous breath. If the pain could be so great at losing a woman he loved only chastely, how great would be the pain of losing a woman he loved with every part of his being? And lose her he would. . . . Cay's body stiffened at the thought of it. But how do you tell the woman you love you believe that?

He closed his eyes as he made up his mind. She did not have to know. It was not her burden to carry. Cay looked up at the ceiling. *Sharing the rest of your nights with me, Sasha . . . could mean the end for you, and I cannot let that happen.*

Sasha felt Cay's body tremble as his chest deflated. She smiled and nestled her face inside the soft cavity before closing her eyes and drifting off to sleep.

Chapter 28

"Will we fly over any other islands on our way back to Magic Key?" Sasha called from the shower.

"Yes, a few," Cay replied.

Sasha stepped out of the shower and began to dry herself. She felt silly and buoyant, like a young girl in love for the first time. She looked in the mirror. A smile was plastered on her face. Sasha stopped with the towel held against her and listened to the sounds Cay made as he moved around inside the suite. They were some of the sweetest sounds she had ever heard.

When Sasha had awakened that morning Cay was already in the shower. It surprised her. But being the assertive businessman that he was, she assumed he wasn't accustomed to sleeping late. Still, Sasha had to admit there was something about the way he was acting that nagged at her. He was too quiet. But of course, Sasha chided herself, she didn't know if that was his normal morning behavior. She had never spent the night with Cay before.

Perhaps he was one of those people who were moody first thing in the morning and remained that way until they had their first cup of coffee. Or perhaps—she tried not to think this—he was already having misgivings about their budding relationship.

Sasha folded the towel and placed it on the counter. *I'm not going to do this to myself,* she declared. *Why should he be having misgivings? We had a wonderful evening and night together. There was nothing to have misgivings about.*

Sasha hummed as she dressed. The tune turned into a song, a song her mother had sung to her when she was a little girl.

Cay listened attentively through the bathroom door. Sasha's voice was full of contentment. It was so vibrant and alive, and the message within her song told him her dreams. A lump appeared in his throat. He did not want to hurt her, but what would be worse, hurting her by backing away or being the one to bring about her early death? It would be so easy to totally open his life to her. She filled a space that he'd never realized was empty. A place that had never been filled before. Cay believed he could be happy with Sasha for the rest of his life, but he also believed that was impossible.

He looked out the window at the peaceful water below. If he told her what he was thinking, it would be out of selfishness. He would be a man who had plucked the most beautiful rose to enjoy it for only a moment, knowing that if he had let it be it would have enjoyed a natural lifetime of beauty.

Cay closed his eyes and held them closed. He wasn't getting any younger, and he realized how much he longed for a balanced life with a wife and children. Yes, children. Something he was finally admitting to himself.

"Ah-h, that shower felt good." Sasha emerged from the bathroom wearing jeans and a T-shirt that said "I've been to the Bahamas . . . Nan-nan-nan-nan." "I'm starved. What about you?"

"I could eat a bite or two," Cay replied as he gathered up his wallet and bracelet.

They looked at each other from across the room. A big grin spread across Sasha's face. "Before you ask me about this stupid grin, I already know how it looks. I just feel so good this morning," she confessed.

Cay thought Sasha looked much younger than her thirty years. He had to smile, but it was all too short. "Let's have breakfast downstairs. That'll be the quickest way to get something to eat." He looked at his watch. "I've got a meeting at noon that I don't want to miss."

Sasha hoped her disappointment did not show. She knew they had to return to Magic Key, but at the moment its troubles seemed so far away. She wasn't in a hurry to get back, but Cay, who was thinking about business, apparently was.

They enjoyed a breakfast buffet before taking off in the seaplane. Sasha had become somewhat accustomed to the motion of the small craft, but she was far from liking it.

"What you see way over there"—Cay pointed and spoke into the mike attached to the headphones—"is Grand Bahama Island. But the island that is almost beneath us now is Mores Island."

"It's rather small," Sasha commented into her own headset.

"There are over two hundred islands that make up the Bahamas. To the left of Mores Island is an even smaller one. Gorda Cay."

They were flying so low that Sasha could clearly see the buildings and vehicles on the islands. Once they flew over Mores Island there was nothing but water for minutes on end.

"We've been flying over the Northwest Providence Channel for a while now. We're about to approach Bimini Island," Cay informed her.

"Bimini Island . . . The street the Bethel House is on is called Bimini Lane."

"Officially, that house sits on Route Nine," Cay replied softly.

"I know that, but Baltron and everybody else say the address is three-forty Bimini Lane," Sasha countered.

"The address of the property was changed rather recently."

"Who changed it?" Sasha found it very curious.

"Precious had it changed."

"Really." Sasha looked down through the window. "I wonder, did she name it after this island?" she said, continuing to look down. Her eyes scanned the land below. It was uninhabited, resembling a lush green emerald. A part of Sasha disliked how much Precious dominated her thoughts—and Cay's. She felt it was unhealthy. Yet there was something about her, even in death, that was comforting, inviting. The image of Hazel and Precious beckoning to her surfaced in her mind.

"Hey! Look at that!" She pointed. "That looks like a walkway beneath the water. Those stones are so huge they remind me of the ones on Guana Estate," she commented with awe. "Do you see them? They look like a road or a lane under the ocean."

"Yes." Cay's hands tightened around the yoke, and his face became drawn.

Sasha stared at him before looking down again. "I guess this kind of thing doesn't excite you anymore."

Silence filled the plane. Sasha waited for Cay to speak, but when he didn't she asked, "Is something wrong?"

"That is the first time I have seen the Bimini Road with my own eyes," Cay spoke slowly.

"But you had heard about it?" Sasha questioned.

"Yes. From Precious. The week before she died. The week she changed the Bethel House's address to Bimini Lane." He let go a tremulous breath.

"So she *did* name the road after this island," Sasha concluded.

"Apparently so." Cay paused. "I was out of town when she hired a private plane to fly over these waters. Precious came back believing she had seen proof that Atlantis actually did exist. And that it had sunk right here in the Atlantic Ocean."

Cay continued. "When I returned home she was erratically excited. She couldn't sleep. Precious told me she had found the proof she was looking for, and she wanted me to fly here that night to see it. But I had to fly out to a conference the next day. So I promised her I would go when I returned. It was the beginning of the end," he said quietly.

"Olive said from that day on Precious wouldn't eat and she barely slept. She roamed Magic Key and the area around the Circle of Stones until late at night. Like you, she believed the stones resembled Bimini Road." He glanced at Sasha before he looked straight ahead. "She was looking for proof that the natural spring was also connected with Atlantis."

Sasha sat in stunned silence as Cay brought the seaplane down, her mind in overdrive. She had seen Bimini Road and she had walked within the Circle of Stones. The magnitude of what she had seen filled her as she said, "Perhaps Precious was right, Cay. Perhaps that road was a part of the sunken continent of Atlantis." Her eyes became wide as a smile spread across her face. "Do you realize what that would mean?" Sasha welled up with joy. "It would mean humankind has a history as old as the stars. That our beginnings are far greater than we ever dreamed and there is nothing that we cannot accomplish if we set our hearts and our minds to it. We're not just some species that's a few steps away from being apes. The human story is much grander than that, a ten on the evolutionary scale."

Cay looked down at the controls of the seaplane. "So it would prove the impossible is possible," he said slowly.

"Yes. That's exactly what it would prove," Sasha agreed.

"And along with our ability to create wondrous things we would be able to create those things that are the results of our darkest dreams." Cay stopped her dead in her mental tracks. "They are both true, Sasha," he announced with a final acceptance. "And that's why I cannot be with you again."

"What?" She couldn't believe what she was hearing.

"If I truly love you, and I do"—he looked deep into her eyes—"I have to break this off now. I'll make you a generous offer for the Bethel House. You should take it and go away as far as you can."

"What are you telling me, Cay?" Sasha held her breath.

"I'm telling you that getting involved with me could be the most life-threatening thing you've ever done. The Ellis family lives under a curse, Sasha. I am cursed."

Sasha sat back in her seat. "So you're saying what we have is over?" She tried to grasp the situation.

"Yes," Cay replied. "It is the best thing to do."

"You're dumping me," she said slowly. "And why?" The question hung between them inside the small plane. "Because your family is cursed." Her gaze beamed with incredulity. "I have never heard such bullshit in my life. I don't believe a word of it."

"Yet you do believe in the possibility of Atlantis. One isn't much different from the other."

"Is that all you have to say after you just took me to a hotel for one night, and now you tell me you can't see me anymore! That's all you have to say?" She tried to laugh but it turned into a choking sound. "You know what I think, Cay? I think this was one big game for you. A diversion from your normal routine. You took me to the Bahamas to play out whatever scenario you had in your mind. You know the rich, like God, play games with other people's lives." She shook her head. "I don't believe the Ellis family is cursed. I just believe you're some low-down rich bastards who don't care about anyone but yourselves."

The harsh statement settled between them.

"Well . . ." Cay turned his head and looked out of the window before he fixed Sasha with a look she would never forget. "As long as you are not involved with me or this family you'll never have to find out the truth."

Sasha sat there looking at him before she said, "I already know the truth." She fumbled with the door handle and leaped from the craft.

Chapter 29

"Good morning, Mr. Williams," Jason's secretary chimed as he walked through the door to his office. "You've got a couple of messages." She handed him the short stack of papers before she stopped and studied his face. "Is everything okay? You look rather tired."

"I had a long night." Jason didn't look at the young woman.

"Well, it's been pretty quiet for a Friday morning. If it remains like this until noon, we may have a noneventful Friday."

"That's just what I need." He glanced at the top phone message as he headed toward his office. "I could use a breather."

Jason closed the door and slowly walked over to his desk. He sank down in his large leather chair. That he'd had a long night was only part of the reason he felt drained. It was hard to believe how quickly his life could be turned inside out. He pulled open a bottom drawer and took a couple of swallows of Mylanta.

Wiping the chalky stain from his mouth Jason opened his daytimer. There were only two appointments, both of them in the afternoon. He sighed with relief. It seemed like someone was looking after him. Maybe there was a God after all, although he doubted it.

"Goddamn that Sherry." He cussed under his breath. From the moment she entered his apartment the night before, she did what she did best, and that was work her way with him. After Sherry called and said she was on her way, he tried to prepare for her, but it pissed Jason off that after all those years her affect on him was the same. And no one knew that better than Sherry. It was written all over her face when he opened the door.

"Are you just going to leave me standing out here?" She tugged at the belt of her trench coat.

"Of course not," Jason stepped to the side, "by all means, come in."

Sherry advanced slowly, making sure she brushed up against him. "My goodness, things have definitely changed for the better, haven't they?"

"You were the one who didn't believe they would," he closed the door. "I told you I was going to make a good living, and I haven't reached my peak yet."

Sherry smiled at him. "I guarantee that you will before the night is over."

It frustrated him, but Jason could feel himself growing just from the look on her face.

"Got anything to drink?" she asked.

"Sure. Are you still partial to Slow Gin Fizzes?"

"Slow Gin Fizz," Sherry laughed and threw her head back. "Take me back. I haven't had one of those things in aeons."

"So you're above that kind of drink now, huh?" Jason's face tightened.

"Don't get yourself all riled up, Jason. I didn't say that. I'd love a Slow Gin Fizz." Sherry stood in front of a frosted table lamp and slid her coat off of her shoulders, revealing a white chiffon dress. Jason wondered if she knew he could see right through it.

"I think you forgot a few things while you were dressing," he announced, looking at the subtle contours of her breasts and the tiny patch of darkness a couple of feet below.

"Unnecessary items, that's what I call them," she looked into his eyes.

It was hard for Jason to turn his back but he did. "You get a kick out of doing this kind of thing, don't you, Sherry?"

"What do you think?"

"Did the Ellises ever get a peek at the real you?"

"It wasn't necessary. I was able to keep her occupied in other ways," she looked at the crystal bowl on top of the cabinet. "Spending money and living unconscionably well."

"You know you didn't have to come over here half nude." Jason said over the sound of clinking glasses. "I had already decided to give you what you asked for."

"How sweet of you," Sherry put her hands on her hips. "Can you tell me what convinced you to be so accommodating?" A knowing gleam entered her eyes.

Jason just looked at her.

"This really is a lovely place, Jason." Sherry reiterated, looking out over the water.

"What did you expect? That I was living in the swamps and you would be forced to leap over frogs and lizards to come see me?" he held out the cocktail.

She chuckled lightly. "Do you own it, or are you just renting?"

"That's none of your goddamned business," Jason replied.

Sherry took the glass and sat down on the sofa. "Ah-h, you're so tense. Why don't you come and sit beside me," she patted the white surface.

"I am not your toy, Sherry. Not anymore I'm not." Jason looked at her with restrained desire.

Sherry's red lips turned up softly against the glass. "I never thought you were."

"You've already . . . paid me for my mother's things," he hoped his point was condescendingly clear. "The only reason I'm letting you have them is because they are absolutely of no use to me."

Sherry bit her finger and shook it in feigned pain.

Jason shook his head. "I'll be right back."

He went to the closet where his mother's things were stored. The mid-sized trunk was near the front. Jason rifled through the objects in the cedar box until he came across a shoe-box that contained a collection of objects.

Among them, a small glass bowl, a kerchief, a coin and the old Sprite bottle that his mother used during her rituals to spray spirit water from her mouth.

Jason picked up a couple of candles and dislodged a wad of cloth held together by straight pins. He started to close the chest but a glimpse of his mother's handwriting stopped him. A repetition of the words, *my son*, *Magic Key*, and *his land* were scrawled from any angle that the small section of now yellow space would allow. Jason stared at his mother's doodling, and a dawning thought emerged. Could it be true? Was he one of the many bastard children Cay Ellis Jr. fathered? After all these years of being jealous of the family that had kept Sherry away from him, was he actually entitled to the Ellis fortune? Jason squeezed his forehead.

"Do you need any help in there?" Sherry called in a syrupy voice.

"No. No. I'm coming right out." Jason closed the lid of the trunk.

"Are you sure?" The click of Sherry's heels against the wooden floor grew louder.

Jason stuffed the paper in his pocket. He placed the candles and the pins inside the shoebox and stood up. "Positive."

"So what all did you find?" Sherry came and stood beside him.

"A few things," Jason started out the room.

Sherry looked at the bed. "You sure you want to leave?"

Jason's eyes cut towards the closet before he answered. "Yeah. Let's go up front." He headed down the hall before she had a chance to refuse. He placed the shoebox on the cocktail table and went into the kitchen.

"It seems like all of a sudden you're in a big hurry?" Sherry looked perturbed as she examined the objects.

Jason was so preoccupied he didn't hear her.

"What is this stuff" She looked at a package of herbs marked with a skull and bones.

"I don't know anything about it. You asked me for them and I'm giving them to you. That's as far as my involvement goes."

Sherry looked toward the kitchen. "I can't imagine how this pile of junk can do anything." She laughed condescendingly.

Jason dug a plastic bag from underneath his kitchen sink. "Call it what you want, but *my mother* didn't think of it as junk, and I don't think too many of the people she worked on did, either. You can put them in here." He handed the bag to Sherry.

"Is this your way of telling me it's time for me to go?"

Jason closed his eyes before he spoke. His head was about to explode. "Look, it's rather late and I've got to prepare for a couple of court cases tomorrow."

"You're not getting off that easy." Her eyes flashed as she took his hand and pressed it against her.

"Not now, Sherry," Jason protested.

"Why not now?" She moved against his hand.

"I've got a lot of things on my mind."

"So do I, but I didn't come over here not to get what I wanted."

"You've got them." He indicated the shoe box.

"But I want more." She unzipped his pants.

"Please . . ." Jason shook his head as Sherry started to manipulate him.

"Just once, Jason." She kissed him lightly. "You know you've never been able to resist me." She lifted her dress.

Jason felt like a pawn, and he realized he would always be a pawn in the big chess game of people like Sherry and Mr. Ellis. That's what they wanted him to be and he hated them for it.

Minutes later Jason zipped up his pants and turned his back.

"Do you think you'll have word on the Bethel property tomorrow?" he asked, standing by the door.

"I might," Sherry replied cattily. "But tomorrow is Friday, and it may be Monday before I can get back with you."

Jason's lip tightened. "I won't be available tomorrow. If you need to contact me you have my beeper number." He opened the door before he said, "No matter what you do, Sherry, I just want you to know I intend to stick it to the Ellises."

"You already have, dear." Sherry patted his cheek as she walked out.

Chapter 30

"Where is my father?" Cay burst into the kitchen.

"You're back," Olive declared, startled by his abrupt entrance.

"I said, where is my father?"

"I guess he's in his room, Cay," Baltron replied. "Is anything wrong?"

"Yes, the same thing that has been wrong for years," he replied as the door swung wildly. His voice waxed and waned with the movement.

"Go, go, go." Olive motioned toward Baltron with her hand. "Don't let him do anything he will regret."

Baltron followed Cay into the hallway. "I wouldn't say anything that would rile him, if I were you. His mood hasn't been too good over the last twenty-four hours."

"I think I can count the times on my hand when my father's temperament was good." Cay strode toward the stairs. "So if I waited for that, the time would never come for me to say the things I need to say."

Baltron touched Cay's arm as he started up the stairs. "I'm serious, Cay. He seems more touchy than I've known him to be. I think he hasn't been feeling well but he's afraid to say it."

Cay looked into the eyes that had shown him kindness through the years. "All right, Baltron, I'll keep that in mind."

Cay walked up and rapped on the bedroom door. "It's me, Father. May I come in?"

"Is it important? I've got business to take care of and I don't want to be late," Mr. Ellis called back.

Cay could feel years of anger rising inside of him. "I'm not some servant in this house, Father, or some associate of yours who needs to make an appointment before I get to talk to you."

The door opened slowly. Mr. Ellis looked at him with an expression Cay had seen all of his life. Someone else would have called it a snarl. "I guess it is important." He walked back into the room, sat down in a chair, and continued to put on his socks. He glanced up. "What's got you so fired up this morning you want to come in here and raise hell with me? That woman must have put some high octane in your tank."

"You can call it that." Cay closed the door and sat down in the opposite chair.

"You intending on staying in here a long time?"

"Until I get some real answers."

Mr. Ellis eyed him, then went back to dressing. "What kind of answers?"

"The kind you should have volunteered to tell me if you had been any kind of father."

"Hold on there, boy. I am still your father, and I don't have to tell you a goddamned thing."

"I think you do have to tell me. You owe me that much. You owe this family that much."

"I intend to do what's right by this family, and I don't need my son telling me how to do it."

"That's all well and good, Father, but I intend to know the real history behind this family. The whole story. How we got into the mess we're in now."

"The whole history. I don't have time to tell you all of that." Mr. Ellis's hands shook as he pulled at his second sock. "And what do you mean, mess? We got one of the largest fortunes in the Keys and we're living large down here. People respect us. You got money to buy anything and everything you want. I don't see anything wrong with that." Mr. Ellis kept up his bravado. "And I haven't seen you complaining until now."

"I'm not talking about the money—I'm talking about the reason all of our lives, our *personal* lives, are in a shambles. Look at us. Wally died a drunk. The only woman I ever married chose death to the realities here. You have chased every woman along the seven-mile highway and never settled down with anyone, and now I've finally found someone I want in my life worse than life itself, and I can't have her because of who I am."

"Is that what this is about? You wanting that woman, Sasha Townsend? I assumed it was her you had run off with for the last day and a half. You didn't get enough of her then?"

"Yes, this is about Sasha. But it's about much much more. I want her in my life, permanently. But I can't have her without destroying her life, can I? Either by my death or by hers. From the time we came out of the womb, you and Grandmother set out to control my life and Wally's life. Why? What was the reason?"

"A lot of this stuff was laid down before your grandmother was even born. So don't put all the blame on us."

"And that's why I'm sitting here right now. I want to know the truth. I am entitled to know." Cay's voice vibrated with determination.

"There ain't much to it. It was the way of our ancestors who lived on Cat Island. We just inherited it. Who knows, they may have inherited it from our Ibo ancestors." Mr. Ellis looked at his son from beneath bushy eyebrows. "I've told you some things through the years."

"I wouldn't say that." Cay pinned his father with a dark stare. "You frightened me when I was a little boy, and you threatened me when I got older, but you never explained anything. You simply said it was the way things were and there was nothing I could do to change it. Once you mentioned my great-

greatgrandfather had started it all. But that's all I recall.''

"Well, he did. He messed over that woman, Sasha Townsend's great-greatgrandmother, who was also heavy in the *obeah*, and he simply met his match. From what I understand he tried to use her and disrespect her in front of everyone they knew, and she would have none of it. One by one members on both sides of the family ended up dead or crazy, until they had harmed so many that they had to call a truce.''

"And the Bethel Agreement is part of that truce?''

"As far as I know. But there were other things.''

"What were they, Father?'' Cay insisted. "No, let me guess. What did you tell me that day I was no more than six years old and you were so angry? You had been drinking, too.'' Cay squinted, remembering the past. "You said, 'Anything you love, boy, is going to die. It's in your blood. In your genes. And there is nothing you can do about it.' I'll never forget how I felt when you said it. Over the years I tried, but I never forgot.''

"I guess that was a little harsh. But it was the truth.'' Mr. Ellis shook his finger. "You needed to get accustomed to not holding on to people. The curse Bethel Obeah put on this family was a black curse. I tried to prepare you for the effects as best I knew how. It wasn't easy, you know. That's why I handled you and Wally with a long-handled spoon. I didn't want you to get attached to anyone. I wanted you to be tough. It's also why I meddled in your marriages. I was thinking about the children you might have. I wanted to raise them at Guana Manor like you and Wally were raised here. I was counting on that damned Sherry to keep the Ellis line going. Precious being the way she was a strange kind of blessing. Too many children would have been too much."

"So you considered all of that?" Cay stated, dumbfounded. "But why did you choose Sherry to be a part of this family? In the beginning it didn't seem to matter to you if she married Wally or me. Why Sherry, Father?"

"That didn't have anything to do with the Bethel Curse. Maybe it was a curse of another kind." Mr. Ellis gave a half laugh. "At the time I was thinking about your grandmother. Back in the islands, many black folks thought lightening up our families was the thing to do. Your grandmother had drummed it into my head that she wanted her grands and great-great-grands to be fair-skinned. From my perspective, Sherry was perfect. You know when you look at her you can't tell if she's black or white." One bushy eyebrow lifted as he nodded his head. "Mother wouldn't stand for us crossing the color line, so damn near white was the best choice."

Cay just looked at him.

"I'm just telling you the truth. But, of course, now I know choosing Sherry was a mistake. She is more of a manipulator than I am. But as far as the rest of it goes . . . you wanted to know your history. There it is. You can't run away from it. No matter how you might try."

"So you're saying what happened to this family is the result of a curse put on us by the Bethels generations ago? And that is how the feud between the Bethels and the Ellises began?"

"Yes. It started with your great-great-grandfather doing what we Ellis men do best. Screwing around." His lips turned a cynical smile.

Cay asked, closing his eyes, "What if I wanted to end it now?"

Mr. Ellis looked at Cay's anguished face, and his son's pain broke through his bravado. He wanted to reach out and comfort him but he didn't know how. "From what I understand, it's not possible. The people who put down the curse have died. No one else can remove it."

Cay was silent before he said, "I can't believe that. There has to be a way to break it," he insisted.

"We've been living with it for generations. That's the way it is, and the way it will always be."

Cay stood up and looked at his father. For the first time since he was a child his heart called out for an end to the pain and sadness that haunted his family. Suddenly, a strength filled him that he had never known before, and Cay declared, "Not if I can help it."

Chapter 31

"I had to get out of there. I haven't seen so many long faces in my life." Olive fanned herself with her hand. "I hope you like conch fritters." She placed the tinfoil bundle on the table. "And key lime pie. It's as good as it gets. I used some of the limes from the orchard back there."

"I love key lime pie and conch fritters," Sasha replied, a little flustered by Olive's impromptu visit. She was still reeling from what had transpired with Cay.

A car passing on the road made Sasha look through the screened door. She caught a glimpse of a black-topped car. She was disappointed it was not Cay's white SUV turning onto her property; Cay coming to apologize because he realized he made a mistake.

"That's probably Mr. Ellis." Olive strained to see the vehicle. "On and off during the evening he kept saying things like 'Nobody takes advantage of the Ellises' and 'I'm going to fix that little red wagon.' Stuff like that. He's got something going. Lord help whoever it involves." She sat back in the chair. "Considering the way Mr. Cay looked when he asked if his father was at home, it appears everybody's got some score to settle."

"So Cay is still at home?"

"He was there when I left the house." Olive shrugged her shoulders. "He didn't say anything to me about leaving."

Sasha looked at the clock. It was twelve-thirty. Cay had said he had a business meeting at noon. He had lied.

"Is something wrong?" Olive asked.

"No." Sasha looked up furtively from downcast eyes.

"Do you mind if I ask you something?"

"I guess not," Sasha said hesitantly.

"It's obvious there's something going on between you and Mr. Cay. Were you two together when he left early yesterday morning? He didn't tell anybody where he was going so we had no idea where he was."

Sasha thought before she responded. What difference would it make if she told Olive the truth? There was nothing between her and Cay now.

"Yes," Sasha said softly, "we were together."

Olive leaned forward. "Well, I'm pleased. I think you would bring some spark back into his life. He acts like he's walking a tightrope that could break at any moment."

Sasha looked down again. She didn't feel like explaining what had happened.

"But you know, it just doesn't make any sense."

"What doesn't make any sense, Olive?" It was hard for Sasha to concentrate.

"I thought with you two going off together like that it would mellow him out a bit." She shook her head. "I just don't know what it's going to take to help Mr. Cay find peace. The Ellises have their problems, that's for sure."

"Did he seem upset?" Sasha asked hopefully. Maybe, just maybe, he was hurting, too.

"If *upset* is a strong enough word," Olive declared. "All I know is whatever had him going involved his father. I swear, every member of that family must be going through some kind of crisis. One moment Sherry is her regular stuck-up self, the next she is as sweet as a lamb. Mr. Ellis walks around as if he's in a world of his own, but when he comes out of it he's surlier than a bull, and Mr. Cay ... I don't know." Her eyebrows knitted together. "Out of all of them, he's been the one who has tried to do the right thing, even though it wasn't always easy for him. Years of working for folks who never seem to be happy gets a little heavy sometimes. But lately things appear to be coming to a head, like a boil. Maybe it's the dark before the light, as my mother used to say. You know, folks say there are always signs foretelling change, but you've got to be aware enough to read them."

Sasha remained quiet. It was hard for her to consider the things that had occurred as positive signs.

"On a few occasions," Olive continued, "while Precious was alive, I would come to the Bethel House to get away. Being here comforted me. It still does." She looked around.

"How did you and Baltron come to work for the Ellises?"

"Oh-h, that was a long time ago, and it began with quite a stir. Mr. Ellis had been drinking and he was about to get himself killed over another man's woman. The man was his gardener." She tugged at her nose. "Baltron happened to be around to talk the man out of it, and he ended up taking Mr. Ellis home. That night Mr. Ellis offered Baltron the gardener's job. Baltron needed the work, but he told Mr. Ellis he would take the position under one condition."

"What was that?"

"That he'd never try the same thing with me that he tried with the first gardener's wife." Olive's eyes brightened.

"Oh-h." Sasha nearly smiled.

"Mr. Ellis said it was a deal and that he would make it easy for Baltron to keep an eye on me if he wanted to. He said they could use my help in the kitchen." She laughed. "It wasn't long before the cook was gone. She wanted to go home, back to the islands." Olive looked ill at ease. "I hope my popping in like this didn't cause you any trouble?" she repeated for the third time.

"No. No trouble at all." Sasha couldn't admit the truth. "I'm looking forward to eating these conch fritters after I take a walk on the beach."

Olive patted her poofy hair. "You know, there's a shortcut to the beach from the back of the house here." She pointed.

"I noticed the trees thin out at the bottom of the slope, and I wondered about that," Sasha replied.

"It's really simple. All you have to do is follow the path."

"Oh, so the path leads to the private beach?" Sasha thought about the possibility of running into Cay. She didn't want to see him if he didn't want to see her.

"It's the private beach, but you'll be coming out close to where the public property begins," Olive said with nonchalance. "I don't care how much money you have, you can't divide up the ocean," she quipped.

"No, you can't," Sasha agreed, and became pensively quiet. "I think I'm going to walk down to that stand that sells old-fashioned Sno-Kones. I've seen it from the road. I haven't had one of those since I was a little girl. My mother used to give me money so I could buy one whenever she knew I was sad." A wistful look crossed her face. "And I'm craving one right now."

"They have some good ones. Mr. Smith, an old fella that patrols both beaches, has been running that stand for years. He knows some of everything about everybody. I don't know how he sits out there under that umbrella day after day. It's got to get really hot sometimes." Olive sighed. "But you know, on the other hand, I guess I do know how he could do it. The man must be at least eighty years old. It's a good way to stay in touch with people and earn some money to boot. But at my age I can't even eat a Sno-Kone. They give me a headache real quick." She patted the top of her head.

Sasha's thoughts had left Olive again. She was thinking about Cay, the Ellis family, and their troubles—the jumbled events that had occurred since she moved to Magic Key.

"Well, I guess I better be going." Olive looked at her watch.

Once the elder woman took her leave, Sasha went into the bedroom, where she threw on a large airy dress and some beach shoes. A walk along the water could do her good.

Olive turned out to have been right about the shortcut. Within minutes Sasha was on the Ellises' private beach. She walked along the edge of the water, virtually alone. She was thankful for that as she focused on the colors in the distance. As Sasha drew closer they transformed into beach umbrellas and beach-goers.

The walk was sobering. She had not planned to cry, but as the salty breeze touched her face, she felt the loneliness of a woman alone in paradise. Inevitably, the tears began to fall. No matter how she had tried to condition herself, Sasha realized there was no way to prepare for this kind of hurt. Cynically, she thought, age had nothing to do with it. Love was still blind. Forever hoping for the best, no matter the size or color of the warning signs.

Sasha threw back her head and laughed while the tears streamed down her face. No one ever could have told her she could hurt like this.

The pure blue water was warm against her ankles. Somehow trudging through it with the sun barreling down on her face helped her accept what had happened. But it didn't explain why. She had tried to keep her distance from Cay, but her heart hadn't let her. Why was she allowed to feel so deeply, only for it to be snatched away?

When Sasha reached the Sno-Kone stand she got in line behind a young couple. The young tanned man couldn't keep his hands off his shapely young woman. Sasha watched him constantly whisper in the woman's ears. The woman giggled in response and laid her head against his chest. It was so obvious they were in love.

Sasha felt a pang of jealousy. She didn't recall ever having what this couple had, the freedom to love openly and wholeheartedly, and she wondered if they realized the magnitude of the gift. Sasha watched as they bought one Sno-Kone and walked off slurping it out of the paper container at the same time.

"May I help you, little lady?" the spry man behind the icebox inquired.

"You sure can," Sasha replied. "Can you give me a dose of what those two have?"

He leaned over the small cooler-counter and studied the couple as they walked away. "I tell you, I see it every day. If you went by what happens on this beach, you would think everybody in the world was in love," he quipped. "But sorry to say, all I can give you is the same flavor Sno-Kone."

"I guess that will have to do," Sasha replied.

Mr. Smith positioned himself to dish up the crushed ice. He looked back at Sasha, who was staring off into space. "Did you know we're having an oyster roast tonight?"

"No, this is the first time I've heard about it," Sasha replied in a scattered fashion.

"We have it once a year." Mr. Smith packed the ice into the funnel-shaped cup. "It's a good time. We start at seven and go until eleven, if you're interested."

"I don't know," Sasha said, her thoughts far away. "I might come."

Mr. Smith made circles with his arm as he maneuvered the ice beneath the flowing syrup. He glanced up at Sasha. "What's the world coming to when a pretty lady like you has to ask me, an old geezer selling Sno-Kones, to give her a dose of love?"

"That's a good question, isn't it?" Sasha began to bat her eyes far too frequently.

"You know what I've learned selling Sno-Kones here for years?"

"No. And believe me, I couldn't guess."

"I've learned people have to truly open themselves to love. They've got to believe in it. They've got to want it." He wiped off the paper cup. "And if there is nothing blocking that space, love will come. I guarantee it." He handed Sasha the Sno-Kone.

She took the treat and smiled. "Well, who could resist a red Sno-Kone with a guarantee like that?"

Chapter 32

Sherry found Cay in the library. His fists were balled up at his sides, his back muscles tensing beneath his silk shirt. She thought of how it would feel to have Cay's arms around her, wanting her, bestowing on her the position of mistress of Guana Manor. It was a feeling she had anticipated for a long time. A very long time . . . and she was growing tired of waiting. Yet Sasha Townsend had experienced some of that, Sherry was sure of it. Sasha Townsend, who, in Sherry's opinion, couldn't touch her with a ten-foot pole.

"So did you have a good time?" she asked as she entered the room.

There was a long pause before Cay answered. "This isn't a good time to start up with me, Sherry," he replied without turning to face her.

"I would have assumed it was an excellent time. Now that you've finally quenched that celibate sexual appetite of yours. I would think you'd be in the best of moods." She sat on top of the desk and crossed her legs. "Or was it a disappointment because the woman you chose to lie down with is so far beneath you?"

Cay gave Sherry a dark, ominous look. "You only wish."

"Oh, my, my, my. That's a look I haven't seen before." Sherry leaned back. "It appears she's been able to melt the Ice King. I wonder why is it that lower-class women tend to be able to do that for men of your status? Is it because they're less inhibited? Or because they are tramps by nature?"

"Who's worse, Sherry? A woman who lays down with a man because she cares for him? Or a woman who wants to lay down with her dead husband's brother?"

"Touché." Sherry's eyes gleamed. "She's really gotten to you, hasn't she? Ms. Townsend must be good at that. Now she has you *and* Jason Williams dangling from her beckoning finger."

"What does Jason Williams have to do with this?" Cay's tone was razor-sharp.

"Of course, he is her so-called attorney," Sherry said lightly as she picked up Khalil Gibran's *The Rubiyat* from the desk. "But I think the real importance lies in her bedding the two of you as part of her MO. She's never been coy about being a woman who knows her way around. So"—she stroked the book's burgundy leather cover—"she may be low-classed, but I have to admit she is also smart. She's got all her bases covered. Ms. Townsend's banking on you to buy the Bethel property for an enormous sum, or if not, she's got Jason's nose wide open, and he's prepared to sue you for a similar amount. Sue you for the pain and suffering she's been through. The anguish.''

"Sasha doesn't want the money. When she arrived here she didn't even know about the Bethel Agreement. Sasha wants the property so she can start her own business. She's a very independent woman. But that's something you wouldn't know anything about," Cay retorted.

"That's the story she gave us, that she didn't know about the agreement. I think she did know and she has been manipulating all of us." Sherry paused to let the seed settle in. "Tell you what. Why don't you see if I know what I'm talking about? Call Jason Williams. Ask him how long he's been in her employ. If he tells you more than a month, you know she was lying."

Cay glanced at the telephone on the desk.

"Come on, Cay, call him. Or are you afraid to find out that for once you've been somebody's toy?"

The image of Sasha in Jason Williams's arms appeared in his mind. Memories from the night before, and the pain of having to let her go, intensified the scene. Sasha was a passionate woman. It was hard to imagine her living a celibate life.

Years of negative conditioning toward women stirred. Cay could hear his father saying, "A woman cannot be faithful, Cay. So you should never become attached to one. If you do . . . make sure she's damn near an angel; it's the only way you can be sure of her."

"Sasha made her relationship with Attorney Williams clear at dinner the other night. I didn't hear him disagree with her," Cay said, fighting to keep his equilibrium.

"No, he didn't." Sherry wet her lips. "It wouldn't have been in his best interest. But I noticed he was unnecessarily aggressive with you, and he carried a rather strange air about him the entire evening. Almost as if he were holding something back. I think they have something going. We women have a sixth sense about this kind of thing. You can ignore it if you like, but how can it hurt you? Call Jason, Cay. Tell him for settlement purposes you need to take the entire picture into consideration."

"I don't have Williams's phone number," he admitted with a tight jaw, embarrassed by the force of jealousy that churned within him.

"Here you go, brother-in-law. I thought this might come in handy." Sherry was leaning toward him with a business card between her fingers.

Cay caught a whiff of her expensive perfume when he took the card, and it sickened him. He moved to the other side of the desk and dialed the number. Watching Sherry as closely as he would watch a black widow spider, Cay spoke into the receiver. "I want to speak to Attorney Williams. . . . He isn't? When do you expect him? Yes, I would. Tell him that Cay Ellis the third called and that I would like for him to call me as soon as possible. Thank you," Cay said and hung up.

"He wasn't there?" Sherry looked exasperated.

"No, he wasn't."

"Well, I think you should make Ms. Townsend a reasonable offer for the Bethel property and see what she says." Sherry flipped through the gold-edged pages of the book.

"I told you, money isn't everything to Sasha," Cay said. "She's not afraid to admit she needs it, but it's not her driving force. Not at this point in her life."

Sherry made a clicking sound in her throat. "What a ploy. Claiming she's the ultimate independent woman. It seems to work, though." She shrugged. "Makes a man like you want to reel her in. I wish I had thought of that one." She grinned mockingly. "You see, Cay, you thought you were the fisherman and Ms. Townsend was the fish, but I can see it was the other way around."

"I've heard enough." Cay walked across the room.

"If you don't want to make her an offer, I will. Just tell me the amount," Sherry volunteered, pushing to end the tie between Cay and Sasha.

"If there is any offer to be made I'll make it myself," Cay replied.

"Just trying to help." She slid off the desk. "And Cay . . ." Sherry called.

"Yes, Sherry?"

"You will let me know what you find out, won't you?"

"It will be my pleasure."

Sherry turned away with a smile, but inside she felt tired. She wondered how it would feel to just let go, to not have to fight for what she wanted. Sherry closed her eyes. She wouldn't have to fight with Jason. Jason still loved her. She could tell. But she opened her eyes and willed the thought away.

The telephone rang as Sasha walked through the back door. She ran over and picked it up, then carefully made her way back to the rug. She began to wipe the sticky sand from her feet. "Hello-o."

Cay didn't know what he had expected, but the merry hello that echoed from the receiver certainly wasn't it. "Hello, Sasha. This is Cay."

"Cay"—she tried to calm the excitement in her voice—"I didn't expect to hear from you so soon."

"Are you alone?"

With furrowed brows Sasha looked down at the receiver. "Yes, I am. What is it, Cay? What does my being alone have to do with anything?"

"I . . ." He drew out the word. "I have some business to discuss with you of a private nature. I didn't think you would want to discuss it in front of anyone . . . maybe your attorney"—the title was clipped—"but no one else."

Sasha looked at the phone again. Cay didn't sound like himself. There was a strange edge to his voice. "No, it's okay. Go ahead."

"I've been thinking about the issue that we

have lying on the table concerning the Bethel Agreement. . . ."

"Yes." Sasha pulled out a dinette chair and sat down.

"As I told you on the plane, I've come to the conclusion that I do want to make you an offer for the property."

Sasha couldn't believe he was going forward with it. That he'd called to talk about business and nothing else. "I see." Her chest felt heavy.

"I'm very aware of property values in these parts, and I know what I'm about to offer is a very good deal. I'm prepared to pay you two hundred and fifty thousand dollars for the house."

"Two hundred and fifty thousand dollars," Sasha repeated with disbelief. "That's a lot of money," she whispered into the phone. "Getting the Bethel property back must mean an awful lot for you to offer me so much."

"Let's just say I'm a fair businessman."

"Is that what you call this? A fair business deal?" Sasha swiped away the tear that tickled the bottom of her face.

"What would you call it?"

"I don't know." There was silence on the line. "I'm going to have to think about this," Sasha replied in a deadpan voice.

"What's there to think about? You just said it's an awful lot of money. It is," Cay pushed.

"It may be." Sasha managed not to sniff into the phone. "But if you're willing to offer that much, being the businessman that you are, there's no telling how much you think this place is really worth." She turned the receiver up and wiped her face on her dress. "I'll just wait for your official offer. You can make that through my attorney, Jason Williams."

The silence sizzled.

"So that's the way it is?" Cay's voice could have frozen her.

"That's right." Sasha's lips trembled.

"We'll play it your way."

The line went dead.

Still holding the receiver in her hand, Sasha walked over to the refrigerator, where Jason Williams's number was visible on a Post-it. Her hand trembled as she dialed the number. "May I speak to Attorney Williams, please. This is Sasha Townsend calling."

"I'm sorry Attorney Williams isn't in," the secretary said with a practiced voice. "May I take a message?"

"Oh." It had never crossed Sasha's mind that he wouldn't be available. "I guess not. No, maybe I will. Just tell him Cay Ellis made me a substantial offer on the Bethel House."

"Yes, ma'am. Is that all?"

"Yes. Will Attorney Williams be back in his office today?" Sasha found herself fighting back the tears.

"No, ma'am, he won't. But I'll be sure to get this message to him as soon as I can."

"Thank you," Sasha said before she pressed the button and cut off the professional voice.

In a daze, she walked over and placed the

phone on the charger. Stunned, she sat on the couch. Moments later Sasha crumpled into a heap, her chest heaving. She was crying more tears than she thought she had within her.

Chapter 33

"Hey! So you decided to come out and join us." Mr. Smith said as he continued to pump syrup.

"I didn't have any better offers," Sasha replied, "so I decided eating piping-hot oysters cooked by somebody else was better than sitting at home alone."

"That's for certain." Mr. Smith passed the yellow Sno-Kone over the counter to an impatient boy. "Here you are, little man." He smiled at Sasha.

"This is a pretty big to-do, isn't it?" Sasha looked around at the large crowd.

"We think so, and it gets bigger and bigger every year. Thank you, ma'am," he said to a woman in a thong bikini. He leaned toward Sasha and whispered, "That's one of the fringe benefits of the Sno-Kone business."

"Do men ever change?" Sasha had to laugh.

"No. Never," he replied.

"God help us."

"Hey, there's no need to bring God into this. Can't a guy have a little fun without feeling guilty?'' He smiled an infectious smile. ''Have you tried the oysters?''

''No, not yet. I just got here.''

''Well, I suggest you get started, because with a crowd this size they can go pretty fast.''

''I don't have to be told twice.'' Sasha waved as she followed his advice, although her appetite had really not returned.

After standing in line for ten minutes, Sasha took her food to the edge of a concrete platform and a stair. Carefully, she settled down on the empty stair with her tiny bucket of roasted oysters, fries, hot sauce, and ketchup. Time passed fast enough as a local band played and the people around her amused themselves with the food and music. It wasn't a lot, but it was enough to keep her from thinking too much.

''What are you doing sitting over here all alone?'' Mr. Smith was balancing a container of steaming oysters. ''Mind if I join you?''

''Absolutely not.'' Sasha wiped her fingers on a paper napkin. ''I could use the company.'' She began to scoot to the edge of the stair.

''No, that's okay,'' Mr. Smith protested. ''I'll put my plate right here''—he placed it on the platform—''and sit down right beside it.'' He pulled himself up onto the platform. ''Boy, it's been a long day.''

''I bet it has. Are you done for the night?'' Sasha munched a fry.

''Yes, I'm done. I'm sure I could make some more money''—he looked around at the crowd—''but my body tells me it's not willing to help me.'' He popped open one of the oysters to let it cool. "Do you live around here? Or are you visiting?"

"I live here." Sasha looked down at her plate. "I have a place on Magic Key."

"You do?" Mr. Smith looked surprised. "I consider myself a self-made historian for this area, and the Ellises are the only people I know that live on Magic Key. Hazel Bethel used to live in the little house in the middle of Guana Manor, but she died a few months back."

"Yes, I know. She was my aunt."

"Is that right? I knew her and her brother, Amos. She was some special lady."

"So I've heard, but I never met any of them. It was just recently that I found out I had an Aunt Hazel."

"Never?" Mr. Smith's brows furrowed even farther. "That would mean you don't know that Amos . . ."

"It's a rather complicated story." Sasha inhaled. "I—"

"Life can get congested as the years go by. If it's that complicated, we don't need to go into all the details."

Sasha felt relieved. It was her turn to ask questions. "Do you live near here?"

"I live on Big Pine Key. Been living in this area all my life. But I consider this beach as mine. I patrol it, make sure the debris is picked up. That sort of thing. I even venture down onto the Ellises' private property. They've never complained."

"So you know the Ellises pretty well?"

"Not really. Mr. Ellis is the kind of man that

doesn't allow people to get to know him. Of course, I've seen him around many times. From some of the things I've heard about him, I think I'm better off the way I am."

Sasha watched Mr. Smith sprinkle a heavy dose of hot sauce on a large oyster. "I've heard he's lived quite a life, and his sons have as well." Olive's claims that the Ellises had always been troubled nagged at her.

"Yes, that's about what I know to be true. I believe someone could make a movie about that family." He rubbed his hands together. "You see, my people were born here in the States, and we don't have a history that's connected with the *obeah*. But the Ellises have roots in the Bahamas—and, from what I heard, the *obeah*, too," he rushed on. "Now, I'm not saying that's why things have gone they way they have, but I've heard, from reliable sources, that when old Mr. Ellis's mother was alive she ruled Guana Manor with an iron fist. And that she was a really strange woman. One that I wouldn't want for a wife or a mother," he said bluntly. "Somebody told me it had to do with the *obeah*. That she let it run their lives, just about ruined them." Mr. Smith shook his head. "They've had enough tragedy in that family for me to believe something isn't right. But money hasn't been a problem. Still, they have been a troubled family." He stopped and looked rather embarrassed. "I'm sorry. I'm going on about the Ellises and you might believe in that sort of thing as well."

"I don't believe anything that preaches

doom and gloom," Sasha replied, but she couldn't help but think of Cay. Could Cay have been telling the truth? Did he really believe his family was cursed? "I do think, if a person believes in something," she started off slowly, "her thoughts or her will can help bring it about."

"I think there's some truth in that," Mr. Smith replied. "But I know I don't believe somebody can just put a curse on me and *boom*"—he threw up his hands—"all of a sudden my life is altered for the worst."

"Yes." Sasha was in deep thought. "If that were true that would mean they fixed the future. Permanently changed it," Sasha said, seriously considering it for the first time. "And I don't believe any human being on earth can do that."

"I refuse to believe it," Mr. Smith announced. "I wake up every morning and look forward to a beautiful day, and that's what I'm determined to have. And believe me, every year that passes reminds me of just how wonderful each day really is." He began to wave and smile as he looked off into the crowd.

Sasha turned to see an attractive older woman in a red skirt and white blouse wave back. "Is that a friend of yours?"

"Mm-hmm. Someone I hope will become a good friend," Mr. Smith replied. "I think I'll mosey on over there and say hello." He lowered himself off the platform. "Take care of yourself. Hope to see you again, real soon."

"You do the same, Mr. Smith." Sasha watched as he weaved his way into the crowd.

Minutes later Sasha finished her food and headed home. In light of what Olive and Mr. Smith had told her, she thought about giving Cay a call. Once again she unlocked the door to the sound of the telephone ringing. Hoping it was Cay calling her back. She hurried and answered it. "Hello." The sound of someone breathing was the only response she heard. "Hello-o. Hello." Sasha hung up. "I am not in the mood for anybody playing on the phone."

She started the shower and the phone rang again. "Hello." No answer. "Look, I'd appreciate it if you wouldn't call back." She hung up and went into the bathroom. Sasha could hear the phone ringing as she showered, and it did not stop until she answered it. Still, the person on the end of the line refused to speak. *This is beginning to be a problem*, she thought as she put on her nightclothes. Sasha knew it was a problem when the phone rang again.

The telephone continued to ring. She tried unplugging it, but soon feared that was what the caller wanted her to do. If she unplugged the telephone she would be unable to call for help if someone decided to do more than call.

Coming up on midnight, Sasha was nearly exhausted. She thought of calling the police, but wondered what the police could do about harassing phone calls. That's when the telephone rang again, and Sasha's anger rang with it. "I am sick and tired of this," she yelled into the receiver. "I'm going to have the police tap my line and you're going to be arrested for harassment," she threatened.

"The wisest thing for you to do is to move.

Don't expect any money or anything else if you value your life," a deep male voice said with deadly calm before the line went dead.

The shock of hearing someone speak for the first time was numbing. But what he said chilled Sasha to the bone. He had told her if she valued her life she would move! Sasha's knees went weak, and she slumped into the chair. Someone had just threatened her over the Bethel property.

"That wasn't Cay's voice." Sasha trembled as she spoke.

The phone rang again, but this time Sasha did not answer it. In a panic, she pulled on a pair of jeans and a T-shirt over her night-clothes and headed for the door. Her hands trembled as she attempted to lock up, and the keys tumbled to the ground. When Sasha stooped to retrieve them a silver object caught her eye. It was an advertising magnet: "Rental Sloops Are Our Business. HAPPY TOURISTS Are Our Goal. (800) 238-7735." It was the same magnet she had seen in Cay's SUV and in the seaplane.

Frightened and with tears stinging her eyes, she drove down the dimly lit road toward Big Pine Key. It was hard for her to accept what the occurrences within the last few hours meant, but there was no way to deny them. The man on the telephone had not been Cay, but there was a high possibility he was some-one Cay had hired. Perhaps he was the same person who had poured bleach throughout her home nearly two months before. In truth, it did not matter. What did matter was, it was clear to Sasha she was not wanted in the Bethel House or on Magic Key.

Sasha pressed down on the gas as her mind raced. She rounded the bend to cross the small bridge and nearly collided with a car that was driving on the wrong side of the road. Quick reflexes were the only thing that saved her. Moments later she came to a screeching halt. "Oh, my God." Her head yanked forward. Breathing heavily, Sasha turned to see if the oncoming car had stopped. To her surprise, the driver had continued on his way. "Who in the world was that?" She watched the red taillights grow smaller as they headed farther into the interior of the Key.

It took a few minutes for Sasha to collect herself before she went on. About fifteen minutes later she pulled up in front of a motel.

"I'd like a room," she told the man standing behind the counter.

He looked down at Sasha's waist, where part of her nightgown hung out of her jeans. She stuffed the material back inside her pants. "That will be ninety-five dollars. Cash," he stressed.

"Cash!"

He slid a sign between them: NO CREDIT CARDS. NO CHECKS.

"I don't know if I have cash." Sasha rummaged inside her bag.

"Can't give you a room if you don't, ma'am." The man crossed his arms.

Sasha could feel panic rising. What if she didn't have any cash and all the motels adhered to the cash-only policy? Suddenly, she remembered her emergency hundred-dollar bill. It had permanent creases when she handed it across the counter. Minutes later Sasha was opening her motel room door.

She looked at the phone and considered calling Jason Williams, but it was a quarter to one in the morning. She had never used his home number before, and she didn't think calling him in the middle of the night would be a good time to start. Sasha sat back on the bed and looked around the impersonal room. She believed she would be safe until daylight.

Drained, Sasha peeled down to her nightgown and looked at the sign on the nightstand: CASCADE MOTEL, ALMOST LIKE HOME. She thought of the man who wasn't going to give her a room if she didn't have cash. She thought of the last thing Cay had said to her on the plane. She thought of what had happened at the Bethel House. Sasha turned the sign facedown. "No way is this place like home. No way at all."

Chapter 34

Cay stood in the attic and saw Sasha's car lights flash on. She drove off the property so fast the Mazda nearly went into a tailspin. He looked at his watch. It was almost twelve-thirty in the morning. There weren't that many places for a woman to go on Big Pine Key at that time of night, and Sasha was in a big hurry. Cay could come up with only one solution: She was going to see Jason Williams.

Despite all the influence the Ellis fortune had, and the power behind it, Cay felt powerless. It was like one grand show on the outside, but inside he was a prisoner of the past. He didn't want to believe the things that had been intricately woven into his life, his psyche, since he was a little boy, but the truth was, when he looked at his life, at the Ellis family's history, reality proved those beliefs to be true.

Feeling heavy, he sat down on the torn upholstered seat. His hands rubbed the familiar carvings etched into the arms of the chair. He recalled a time when his hands could not span the round lion faces. Then the chair had been a throne, a boy's throne.

Cay smiled wistfully. He had granted many favors to loved ones seated here, and righted the wrongs he and Wally endured inside Guana Manor. As an adult he wished the magic worked as well.

Cay looked around the attic. He was no longer a frightened boy seeking refuge, but perhaps as a grown man he was even more afraid, because he knew how fleeting happiness could be and how much damage an unkind word could yield.

Again, Cay looked out the window, but now there was nothing but darkness. It illustrated how his life had been for a long time. Maybe it was the same for his father, who had tried to disguise the bleakness with liquor and women through the years. Cay realized that his father had managed to bury himself beneath a facade of anger and a mean spirit. Buried himself because he was afraid to claim sovereignty over his own life. He tried to remember a time when he'd believed his father was happy. It was very difficult to do.

He took his foot and nudged a pile of curtains mixed with boxes. One of the box lids tumbled aside, and several articles spilled out. Cay's eyes examined them, but his thoughts churned, looking for a way out.

There was costume jewelry, long black gloves, a music box, and a cloth-covered scrapbook. It was on the music box that Cay's attention focused. It had belonged to his grandmother, and although it had sat on her dresser for years, he had never heard her play it. Cay wound the ballerina-topped box, and a stilted version of music from *Swan Lake* began to play. He placed the scrapbook in his lap and closed his eyes.

It was hard to imagine his grandmother listening to and loving such a beautiful tune. Yet it was easy to visualize Sasha embracing it. Precious would have allowed it to carry her away, never to return.

Cay opened the scrapbook, and the faded image of a beautiful woman looked back at him. At first he did not recognize her, but written underneath the photograph, in a steady hand, was his grandmother's maiden name, Cecilia Rose Marsh. As Cay turned the pages, he realized that the contents of the scrapbook were from his grandmother's life prior to his father's being born. There were remnants of an elementary school play, a blue ribbon from a foot race, and a glee club name tag. At the back of the book, tucked behind a Valentine's heart made from construction paper, was a picture of a man. The name Louis J. Bethel was printed at the bottom. "Love, L.J." was written on the back.

An erratic glow of weaving headlights beamed up the road toward the house. Cay looked out the window when the car was in floodlight range. He recognized his father's black Cadillac. He guessed his father had drunk too much when he saw him park the car in the middle of Sherry's favorite flower garden.

Chapter 35

"Mr. Ellis must have tied one on last night." Olive looked out the window at the Cadillac, then let go of the curtain. "Ms. Sherry's going to have a fit about her flowers." She looked at Cay and crossed her arms. "You sure are up early for a Saturday morning."

"I had trouble sleeping last night." Cay sat down at the kitchen table.

"I haven't had time to fix breakfast. Do you want some coffee?"

"Yes, I could use some." He rubbed the stubble on his face.

Olive wiped out a couple of mugs with a towel. "I don't know what time your father got in last night." She poured the coffee. "Here." Olive set the hot mug in front of Cay, then took a seat beside him. "So I guess I missed the fireworks, if there were any."

"Morning." Baltron interrupted the exchange as he entered the kitchen.

"Morning, honey."

"Good morning, Baltron." Cay turned toward Olive. "I don't know. Father was asleep by the time I came downstairs from the attic."

"What time was that?" Baltron inquired, pouring himself a cup of coffee.

"About one."

"So I guess he must have fallen out. He was in pretty bad shape last night." Baltron sat down beside Olive and took a sip of coffee. "So, what were you doing in the attic?" He looked at Cay.

"Just nosing around," he replied.

"You used to go up there all the time when you were a little boy," Olive recalled. "I didn't realize you still did."

"As of late I've found myself up there on a couple of occasions. I don't know why," he fudged the truth. "Maybe I'm trying to recapture the past. Who knows?"

"Have any luck?" Baltron leaned back in his chair.

"Maybe. I found a picture of a Louis J. Bethel. Does that name sound familiar to either one of you?"

"Nope." Baltron shook his head.

"No-o, I can't say it does." Olive's brow wrinkled. "But it seems like . . . no, I can't say it does."

"I found the picture in a scrapbook Grandmother must have made before my father was born. The things that were in there looked like they were from her school years."

"That sounds rather sentimental for Mother Ellis. She was a stickler about throwing things away that had no use, as she called it," Olive replied. "She never gave me any indication that she would be into that sort of thing."

"From what I remember about her"—Cay gazed off—"I thought the scrapbook was rather out of character. The picture was in the back of the book, tucked beneath a hand-made Valentine's card. The name was printed on it, and on the back it was signed 'Love, L.J.' "

"It might be one and the same ..." Olive murmured.

"What might be one and the same?" Baltron replied.

"I recall Mother Ellis talking about someone called L.J. during her last days. You know, things had gotten pretty fuzzy for her by then. But I remember her calling on an L.J. As it got closer to her time she was talking to him. Still, you know what they say, a dying person has one foot in this world and one foot in the other. So, I only half listened to what she had to say."

"Half listened." Baltron made a face. "That's impossible."

"I mean I wasn't just sitting there waiting for everything she said," Olive retorted. "Of course I heard some things. But in my opinion she was babbling, so how seriously can you take that?" Olive looked offended as she sipped her coffee. "As I think about it now, she had been sweet on this L.J., and I guess he was sweet on her. At least from her end of the conversation that's what I gleaned. Still, something must have happened, 'cause one night she was crying her eyes out and pleading with L.J. not to go."

"Is that right?" Cay sat up, holding the mug between his hands.

"That's the way I recall it," Olive replied.

"Did you ever hear her talk about my grandfather?" Cay asked. "When I think about it, I don't know much about my family. Father never talked about my mother, and I've never heard him mention his father."

"I never heard her say a word about him," Baltron said, and Olive shook her head. "But some years ago there were some folks visiting here from the islands. They were relatives of the Myerses, who own that restaurant on Big Pine Key." Baltron sipped his coffee. "They were talking about how well some of the islanders who migrated here were doing. Of course, your family was mentioned. One man claimed he knew Mother Bethel a long time ago, and that he knew your grandfather. He claimed he was a real dark-skinned man. Tall. Good-looking. Said he was dead now, but while he was alive he had been a good fisherman."

Cay placed his mug on the table. "The Myerses who own the seafood restaurant?"

"Yes, on Oceanside Drive." Baltron thumbed over his back.

"I'd like to see the picture you were talking about," Olive jumped in. "It seems weird to think of Mother Ellis being in love. No offense." She placed her hand on Cay's shoulder. "But I just can't see it."

Cay pulled out his wallet and removed the old photograph. "Here it is."

"This is him?" Olive moved the picture closer to her face.

"Cay said the name was printed on the front, Olive," Baltron chided his wife.

"I know what he said *and* I can read," Olive retorted.

"Well, why did you ask if that was him?" Baltron mumbled.

"You look at it." She put the picture on the table in front of him.

Baltron adjusted his glasses, then leaned forward. "This looks like a white man." He turned the picture over.

"You said it. I didn't." Olive looked satisfied.

"I think he is white," Cay replied.

The room went silent.

"But you know how Mother Ellis felt about that." Olive's eyebrows went up. "According to her she wasn't having none of that in her family."

"So I've heard," Cay replied, "from what you've told me and what Father has said too many times. But the truth is, out of all the people I know, Grandmother and Father really had a problem with color. Father still does."

"It doesn't make any sense," Olive declared.

"Louis J. Bethel," Baltron said as he continued to study the photograph. "It seems like a strange coincidence that his last name is Bethel. But he can't be a relative of *the* Bethels because he's white." Baltron scratched his head. "Then, on the other hand, he could be."

"I've told myself the same thing," Cay replied. "But there's got to be a connection.

There's got to be. I think it would be interesting to find out just what that connection is." He stood up. "I think I'll make a run to Big Pine Key."

Chapter 36

"What's going on?" Jason Williams leaned forward and placed his hand over Sasha's. "You looked aw—" He stopped short of saying "awful." "You look like you had a pretty rough night."

Sasha stared down into her teacup. She knew what she wanted to say, but it was difficult to form the words. "Somebody went through a lot of effort to frighten me last night. And I tell you"—she swallowed hard—"they really accomplished their goal." She bit her lip. "Now when I think about it, I get so angry."

Jason patted her hand. "Start from the beginning and tell me exactly what happened." The waitress placed a plate of bacon and eggs in front of him. "You sure you don't want anything to eat?"

"No." Sasha shook her head. "I couldn't eat anything if you paid me."

Jason waved the waitress away. "I guess that's understandable. So what happened?"

"It may not sound like much to you. But while it was going on—" Sasha looked down, searching for the right words to convey the event.

"Stop." Jason said softly and raised his palm. "You don't have to make any excuses for how you feel. Just tell me what happened and let me be the judge of how serious it was."

Sasha folded her hands on the table. "Somebody started calling my house the minute I stepped through the door from the oyster roast last night."

"What time was that?"

"About a quarter to ten."

"Okay. Go ahead."

"Well, he started calling and he wouldn't stop." Sasha shook her head. "He called for over two hours."

"Did he say anything?"

"No. I mean, yes. During the last phone call someone spoke. It was a man with a very deep voice. He threatened my life and told me I better move."

Jason put down his glass. "This man told you he was going to kill you if you didn't move out of the Bethel House?"

"He didn't use those words, but the message was very clear." Sasha's face looked strained.

"Oo-o-we-e. Cay Ellis must be losing his mind. I can't believe he did something like this. It's absolutely bizarre," Jason proclaimed.

"And that's not all," Sasha said in a small voice.

"There's more?" Jason held a fork full of grits in front of him.

"I found an advertising magnet on my front

stoop as I was leaving for the motel."

"An advertising magnet? I don't see how that's important."

"It's one of the promotional gadgets Cay uses to advertise his charter business."

Jason bit down into another piece of bacon. "I told you not to get involved with him."

"I know." Sasha sighed. "That was easier said than done." She became quiet. "But what can I say? For some reason, my instincts told me I could trust him."

"Well, so much for your instincts," Jason replied. "What time did you get to the Cascade Motel?"

"Around one." Sasha looked up suddenly. "How did you know I stayed at the Cascade Motel?"

"You told me." Jason mopped his plate with a corner of his toast.

"I don't remember telling you that." She sat back in the booth.

"That shows what bad shape you're in, mentally and emotionally. Oops, there goes my beeper." Jason looked down at his waist. "Two, two, nine, five. I don't recognize this number."

"That's Cay's cell phone number." An alarm went off inside Sasha, and she was reluctant to tell him anything else.

"Can you believe it? Rich guys have such big balls. At least they think they do," he leaned back in his seat. "See, he knows you didn't stay at your house last night because he had someone watching you. And"—he cleared the pager—"he knew you would get in touch with me. I bet he's calling to see how well his fear tactics worked. See if you're ready to drop the entire thing. It's a pity he doesn't have anything better to do with his time." He downed the rest of his orange juice.

"I can't believe it." Sasha felt uneasy. "So you think this is all about power and playing with other people's lives?" For Sasha, it didn't ring true.

"That's it. It's not the money. It's about controlling the lives of the little people around them." Jason spoke passionately. "But I tell you what, this time the Ellises have overstepped their bounds. Threatening someone's life is a crime, and we've got a motive: They want possession of the Bethel property," he pointed out. "And that incident with the bleach can be tied in real well. The way I see it"—his eyes gleamed—"we're going to come out on top. And besides going deep into their pockets, the Ellises will have a real embarrassing situation to deal with. It would be great if I could lock one of them up, if only for twenty-four hours."

"It's starting to sound like a personal vendetta for you, Jason, instead of your looking out for my legal interest."

"I can smell victory, that's all." Jason wiped his mouth. "Let's give Mr. Cay a call and see how much further he will incriminate himself. Shall we?"

Sasha folded her arms and nodded. With a cold cup of tea in front of her, she watched Jason punch in the number on his own cell phone.

"Hello. Cay Ellis?" Jason began to nod. "You called my office about five minutes ago."

Something was wrong, Sasha thought as she watched a mother and child walking hand in hand down the street. She knew she had not told Jason the name of the motel, no matter what he claimed. "Why do you ask?" Jason's tone made Sasha look at him. "I don't think you are in a position to demand anything," he continued. "What if she is? I don't think a meeting would be appropriate at this juncture. After what happened last night I've got enough on your family to nail you Ellises to the wall." Jason stabbed his plate.

Sasha watched him with a growing sense of unease. The aggression in his eyes was not about her. She was sure of it. Somehow she was caught in the middle of something else, Jason's personal agenda, and Sasha knew with every part of her it wasn't a safe place to be. "I want to meet with him. I want to meet with Cay Ellis face to face," she spoke up quickly.

"So you need to crank that Ellis fortune up—"

"Did you hear me?" Sasha asserted.

"One moment." Jason covered the phone with the palm of his hand. "What is it?"

Sasha squeezed her hands below the table. "I want to meet with him."

"I don't advise it."

"I can see why you wouldn't." She didn't want to cross him. "But on a personal level, I need to settle this." Sasha leaned forward conspiratorially. "I want to see his face when he realizes how much trouble he is in. And as my attorney I would like for you to be there." She hoped Jason would buy into it.

He took a deep breath before he spoke into the phone again. "What time do you want to meet? An hour from now?" Sasha nodded. "We'll see you then." He flipped the cellular phone closed. "I have to say, it's this kind of impulsiveness that got you entangled in this mess. If you had kept your distance like I advised, you wouldn't feel the need to go and confront Mr. Ellis. You would confront him in court, and that would be that."

"You may be right." Sasha attempted a smile. "But he led me on, and it's something I need to do. I come from a side of town where people settle their differences just one human being to another." Jason's eyes brightened. "Don't get me wrong," she said to appease him. "I want you to go after the Ellises, but there are some things a court just can't settle."

Jason threw up his hands. "We're to meet at Guana Manor in an hour. I'll drive," Jason said with finality.

Cay hung up the cell phone. Jason and Sasha were together at that very moment. The thought of it made him uneasy, and he was glad he had been able to set up the meeting.

One thing at a time, Cay thought as he sat in his chair in the Myerses' seafood restaurant. For once in his life he felt the pieces were falling into place. The veils were being pulled away from his family's ominous situation, and Cay realized that once looked in the face, truth opened the doors for change. An invisible enemy had been virtually impossible to overcome.

Cay felt as if a weight had been lifted from his shoulders. He'd never thought it would end like this. He looked down at the original Bethel Agreement. His own attorney said it wasn't worth the paper it was written on. The property was Sasha's free and clear. It always had been.

Ironically, he found peace in that. Then Cay's brow furrowed. How could Jason Williams make such a mistake? Was he inept? Or did he have his own personal reasons for allowing the situation to go this far?

"If we're done, Mr. Cay, I really need to get going." Cay's attorney picked up the restaurant ticket from the table. "But I've got to tell you, this was some of the easiest money I've ever made."

Cay took the check. "This is on me, Michael."

"Are you sure? I was planning on eating here today anyway. I love their gumbo."

"Positive."

"All right." The lawyer stood up and extended his hand. "Give me a call if you need me again. I wish all my clients were as easy to take care of as you were today," he said before he walked away.

"Is there anything else we can get for you, Mr. Cay?" Mrs. Myers asked.

"Not a thing. You've done more than you know by sitting here talking with me."

"That's good to hear. Hon and I like talking about the past. Takes me back to my passionate days." She touched her big bosom. "And I was a passionate woman back then, just like your grandmother. The problem is, passion is such an unpredictable thing. When you have it, it feeds your soul, but when it's abruptly taken away, it can change your life."

"Yes, it can." Cay thought of Sasha.

"I was lucky enough to marry the man I was passionate about." She looked at Mr. Myers, who was welcoming some tourists.

"Is your relationship as good now as it was back then?" Cay asked.

"In some ways it's actually better." She smiled. "I can't say we still have the fire we had so many years ago, but the love is definitely there. It's the foundation of my life."

Cay smiled. "Well, thanks again." He reached out to shake her hand.

"No, son, let me give you a hug." She took him into her meaty arms. "I'm just glad to see you, and I'd like to see you more often."

"I believe that can be arranged," Cay replied.

Chapter 37

"Where is Sherry?" Cay closed the front door behind him.

"Sleeping, I guess." Olive separated the gladiolas in the crystal vase. "She came into the kitchen this morning and got herself some cold water. Strange enough she offered to take Mr. Ellis his ice tea. Boy, did she look tired." Olive made a face. "She looked like she needed to go back to bed. Plus, Sherry usually sleeps in on weekends."

"I know, but it's nearly one o'clock, and that's late even for her." Cay walked toward the stairs.

"You look a lot happier than you did earlier." Olive patted the flowers. "As a matter of fact, you look happier than I've seen you in a long, long time."

"Do I?" He touched Olive's chin. "And I think it can only get better."

"What's going on?" She turned as he bounded up the staircase.

"Life is going on, Olive. Maybe for the first time."

Cay walked down the hall and rapped on Sherry's door. "Sherry."

The door opened slowly. Sherry's eyes appeared hollow as she peered out. "Yes?"

"Are you up?"

"Yes," she spoke slowly. "I am."

"I want you to be downstairs for a meeting that's going to start in about forty-five minutes." Sherry's eyes were blank as she looked back at him. "Did you hear me?"

"Is everything else okay?" Sherry asked.

"Everything is fine." Cay looked at her with concern. "I just need you to be downstairs in about forty-five minutes."

A look of relief passed over Sherry's face. "All right."

Cay went on to his father's room. He started to knock on the door but changed his mind. He cracked it and looked inside. Mr. Ellis was buried in the covers. Cay thought he looked so small in the huge bed, and Baltron's comments that morning came to mind. He decided to let him be. His father was getting older, although he was fighting it every step of the way. And there was nothing he could do to change things. The dilemma surrounding the Bethel property was crystal-clear.

Mr. Ellis heard the door close and waited a few moments before he sat up. With thick fingers, he buttoned the first two buttons of his silk shirt lower than they should have been, and the garment bunched unattractively. His dark legs looked like sticks beneath his BVDs when he swung them to the floor and picked up the socks he had worn the night before. Mr. Ellis put on the socks and his best pair of alligator shoes. Looking around as if he thought someone might be watching, he pulled the urine-stained sheets off the bed and rolled them into a ball. "I'm not going to sleep on these sheets another night," he proclaimed. "I don't care what Mother says. I'm not." He pushed out his lower lip.

He reached for the lighter fluid and his cigarette lighter. Accidentally, he knocked over the ice tea sitting at his bedside. Mr. Ellis ignored the mess as he put the articles in his pocket and stuffed the pungent sheets under his arm.

Still acting as if someone might be watching, with his eyes squeezed shut, he opened his bedroom door. Fear mixed with excitement settled on his stubbled face as he peered out into the hall. Mr. Ellis smiled when there was no one there. Giggling under his breath, he took off for the back stairway with a portion of his sheets mopping the steps behind him. He was more than pleased to discover the kitchen empty, and he laughed loudly as he went out the door and headed for his car.

"Where's Papa?" Sherry asked, looking down at her hands.

"He's still asleep," Cay replied, "but we had quite a talk yesterday. And things are finally coming together. Perhaps not in the way that I thought they would, but together nevertheless."

"What do you mean by that?" Sherry's eyes were puffy and dark.

"I've discovered some things that shine a different light on everything." Cay looked into her drawn face

Sherry grew paler. "You've discovered—"

The doorbell toned and Cay turned toward it. "That must be Sasha and Jason Williams."

"You've invited them here?" Sherry tried to grab his arm.

"You said I should have talked first, Cay. Settled things in the family first." Sherry backed up to the staircase as Cay crossed the foyer and opened the door.

"Come in, Attorney Williams." He walked past Cay. "Sasha." Their eyes met, and Cay mouthed, "It's going to be okay." Sasha's turbulent eyes looked relieved.

"Sherry," Jason spoke as he walked inside.

Sherry pressed her back against the baluster at the end of the stairs. "Jason." The name was barely audible. Sherry and Sasha acknowledged one another with nods.

"Let's go into the office." Cay motioned toward the east end of the mansion. Once again his gaze fell on Sasha. "This way please," Cay announced as he walked ahead of the group. When they reached the office Sasha sat in a wing-backed chair. Jason sat on one end of the sofa with his eyes on Sherry, who sat on the other end of the same sofa. Cay remained standing.

"It's a shame things had to go this far." Cay looked at each one of their faces. "It's a horrible thing to live with fear. It can stifle your life, turning you into someone you don't recognize." Cay looked down. "The truth is, I feel this is something that should have been settled privately. But even now there are questions that remain unanswered, questions that I hope will be answered this morning." He looked directly at Jason. "I want to begin by—"

"Excuse me, Mr. Cay," Baltron said as he burst into the office, his breath coming in spurts.

"What is it?"

"I saw Mr. Ellis in the Cadillac tearing down the road towards the interior of the island as if his life depended on it." Baltron gulped, and Sherry gasped. "He nearly ran me over, but I don't think he saw me. If you know what I mean." Discomfort blanketed his features as Olive appeared behind him. She placed a comforting hand on his arm.

"When was this?" Cay replied.

"A few minutes ago. I got here as fast as I could to tell you."

"Look!" Sasha pointed toward the window. "There's smoke coming from the direction of the Bethel House!" She was on her feet. "I think the Bethel House is on fire!"

Sasha ran for the door, and Jason Williams looked at Sherry before he headed out behind her.

"Olive, call the fire department," Cay commanded. He turned to Sherry and Baltron. "Come on. They may need our help."

"But what can I do," Sherry began to shake her head. "I didn't have anything to do with it," Sherry said quietly.

"I didn't say you did," Cay retorted.

"But I wouldn't know what to do," Sherry continued to protest.

"For once think about someone besides yourself, Sherry," Cay admonished her.

"I am." Sherry's voice trilled as she caught up with Cay. "I just—what do you think is wrong with Papa?" she asked, her eyes wide.

"I don't know. But if he set fire to the Bethel House, the Bethel Curse loomed in his mind, it doesn't look very good."

Sasha hesitated as she stood outside Jason's car.

"It's unlocked," he reassured her.

She looked at the smoke rising into the air and jumped inside.

Jason gunned the engine and headed back up the drive. "Maybe it has been Mr. Ellis all this time," Jason started to jabber. "Maybe I had Cay pegged wrong," he continued.

"Maybe." Sasha leaned toward the dashboard. "God, I hope he hasn't had time to burn the house down."

Jason let out a disdainful chuckle. "Yes, it probably was the old man. Everybody knows he's no good. He's been a liar and a cheat all of his miserable life."

It was too much for Sasha. "He's an old, sick man, Jason," she said, feeling tired, "with a childhood that was horrible. Life can do strange things to people. It's not easy for people his age when they're sick and have a fear of dying. It's not easy for them or for the people who love them." Sasha spoke from experience.

"I wonder what pushed him over the edge?" Jason went on. "If he has set fire to the Bethel House, that's arson, and he could do some time for that. I wonder how well his rich, pampered ass will do in jail with the rest of us ordinary folks?" he mused as they approached the Bethel House.

Anxiously, Sasha waited to see the place she had come to love. When it was in view relief washed over her. There was no smoke or flames coming from the structure.

"The house doesn't look like it's on fire," she said as Jason drove up. Before he could come to a complete halt Sasha was out of the car. She could hear Cay's SUV pulling up behind them. She walked up to the house and unlocked the door.

Nervous, Sasha inspected each room, checking for any evidence of a fire. There was none. When she returned to the front room, Cay was standing inside. "The Bethel House isn't on fire," she heard herself say as confusion blended with relief.

"Thank God." Cay put his arms around her. "This is your home, Sasha. The place that will keep you close to me until I can bring you even closer," Cay said, looking into her eyes.

"What?" Sasha pulled back. She couldn't believe what she was hearing.

"I met with my attorney today. The Bethel property is yours. It always has been. That's what I was going to announce at Guana Manor."

"Honest?"

He nodded.

"Then you never tried to scare me away from Magic Key?" she asked, searching the depths of his gaze.

"Never," Cay replied, pulling her into his arms again. "Why would I want to scare you away when I love you?" Sasha's eyes closed as she rested against his chest.

"Hey!" They heard Baltron yell. "The smoke is coming from the other side of these trees." Sasha and Cay emerged from the house together.

"I think it's coming from the Circle of Stones," Baltron said, pointing due east.

"That's impossible," Sasha protested. "We have to take the main road back past Guana Manor in order to reach the stones."

"That's not true," Cay informed her. "Grandmother wanted it to seem as if the Bethel property was much farther away from the main house than it actually was. So the main road circumvents the Key. The stones are on the other side of this wall of trees. It's all an illusion, Sasha. All of it."

Amazement surfaced on her face before she crinkled her nose. "The fire must be getting bigger. The smell of smoke is stronger now." Once again she feared for the safety of her property.

"I can smell it, too," Cay replied, then pointed over her head. "The quickest way to get to the stones is right through there."

"What's going on?" Jason stepped away from Sherry.

"That's what I'd like to know," Cay replied. "I was told your interest in this whole thing goes beyond representing Sasha." Cay looked at Sherry, who was standing stiffly behind him. "And I intend to find out what that interest is."

"I don't know what you're talking about," Jason defended himself. "Sasha, don't let him fool you. You've got enough against the Ellises to sue them for millions. Don't let him talk you out of it."

"Sasha doesn't have to sue me to get my money. If things work out the way I want them to, all of this"—he made a sweeping gesture—"will be hers as well as mine." Cay's voice softened as he looked down into her face. "No, this isn't about Sasha, Jason. This is about you."

Jason looked angry and flustered as he stared at them. Finally, he retorted, "You *will* get my bill." He turned to Sherry. "Is this proof enough for you? Your man Cay has made his intentions plain. Are you going to stay here or are you coming with me?"

"Coming with you?" Sasha repeated, confused.

Sherry's eyes grew wide as she looked from Jason to Cay. "Cay . . ."

Their gazes met before he shifted his focus to Jason. "Give me your keys, Jason. You're not going anywhere until I find out the whole truth." Cay stood threateningly close. "Somehow I think you are the key to this entire thing."

Jason looked up into Cay's face towering above him. "I guess I have no choice, do I?"

"I would say you don't," Cay replied.

"You're not going to find out anything." Jason handed over his keys. "But I'm going to take you to court for harassment," he threatened. "Maybe even kidnapping."

Cay ignored his threats as the group made their way through the barrier of trees. Minutes later they emerged on the other side. There was a profound silence. Perhaps it was the shock of what they saw, for in the middle of the Circle of Stones, beside a smoking mass that reeked, sat a nearly naked Mr. Ellis.

Chapter 38

~

"Hazel, is that you?" Mr. Ellis asked as he looked at the befuddled group. "Come here. Come here," he repeated, moving his index finger like an inverted inchworm. "I want to show you something."

Sounds of shock, discomfort, and confusion undulated through the group before Jason laughed. "He's as crazy as the day is long."

Sasha had to hold Cay's arm to restrain him. "And you think that's funny?" She studied the man she had trusted to handle her affairs. "I don't find it funny at all."

"Why are you talking to him, Hazel?" Mr. Ellis spoke again. "I want you to come over here with me."

Sasha pointed to her chest. "He thinks I'm my Aunt Hazel."

Mr. Ellis beamed a wide smile in her direction, his spindly legs sticking out from beneath his untidy silk shirt like spikes. "Hurry up and come over here before it goes away. It's a little rainbow." He pointed toward the silver object

357

on the ground. "You always used to tell me to look for the rainbows."

"Poor Mr. Ellis," Baltron said with tears in his eyes.

"Poor Mr. Ellis," Jason mocked. "This is irony at its best."

Cay took a step toward his father. "Father," he spoke gently.

"Who are you?" Mr. Ellis looked at Cay suspiciously. "Is that you, Papa?" His eyes widened with fear. "Papa"—he pointed and tucked his lips—"you stay away."

Sherry cringed to hear the term she used being used by Mr. Ellis in reference to his own son. Silently, she began to cry.

"You stay away, you hear," Mr. Ellis continued. "Mother said you were a mean man and that I was going to grow up just like you. She said I had to learn to control myself. 'You have no control,' that's what Mother said." He kicked the smoking heap of limbs and sticks covered with smelly sheets. Sparks flew up into the air and a few twigs caught flame.

"Isn't this a classic?" Jason piped up again. "Now that he's a stark raving lunatic, he doesn't claim you." He laughed boisterously. "Just look at him. The great Mr. Ellis, head of the Ellis fortune, sower of bastards from one end of the Big Pine Key area to the other. But he doesn't claim them all."

"We've got to do something about this before he sets himself afire," Baltron warned. "That's his lighter fluid can he's got down there on the ground. He'll be in a helluva lot of trouble if the top isn't closed tightly and it ignites."

"You're right," Cay replied. "Sasha, we're going to need your help."

"Yes." She looked at Mr. Ellis with renewed concern.

"He thinks you're Hazel, and he trusted her. Perhaps you can persuade him to move away from the fire. I'll try and handle it from there."

Sasha nodded and began to approach Mr. Ellis slowly. "I'm coming over now . . . Ca-Cay. I want to see what you have to show me." Her voice sounded strained. "But I have something I want to show you. And you have to come with me to see it."

"See! It's a rainbow," Mr. Ellis repeated, smiling down at the canister. "You said you and Precious believed rainbows were a sign." He smiled wistfully. "It's there just like my love for you was always there," he said softly. "See, it's a—" He tried to get up on his knees but he lost his balance and kicked the lighter fluid can. "Aw-aw, it's gone," Mr. Ellis lamented, picking up the canister. A clear liquid poured out. It flowed over his legs, onto the sheet, and down to the ground. A mighty whoosh followed. The sheets and Mr. Ellis's lower legs went up in flames.

"Oh, my God," Sasha cried, but the next thing she knew Cay was at his father's side, pulling him away from the pyre. With his own body he smothered the blaze that burned his father's thin legs. "Get some water," he yelled, taking off his T-shirt. "Quick! Somebody get some water from the pond over there."

Sasha grabbed Cay's T-shirt and ran toward the natural spring. She could hear Cay saying, "You're going to be all right, Father. Don't worry, everything is going to be fine." Mr. Ellis groaned with pain.

Sasha allowed the moist earth to lead her to a shallow pool among the plants. She immersed Cay's T-shirt, then ran back toward the center of the stones. Nearly out of breath, she handed the dripping cloth to Cay.

He stared at his father's badly burned legs and prayed as he wrapped the shirt around them. "Oh, God, I'm so tired of this family dealing with tragedy and death. I thought things were looking up for us. We're ready for it. It's time. And I'm asking you now to give us grace," he pleaded as the entire group hovered close by.

Mr. Ellis lay as still as death, and nobody moved.

"Is he going to be okay?" Sasha had to say something as she looked at Cay's stressed face.

"His burns look real bad." Cay gazed up at her.

"Look," Sasha said, "he's coming to." Mr. Ellis's eyes began to flutter.

"Did I hear somebody say okay?" Mr. Ellis said softly. "I better be okay." He looked at the people standing above him. "What the hell am I doing here?" he asked, bewildered.

"What's going on?" Mr. Smith called as he walked toward them. "I saw the smoke when I was patrolling the beach. Is there anything I can do?"

"There's been a fire. But there's nothing you

can do. We're waiting for the emergency vehicles now," Cay replied. "I think I hear them in the distance."

Mr. Smith studied the situation, then looked at the people gathered in the circle. He nodded to everyone and acknowledged Sasha with obvious pleasure. "Didn't think I'd see you so soon."

"How are you, Mr. Smith?" She managed a slight smile.

"Doing just fine. Things have been interesting, haven't they?" He looked down at Mr. Ellis again. "But I see things are looking up for you. You finally got together." He motioned toward Jason.

"Beg your pardon?" Sasha replied.

"You and your brother, Jason."

There was a stunned silence.

"My father is right there," Jason pointed accusatorily.

"Mr. Ellis is not your father," Mr. Smith looked surprised. "Amos Bethel was. He told me so himself. He was proud that he had a son that had become a lawyer."

Jason looked at Sasha. "This can't be true."

"But it is true," Mr. Smith persisted. "Seeing you together like this, I thought you knew. I didn't mean to start any trouble."

"You haven't caused any trouble, Mr. Smith. I guess we would have found out at some time or another." Sasha stared at Jason. "So you're my half brother? But all this time you thought you were Mr. Ellis's son."

Jason shook his head. "I really didn't believe it until the other night when I read something my mother had written." He looked bewildered.

"Jason is the one who threatened you," Cay said as he held his father's head in his lap. "He wanted to buy the property out of Probate Court, but when you came along, the situation took an unexpected turn, and somehow he got you to choose him as your lawyer."

"He put a flyer advertising his firm in my mailbox the first week I moved here," Sasha said. "When Sherry summoned me to Guana Manor I needed a lawyer quickly."

"Yes." Cay nodded. "You see, he wanted to represent you, even though he knew all along the Bethel Agreement didn't have a legal leg to stand on. Something that even I never knew until now." Cay's eyes brightened. "Because no one had ever challenged it. He thought he could use representing you to his advantage. And he did. He made it seem as if my family was behind all the things that had been happening at the Bethel House, but Jason had been responsible all along."

"I told you you couldn't trust attorneys," Mr. Ellis added. "But the Bethel Agreement isn't legal?" His gray brows knitted in consternation.

"No. It isn't worth a cent, Father," Cay told him. "It was part of Grandmother's obsession to make the Bethels pay for what she felt they'd done to her. You see, once she was in love with a white man named Louis J. Bethel. But when she wanted him to marry her, he rejected her because she was black.

"But Grandmother wasn't the only island

woman he had been involved with. Hazel and Amos's mother was another. She was the one he cared for the most. It was Louis J. Bethel who provided the money for their mother to start a life here on Magic Key, and Grandmother hated her for it.

"The money my grandfather made through fishing on his fishing boat in the islands initially paid Grandmother's way here. It was his money that helped to start the Ellis fortune and buy Guana Estate, which even then surrounded the Bethel property.

"The Bethel Agreement was a fabrication." He looked down at his father. "We never owned the Bethel land. It was a lie perpetrated by a woman scorned."

"But it's quite a coincidence that my birth father's and my Aunt Hazel's last name is Bethel, and Louis J. Bethel's last name is Bethel, too," Sasha stated.

"It's not a coincidence," Cay told her. "When their ancestors were slaves, Louis J. Bethel's ancestors were their masters. Your ancestors took on the name of their slave masters, like all slaves did." Cay turned a cynical smile toward Jason. "So this *is* your history as well. You just decided to be a member of the wrong family."

"This can't be right," Jason continued to protest.

"But it *is* right, and you were caught up in it just like we all were. You wanted to use Sasha to get to our fortune, but you didn't know you were using your own flesh and blood," Cay said. "It wasn't until today that

Baltron and I figured out that you were the one behind what was happening at the Bethel House. Baltron saw your car parked close to the back of the house the day the bleach was poured inside. But it wasn't until this morning, when he saw you driving it, that he identified the vehicle."

"What was wrong with you, boy? Why were you so keen on getting your hands on my money?" Mr. Ellis lamely patted his chest.

Jason looked deflated. "I thought if I could take something away from you . . . your wealth or your dignity . . . by dragging you through court and perhaps even putting one of you in jail, I would feel avenged"—he looked at the ground—"and Sherry would want me. See that I was as good as the Ellises."

"Oh, hell, what does Ms. Sherry have to do with this?" Mr. Ellis grumbled.

Sherry looked into Jason's troubled eyes, and her tears began to flow again.

"Years ago, because I wasn't rich and I didn't have a family name, Sherry chose your family over me. If I had had the money and the status, she would have married me. I know she would have, because I loved her and she loved me."

"Ach-ch," Mr. Ellis moaned. "Women." He shook his head. "All of this for a woman with no scruples, no morals. It's a damned shame. Women." He closed his eyes in pain. "Mother included."

Sherry put her hand on Jason's arm. "I never meant to hurt anyone, Jay. I never meant to hurt anyone. I was just trying to look out for myself. That's all."

The loud sound of fire engines whirred from the other side of the trees. Moments later two firemen accompanied by Olive emerged at the edge of the circle. "Look's like some sort of bonfire," one of them said. "Is everyone okay?" the other called out.

"My father's been burned," Cay replied. "I think he's got second- and third-degree burns, and he needs to go to the hospital."

"We'll bring a stretcher over right away."

Chapter 39

"Let's get some medicine on these burns before we take him in," the paramedic advised. "Everybody please move back and give us some room to work." He looked at Mr. Ellis. "I'm going to remove this t-shirt now. It's bound to hurt a bit, but I've got to get it off."

Mr. Ellis nodded his head and closed his eyes.

The paramedic began to remove the cloth. During the entire process Mr. Ellis didn't make a sound. Once it was done the paramedic leaned closer.

"I thought you said your father had third- and second-degree burns." He looked at Cay. "This man's legs look as if they have barely been burned at all."

"Well, I'll be damned." Mr. Ellis stared with his mouth wide open.

Cay got down on his knees. "But I tell you, his legs were badly burned. I don't understand it. They were totally engulfed by flames."

"They were burned," Sasha said, substantiating Cay's assessment. "We all saw them." A chorus of "That's right" and "I saw them" echoed through the group.

The paramedic gave them an uncertain look.

"It was the water," Cay said softly.

"What water?" the paramedic questioned.

"The water from the natural spring." He looked at Sasha. "The curse has been lifted because I believed." Tears came to his eyes. "I called on God from the deepest part of me and the water healed his legs."

The paramedic stood up. "Look, I don't know what's going on here, but as it stands this man's injuries aren't serious."

"You believed, Cay," Olive proclaimed, slapping her hip. "There's been a healing today because you believed."

"A healing in more ways than one, Olive." Cay put his arm around Sasha, who tentatively looked at Jason.

Cay helped his father get to his feet, and the group looked toward the Bethel House. Cay stayed close to Mr. Ellis's side just in case he needed him.

"Well, I'll be da— . . . blessed," Mr. Ellis exclaimed. "There's a rainbow above the Bethel House. A rainbow with no rain."

The ends of the arched prisms stretched over one side of the Bethel House to the other. Everyone stopped and stared.

"It's a sign," Sherry said. "A sign that things will get better."

"I believe you're right." Sasha looked at the ribbons in the sky with awe. She grabbed Cay's hand. "I think Precious and Hazel were right." She looked into his eyes, and he squeezed her hand reassuringly.

When they reached the vehicles Cay helped his father climb into his Cadillac. Baltron and Olive followed. Sherry stopped in front of the SUV, then turned to Jason, her eyes bright. "May I come with you?"

Jason was quiet for a moment, then he opened his arms and Sherry went inside them.

"I think we're going to have to start all over again," Jason said to Sasha over Sherry's head. "I'm sorry for all the things I've done. I was blinded by my own pain and ambition. I'd like to get to know you as my sister—that is, if you'd like?" He rushed on, "I never would have hurt you, really, and I hope you can forgive me."

Looking up at the rainbow, Sasha replied, "I think I can. And anyway, you're the only family I've got."

"For now," Cay whispered in her ear as Jason smiled. Moments later the lawyer and Sherry drove away.

"What are you going to do?" Cay asked Sasha.

"I'm going inside." She looked at him with steady, dark eyes. "You want to come?"

"Sure." Cay put his arms around her. "I have nothing to hold me back."

"Nothing?" Sasha questioned.

"Nothing in this world or in the next," he replied.

Sasha stopped in the doorway. "You know, I don't think that springwater should be sold. Given away to anyone who discovers it, but sold . . ." Sasha shook her head. "Never. However, I've got that key lime orchard back there. I've heard the key limes are second to none when it comes to making key lime pie. I could sell them . . ." She began to explain as Cay closed the door to the Bethel House.

"I'm sure you could, Sasha. I'm sure you could."

Cay and Sasha lay in spoon fashion on her bed. He tightened his arms around her, and she closed her eyes in gratitude. When Sasha opened them again, she continued to gaze out of the window into the night sky.

"Cay, did you realize when we look at the stars, we are looking at the past?"

"I remember studying something like that in school. About the light having such a long distance to travel and by the time we see it thousands of years have gone by," he spoke softly behind her. "But I don't remember my professor putting it so simply."

Sasha smiled. "But it is true. And so at this very moment we are experiencing the star's past, and how it twinkles in the present, which is also its future. You and I are experiencing every single one of those things right now. It's amazing."

"No one will ever be able to say that I only love you for your looks or for this." He patted her bottom.

Sasha chuckled. "Cay . . ." She turned over to look at him.

"Yes?"

"Did you believe the springwater might

heal your father's legs when you asked for it?''

He paused for a moment. "No, I didn't. I wasn't thinking about that. I wanted to stop his legs from burning, and I knew the water from the spring would be much cooler than the temperature of his flesh. I only wanted to stop the burning.''

"Even when you started to pray?''

"Oh, that. I just wanted the pain and suffering to stop. Not only my father's physical pain, but the emotional and mental anguish my family had been dealing with for as long as I can remember." He paused. "I didn't think the water would heal him. But now I can't help but wonder: If I had given Precious the springwater, would she be alive today?''

Sasha turned her back to Cay again. "I don't think that was in the plan for Precious, or in Precious's plan.''

"What do you mean?'' Cay asked softly.

"I mean, it's obvious to me Precious and Hazel had a reason for being here on Magic Key and they fulfilled it. They were put here to open us up. To encourage us to look outside of what we feel is reality. Expand our perceptions of the possibilities.''

Cay couldn't resist placing a kiss on the back of Sasha's ear.

"Think about it, Cay,'' she continued in hushed tones. "Precious was on a life quest to prove the existence of Atlantis. A place most scholars would simply scoff at if you mentioned the word. And, of course, that in and of itself means most people accept that Atlantis did *not* exist. We never question it. So when someone like Precious comes along, we believe she's strange or a little crazy for believing the opposite. But Precious took it further than simply saying she believed it. She set out to prove it, and she generated plenty of attention in doing that."

Cay sat up on his elbow. "But it would have been different if she had proved it and if she were still alive. None of that is true."

"I know. But she and Hazel had plenty of people talking about positive, magical things. Hazel was also a catalyst because, from a logical standpoint, she was a complete stranger who gave Precious a foundation to build from. She gave Precious her home, the Bethel House. Why would she do that considering the history between the Bethels and the Ellises? Why? There was a bigger picture." Sasha got a little excited. "A bigger plan. So when Precious died in the manner that she did, which she *knew* she would, it caused an even bigger stir. More people heard about it and became aware of her entire story and the things she believed."

"I don't know if she knew she was going to die," Cay replied. "Precious didn't believe in death. She believed we never die."

"Well, maybe there's some truth to that as well, Cay. I never told you this, but Hazel and Precious came to me in a very powerful meditation. That's why I went to the Circle of Stones that night. They asked me to come. And if you remember, I told you I saw a rainbow appear on that stone. Now, after seeing that rainbow above the Bethel House today, I know it was really there. It was a sign that what we believe is impossible sometimes is possible. Like Mr. Ellis's legs healing so quickly. All we have to do is be open to the possibilities of our lives."

"You're a piece of work, Sasha Townsend," Cay told her, bringing her to him.

"Does that mean you want to work on me some more?" she purred invitingly.

"A lover's work is never done." Cay placed a soft kiss on her lips.

"And I'm going to be your greatest masterpiece." Sasha pulled him down on top of her and kissed him deeply.

Feeling satisfied and full of joy, Cay replied, "One that will take a lifetime." He kissed her again.

From best-selling author
Beverly Jenkins
books you will never forget

NIGHT SONG
77658-8/$5.99 US/$7.99 Can

TOPAZ
78660-5/$5.99 US/$7.99 Can

THROUGH THE STORM
79864-6/$7.99 US/$9.99 Can

THE TAMING OF JESSI ROSE
79865-4/$5.99 US/$7.99 Can

ALWAYS AND FOREVER
81374-2/$5.99 US/$7.99 Can

Rita Award-winning Author
BARBARA FREETHY

"A fresh and exciting new voice."
Susan Elizabeth Phillips

JUST THE WAY YOU ARE
0-380-81552-4/$6.50 US/$8.99 Can
Take a romantic journey with Barbara Freethy to
Tucker's Landing, Oregon, where Sam and Alli
Tucker have made a life together . . . a life about to
be tested by the return of the only woman who can
break them up . . . Alli's sister, Tessa.

Also by Barbara Freethy

ALMOST HOME
0-380-79482-9/$6.50 US/$8.99 Can

THE SWEETEST THING
0-380-79481-0/$6.50 US/$8.50 Can

ONE TRUE LOVE
0-380-79480-2/$5.99 US/$7.99 Can

DANIEL'S GIFT
0-380-78181-9/$5.99 US/$7.99 Can

Check these sizzlers
from sisters who deliver!

Wonderful, Sassy Romance
from Nationally Bestselling Author

Susan Andersen

ALL SHOOK UP

0-380-80714-9/$6.99 US/$9.99 Can

A man who doesn't believe in love and a woman who
doesn't trust it find out just how wrong they can be . . .

And Don't Miss

BABY, DON'T GO

0-380-80712-2/$6.50 US/$8.99 Can
"[A] madcap and humorous romp . . ."
Romantic Times

BE MY BABY

0-380-79512-4/$6.50 US/$8.99 Can
"Sexy humor and smoldering passion . . .
Don't miss out!"
Romantic Times

BABY, I'M YOURS

0-380-79511-6/$6.50 US/$8.99 Can
"Sassy, snappy, and sizzling hot!"
Janet Evanovich